The Repulse Chronicles
Book Seven

Aftermath

by
Chris James

www.chrisjamesauthor.net

Also by Chris James

Repulse: Europe at War 2062–2064
Time Is the Only God
Dystopia Descending
The Repulse Chronicles, Book One: Onslaught
The Repulse Chronicles, Book Two: Invasion
The Repulse Chronicles, Book Three: The Battle for Europe
The Repulse Chronicles, Book Four: The Endgame
The Repulse Chronicles, Book Five: The Race against Time
The Repulse Chronicles, Book Six: Operation Repulse

Available as Kindle e-books and paperbacks from Amazon

Copyright © Chris James, 2024. All rights reserved.
Chris James asserts his moral right to be identified as the author of this work. All characters and events portrayed in this novel are a figment of the author's imagination. For the avoidance of doubt, so-called artificial intelligence has not been used at any stage in the writing or editing of this novel.

ISBN: 9798328239479

Chapter 1

19.09 Monday 15 October 2063

Serena took the last few steps to the table. As instructed, she placed the platter in front of the Third Caliph. She moved her arms away and bowed low. As she did so, she drove her right hand up her left sleeve and unclipped the button holding the stiletto in its sheath.

Serena raised herself. In one fluid motion, she withdrew the weapon from her sleeve and plunged the blade deep into the side of the Third Caliph's neck.

Time slowed. Serena held fast and waited only for the welcome release of death. Her work on this Earth was complete.

The Third Caliph's mouth fell open but no sound emerged. He tried to rise, which Serena hadn't expected. She put her weight behind the blade in her right hand and locked her left arm around the top of his head, forcing him back into his seat. A spurting warmth swamped her right hand and watery liquid dripped from her forearm. The Third Caliph began to shudder and a constricted gargle escaped his mouth.

The other men around the lavish table—including Father—rose with looks of incredulity on their dark, Persian faces. Serena redoubled her strength as her prey's struggle intensified. His arms flailed and the strange noise from his throat increased. One of his dirty fingernails caught her forehead and scratched her above her eye.

A florid, overweight man in a cream *kandora* pointed a fleshy arm at Serena and cried, "Computer, kill that slave—at once!"

Tiphanie leapt towards him before he could make another sound. The rest of the men stood frozen, their faces suffused with shock.

Serena closed her eyes and held her prey more tightly. His struggles were already lessening. His warm blood continued to spurt over her arm and spat on the floor, the noise clear and sharp in the silence. She sawed the stiletto back and forth in the flesh to open the wound further, certainty growing that her blade had severed all of the jugular veins and the carotid artery. He would die; nothing could save him now.

She offered up a prayer of thanks to God for allowing her to live long enough to know she'd succeeded.

A new, guttural shriek came to her ears. She opened her eyes to see Tiphanie withdraw her stiletto and bury it in the overweight man's right eye socket. Tiphanie dragged him backwards, glancing left and right, a desperate, animal snarl on her face. His arms also flailed the air in impotence, while his *kandora* fluttered and then billowed as the legs within it jerked and shook in spasms. Indistinct shouts and calls for assistance filled the room.

Behind her, Serena heard the doors open. The Third Caliph's body gave its final twists and twitches as its occupant's soul set out on the long journey to hell, while Tiphanie had bent over almost double to maintain the pressure on the blade buried in the fat man's eye socket.

"Stop," Father yelled, standing and moving around the outside of the table.

The Third Calip's body became limp. Serena allowed it to slide from her grasp and the sticky stiletto came free. The body gave an ungracious gurgle as it slithered off the chair and crumpled in a heap at the foot of the table.

"Computer," called the small man with whom Father had been engrossed in conversation a minute earlier, "Kill all of the slaves in this House this very instant."

Father cried, "No! There shall be no more bloodshed in my House."

Serena heard heavy footsteps approach. Her eyes met Tiphanie's as the Frenchwoman stood erect, gripping her bloodied blade, a snarl of grim vengeance on her face.

Serena called to her, "They will kill us. They must; they have no op—"

A hard, open hand smashed into the top of her spine from behind. The force of the impact drove the breath from her lungs and threw her onto the table. The *Tahchin* that she'd served moments earlier filled her vision, the aroma of saffron still strong. A tingling numbness spread from her shoulder blades and into her chest, and sounds became distant. The large, heavy hand pinned her to the table.

A new voice spoke, but Serena couldn't see to whom it belonged. "Arm the guards. Secure this property. No one can escape. We must contain knowledge of this disaster."

The small man spoke again, demanding, "We must kill all of the slaves now. Later we can decide what to do with this traitorous family of the House of Badr Shakir al-Sayyab."

Serena closed her eyes and waited patiently for death. She had spent much time preparing herself: first to have the courage to do God's will if the opportunity arose, then to imagine her transition to His embrace. As the pain from the hand pinning her to the table increased, a tiny spark of fear flashed inside her. Serena considered that the journey into the one true God's presence would have to commence with far greater pain.

"Everyone, remain still," demanded a different voice from behind her.

"At least the slaves must die—"

"No, not yet."

"But the Third Caliph has been slain this night by the most treacherous—"

"Wait, all of you," the new voice ordered.

A moment's uneasy silence passed.

The new voice spoke again, "His brothers, Waqas and Affan, have now been informed and have issued instructions."

She recognised Father's voice when he spoke in a tone of anxiety. "And what 'instructions' have Waqas and Affan issued?"

There came no answer. A high-pitched squeaking of boots accompanied more hurried footsteps. Indistinct figures passed in the periphery of Serena's blurred vision.

When the new arrivals stopped moving, Father spoke again, a tremor of fear in his voice, "What do you think you are doing?"

The new voice answered, "You are very much under arrest—"

"I demand a fair hearing under Article Three of the Scroll of Justice of the New Persian Calipha—"

"Be silent, Badr Shakir al-Sayyab. In this house—your House, one of your worthless slaves has taken the life of His Highness. Our great leader gave Himself into your care, and you betrayed that trust—"

"This was not my doing, nor the work of any—" Father broke in, his voice betraying fear.

"Be silent," the new voice shouted again.

In the following pause, Serena sensed the powerful hand pinning her to the table begin to tremble. Then, the unmistakable sound of a blade being withdrawn from its scabbard scratched the leaden silence like a metal knife on a China plate. She closed her eyes and concentrated. As the blood coating her skin dried, her flesh stuck to the table when she tried to move.

Soon, she told herself. *Nothing matters now.*

The new voice went on, "Waqas and Affan have ruled that no one is to enter or leave this house. Nothing will change. We will mourn in private. Our computers will keep His Highness alive in the minds of His subjects and in the face of the world of the infidels. Outside this house, the Third Caliph lives and breathes still, and His benevolent rule will continue uninterrupted."

Serena heard and understood the words, but she only wished for the sword to come down on her neck.

"Of course, all of the slaves in this house will be killed at once. Take them away."

The heavy hand lifted from Serena's back and grabbed her hair. The unseen warrior behind her yanked her upwards. The sudden disorientation made her stagger. Around the vast table, the men stared at her with malevolence. From members of the Third Caliph's retinue and the phalanx of warriors standing behind them, a wave of violent intent washed over her.

Then her eye met Father's. She saw regret there, but she had stopped caring about any of these animals. She closed her own eyes and heard Tiphanie breathing close by.

The flat of the warrior's blade arrived on her chest, just below her throat. The brute pressed it harder and asked, "Here, sir?"

"No," came the answer. "This place where our glorious leader has been slain in so cowardly a fashion must not be sullied with the blood of the infidel. Take both of these assassins away and execute them outside. After your men have had their pleasure."

The warrior grunted in confirmation.

Serena came back to her senses in a flash of panic. So, she and her sisters would be raped before their execution. And now they had no stilettoes with which to defend themselves.

Chapter 2

19.27 Monday 15 October 2063

Crispin Webb stood at the ornate washbasin, pulled some paper sheets from a matt-black dispenser in the wall, and dried his hands. He stared at his reflection in the mirror while data from half a dozen feeds in his lens scrolled upwards.

The slow return to some kind of normality in London had brought with it as many drawbacks as benefits. The thousands of NATO troops now advancing deeper into Europe had alleviated the pressure on English logistical nodes. Super-AI controlled road and other networks had greater capacity so ordinary civilians could return to travelling for pleasure once again. More fresh food was arriving in England's ports and the production of medical equipment alleviated the controversial issue of giving wounded NATO soldiers priority over civilians. On the other hand, many pre-war problems had started creeping back in—

A flashing comms icon broke into his thoughts, originating from one of the many contacts he hadn't missed during the height of the drama over the previous two years.

He accepted only because the boss had earlier given him a clear order to do so.

"Hi, Cris," said MacSawley, editor of *The Mail* media outlet.

Crispin choked back an expletive at the truncation of his name, which he loathed. "What do you want?" Crispin snapped, thinking of the things this editor deserved, none of them good.

"We're about to publish a story on mixed up body parts returned to grieving family members—"

"Keeping it nice and cheery, as usual, then."

"And seeing as I'm a reasonable kind of guy, I thought I'd give Number Ten the right of reply before it goes live."

Crispin heaved in a breath and felt his heart rate accelerate. He tossed the crumpled paper in the bin beneath the basin and decided to deflect. "That's Health. Call the department." But before MacSawley could speak, a sudden realisation crystallised in Crispin's mind and he added, "Wait a minute. That's not possible. They've got battlefield management systems. There's DNA records. How can the wrong body parts get sent to next of kin?"

"Er, because it's fucking chaos over there?" MacSawley answered with mock confusion. "Millions of soldiers. Millions of bodies, both civilian and military. Fighting still going on. Sometimes, the super AI catches a cold and fucks up. And then your boss's government looks like it's asleep on the job. Now, I can slant the story so the PM looks as if she's doing her best and this is just an unfortunate slice of bad luck, or I can make the government look like it can't keep tabs on the military and she looks like an incompetent bi—"

"Of course, you can," Crispin replied, his voice even but a fist clenched below the basin to expel his anger. "But you do the latter and I'll make sure the boss does a raft of interviews reminding the great English public how you led the charge out of England when it looked like we were finished."

Silence greeted his observation and Crispin smiled. He had many things still to do this evening and didn't have time for the mouthy editor. On the other hand, the anticipation of satisfaction made him continue: "Where did you run away to when England looked like it was finished? You 'summered' on the British Virgin Islands for eighteen months, if memory serves, wasn't it?"

"The proprietor instructed all key staff—"

"Sure, blame it on the boss, coward," Crispin said with a sneer.

"Don't fucking talk to me like that, you queer fu—"

"Shut up, coward," Crispin broke in, repeating the insult. "This war's changed a lot of things, and the Great English Public remember who stayed and who ran away. What used to work eighteen months ago doesn't cut it now. So, the military's super AI fucked up for a few nanoseconds? You're stupider than I thought if you think you can use something like that to make the PM look bad."

"Okay," MacSawley said, an unexpected note of placation dulling the edge of his arrogance. "How about an exclusive interview with her—"

"Piss off," Crispin spat, the thought of himself and the boss being in close proximity to the vicious editor repulsing him.

"Aren't you the right little fucker today—"

"I've still got work to do, MacSawley. How about you?" Crispin placed his palm on the door of the bathroom, pushing when the click from within announced that the lock had deactivated. He emerged into the broad corridor to see the boss in conversation with Monica. They stood at the entrance to the flat in which the boss liked to hold most of her meetings. Monica's face was set in its familiar frown of uncertain concentration.

"Come on, Cris," MacSawley cajoled, "maybe you give me a half-decent quote and then I won't leak the date and location of the November conference?"

Crispin froze in mid-step. "What did you say?"

"Oh, haven't you heard?" MacSawley replied in mock innocence. "There's going to be a—"

"I know what there's going to be in November, you little fucker," Crispin hissed, appalled that the top-secret information had leaked.

"I'm not sure I appreciate your language, Mister Webb," MacSawley countered.

Crispin controlled his breathing. The need to contain the situation cooled his anger: the boss wouldn't appreciate a new problem with *The Mail* on top of her current raft of issues. Suddenly, the breath went out of his body. He leaned back against the wall, swamped by an abrupt and overwhelming sense of pointlessness pushing his shoulders down like the deep ache he felt years ago after swimming sixty lengths. He resolved to deal with the immediate problem. "Yeah, okay. I'll get a quote from her and get back to you."

"Within an hour, okay?"

"Right. Yes," Crispin gasped.

"Good, and don't think about fu—"

Crispin ended the call with a twitch of his eye.

Napier strode along the corridor towards him and asked, "What is it?"

"Nothing serious," Crispin replied, seeing Monica scuttle off around the corner.

There came a silence between them and Crispin knew that the boss sensed something was amiss.

"Well?" she asked.

"I need to get Joel downstairs to sort out a quote from you for *The Mail*."

"So, that jackal MacSawley has finally started trying to cause trouble again, yes?"

Crispin nodded. "He's got an exclusive and is using it to try to get some leverage."

"Nothing new there," Napier replied, an eyebrow raised. "What else is going on with him?"

Crispin replied, "He claims to know about next month."

"Damn. If that information gets out through an English-language outlet like that, it will make me look bad in front of our allies."

"It means we've got a leak somewhere in Number Ten."

"Many more staff have returned now, Crispin."

He asked in mischievous irony, "Can't we get the British Army's special forces to persuade MacSawley to commit suicide, even if he doesn't want to?"

Napier tucked a strand of auburn hair behind her ear and replied with a mirthless smile, "We can't get away with that kind of thing these days. Come on, let's go to the cabinet office. I'll attend the fresh food conference from there."

Crispin walked by her side as they strode to the lift at the end of the corridor.

She went on, "Still, if there is a leak and you can find out which department or office it came from, do let me know."

"Of course, boss."

The lift door slid open at their approach. They entered and Napier reasoned, "The November conference is going to bring some serious challenges."

Crispin eyed her as she glanced up at the ceiling of the lift.

She mused, "When the fighting's over, the subsequent reckoning with our enemy and ourselves will cause all kinds of problems."

Usually reluctant to correct the boss, Crispin felt compelled to point out, "The fighting is still quite some way from over."

She sighed and faced him. "It won't be long," she said with a hint of suppressed desperation.

"It might be," Crispin countered. "Have you read today's military brief?"

She shook her head, "No. I spoke to Terry this afternoon, and I thought he made things sound worse than they are. Spain is quite far away. I'm sure Terry will be able to manage things. He mentioned that as soon as our own new weapons come into play, the situation will improve. And then, at long last, we can look forward to an end to the fighting."

The boss's wistful tone nonplussed Crispin.

The lift stopped and the door slid open.

She said, "Anyway, we need to concentrate on more important things now, Crispin."

"Sure, boss."

They exited the lift and strode towards the main cabinet office.

"I would like to have some feedback on how the public perceive the government currently. Are MORI up and running?" she asked, referring to the polling organisation.

Crispin checked in his lens and replied, "Not yet. The building that housed their HQ still hasn't been rebuilt. They're aiming to be back in business by the new year."

"Very well," Napier replied with a trace of impatience.

They arrived at the ornate oak doors that opened into the broad cabinet office, the centre of the English government. Crispin nodded to the undersecretary at the desk in the corridor.

Napier stopped before entering the room and lowered her voice, "You probably think I'm being a little vain, needing an opinion poll."

Crispin thought she was out of her mind. He mustered what diplomacy he could and replied, "Boss, the war is far from over. The country is dislocated, broken and recovering. Just today, you've attended five different conferences and meetings in which all kinds of worthy causes were begging the government to increase their allocation of recovery funds. Your ratings are not something that should be top of the agenda—"

"Yes, there are many issues we need to tackle," she conceded. "But if *The Mail* knows about the November conf—"

"I can handle MacSawley. And anyway, he and most of Fleet Street ran away to America when it looked like we were done for last year. Thanks to that cowardice, what they publish doesn't carry half of the weight it used to before the war."

Crispin watched as the boss drew in a considered breath and hoped she wouldn't make any more pointless requests. With a specific nod, he indicated to the undersecretary that she was ready for the conference.

The small man with a pointed face gave a slight cough, stood, and strode with measured pacing to open the doors for Napier. He said in a quiet voice, "Everyone is present, ma'am."

Napier entered without speaking and Crispin caught sight of the handful of cabinet members who'd troubled themselves to attend in person. With a heavy click, the doors closed and the scent of aged, polished oak made Crispin recall times before the war, when a bad news day meant nothing worse than a few northerners drowning because flood defences somewhere had failed.

"Would you like to wait, sir?" the undersecretary asked.

"No," Crispin replied. He turned around and walked back along the corridor. Once out of the undersecretary's earshot, he twitched his eye and said, "Monica?"

A thumbnail appeared in the bottom-right of his vision and the boss's PA replied, "Yes?"

"How much has she been drinking lately, when I've not been around?"

Monica tilted her head, shrugged, and said, "Not as much as when we were about to get invaded. Why?"

"No reason, but let me know if that changes."

"You spend way more time with her than I—"

"Okay, okay. Listen, some of those vultures in the media know about the thing we're not going to mention."

"Oh, you mean next month—?"

"Yes. Any leak cannot be seen to have come from Number Ten. In any circumstances. Got that?"

"Yes, deflect. I know."

Crispin ended the connection and strode on, his feet leaden at the prospect of what November might bring for everyone in the government.

Chapter 3

19.59 Monday 15 October 2063

Field Marshal Sir Terry Tidbury reposed in the Queen Anne wing-backed leather chair at the rear of the mess room under the War Rooms. As he rocked his brandy snifter back and forth, low orange light swept and swirled through the auburn brandy. The soft upholstery caressed his aching hip joints and shoulder blades. The dim light obscured the faces of the three other generals he'd invited, who sat in similar chairs. Several floors above them, staff in the War Rooms monitored the worsening situation constantly.

Flames in the fireplace licked and twisted around blackened oak logs. Suspended on the wall above it, a screen allowed four other NATO generals to join the meeting. Terry's glance refocused from his glass to the fluted Corinthian columns on either side of the fireplace, holding up a broad, marble mantelpiece that was adorned sparsely with two slim candles in gold holders and a small gold carriage clock.

The carriage clock chimed the hour with a soft, metallic strike.

"Ladies and gentlemen," Terry began, glancing up at the screen. "I'm sure you'll agree that it has been an unpleasant few days." He paused, wanting to frame his thoughts with the minimum of negativity. "The enemy has prevented both of our lines from continuing their advance. Unfortunately, since Sunday morning, we have incurred the greatest number of casualties since the start of Operation Repulse."

Concerned faces stared back at him from the men in the other chairs and the four generals attending remotely. None spoke.

Terry went on, "Now we have appraised ourselves of the situation one hour ago, at 19.00 CET, you appreciate the importance of committing—for now—to a staggered withdrawal. The enemy's new weapon has been given the reporting name 'Siskin'. The latest sitrep includes an annex on the enemy machine's improved performance, firepower and tactics. I'm sure you've all at least read the summary, yes?"

All of the heads dipped in nods of confirmation.

"The good news, such as it is, is that the numbers are not as bleak as they might appear at first glance. As long as we can maintain production and deployment of a minimum two thousand Scythes per day, we will be able to manage a slow and orderly fighting retreat, although there remain the usual range of unknown factors."

From the screen, the dour Estonian General Kask asked, "The sitrep was not explicit as to the source of this reversal, SACEUR. Does this mean the enemy's weapons plant at Tazirbu is now returned to full production?"

"I believe so," Terry answered, not entirely sure the question and its answer had any relevance. "The continuing and very public standoff the enemy is engaged in with India has certainly tied down his forces in the eastern half of his empire. Thus, it stands to reason that the tactical advantage we gained two months ago has been neutralised. To a certain extent, we are now relying on the political status quo being maintained. If the enemy reaches some kind of compromise on his eastern flank, we may find our slow and orderly retreat becoming rapid and disorderly in short order. However, there are other problematic issues of which you all need to be appraised. Sir Patrick?"

From opposite him, General Sir Patrick Fox cleared his throat and spoke, "Whether or not the production plant at Tazirbu has been repaired, the fact remains that an eventuality we had anticipated—but which we hoped we might evade—has indeed come to pass. The future of Operation Repulse now relies on factors that, to a significant degree, are outside our control."

Terry sipped his brandy, content to let Fox carry this part of the briefing. Fox's received pronunciation and stiff, aristocratic bearing hid any emotions he might have felt, and Terry knew from experience that many Europeans in NATO still held such affected mannerisms in high regard.

Sir Patrick went on, "We are now in an exposed position. If the Third Caliph should broker some kind of treaty with India which would then free his armies on his eastern flank, he might indeed turn Operation Repulse, and the controlled retreat we face today might well become a rout."

Terry saw the other faces fall in this statement of bald fact.

"However," Sir Patrick said, "as the field marshal mentioned, our production numbers of Scythes have never been greater, and this should allow us some agency. For the present, at any rate." Fox sipped his small glass of port before continuing, "In the meantime, and in addition to the myriad tactical and related issues we must deal with on our individual sectors, another important challenge has arisen.

"In the last forty-eight hours, after the introduction of the Siskin, the enemy followed the attacks with waves of advancing warriors. Thus far in the war, the enemy was content to allow his ACAs to do all of the, shall we say, heavy lifting, before committing flesh-and-blood troops to the battlefield—"

The Polish General Pakla interjected from the screen, "A fact we know only too well after almost two years of this war."

"Quite," Sir Patrick conceded. "But now, it seems the enemy is being freer with his manpower."

"Perhaps," began the Italian Lieutenant-General Lombardi, "this is evidence of his... frustration, no? Maybe he think a bit more like he can lose this war? So, he is more ready to commit troops to the battle?"

Terry watched as Fox tilted his head in consideration of the Italian's comment.

"I agree, up to a point," Fox said with diplomacy. "But it may not be as simple as that. I believe his objective is to attempt to damage our own troops' morale by forcing them into closer combat, including hand-to-hand; something that has been singularly lacking in the conflict until now."

A Czech general spoke from the screen, "Are you saying we need to better motivate our own troops? I can assure you that the soldiers under my command—"

"Not at all," Fox broke in. "But this new enemy tactic has led to another problem we must address. As you will no doubt have noticed, today's sitrep included a top-secret annex with the annotation that only select commanders would be allowed access to it. I will now divulge it to you. Keep in mind that only the eight of us present here are allowed access at this time."

Fox paused and Terry watched his subordinate's eye flicker. For the umpteenth time, Terry wondered what it must be like to have one of those confounded lenses in his eye and to be able to inform his subordinates of important information just with a simple twitch.

A map of Europe resolved on the screen. A dozen or more red indicators flashed over locations on both lines of advance, in western Germany for Attack Group East, and northern Spain for Attack Group South.

Sir Patrick continued, "We have evidence that the enemy has captured NATO troops, some of whom have been briefed on our new Scythes, the Alpha and Omega."

Terry watched the faces of the others, expressions ranging from regret to dismay. A log on the fire slipped from the one below it and threw out a shower of orange sparks in a fizzing crackle.

"We need to recover these troops, with the utmost urgency," Sir Patrick said. "The indicators on this map show the locations of where our troops were captured. You are attending this briefing because these locations are on your and your subordinates' sectors of the fronts."

General Pakla's accented English boomed through the room, "But how do we know if they are even still alive?"

"We do not," Sir Patrick answered.

Lombardi asked, "And if they are captured alive, how can we stop the enemy accessing the data? He is going to do to our troops what we are doing to his, no? Our captured troops must be already dead, like his warriors we caught, no?"

Terry spoke, "So far, our intel from the brain scans show that the enemy has not developed this technology. Possibly because he has never needed to."

Fox said, "Our super AI gives varying estimates on whether the captured NATO troops are alive, injured, dead, or undergoing torture. Detailed percentage figures are available in the annex to the sitrep. Nevertheless, this evening our computers are organising the required counterattacks to ensure that the enemy is prevented—insofar as this is possible—from gaining access to the Scythe Alpha and Omega operational parameters ahead of their anticipated deployment. Wings of X–7s and X–9s are being redeployed from defensive locations. The counterattacks must happen within the next four hours, which is how long the computers assess the probability of maintaining security."

Lombardi asked, "But the encryption on our hardware cannot be broken, no?"

"Indeed, it cannot," Fox confirmed. "But there remains the prospect of physical torture. Most of the captured troops have only gone through basic torture resistance training and can't be expected to hold out for very long."

Pakla asked, "General Fox, how do we know the captured troops are still close to the front line? In a similar situation, we withdraw captured warriors to the rear as soon as possible. Would the enemy not do the same?"

Fox replied, "The SHF burners on the SkyMasters can keep the area immediately above the battlespace mostly free of jamming. Thus, we are able to track their locations. Yes, there are indications that individuals are being taken further behind the lines. This is one of the reasons we must move as quickly as possible. Any further questions?"

Terry sensed the discomfort in the generals in the room and those attending remotely. He addressed them, "Gentlemen, this is a novel development. The war has been a fact of our lives for more than a year and a half. Since we began to push the enemy back two months ago, the impetus has been on our side. However, the shock of the enemy retaking the initiative in this fashion should not come as a surprise. We knew something like this would happen. We just didn't know the when or the how. Now, we do. Therefore, we must react accordingly. The troops under our command—

your command—who will carry out these counterattacks cannot be told more than is absolutely necessary."

Pakla spoke again, a cynical edge to his question, "When you say 'counterattacks', Sir Terry, do you not mean 'rescue operations'? And if that is the case, what should *our* troops do if those who have been captured cannot be rescued?"

Terry paused. He valued the Polish general, but no single one of them was indispensable. Pakla had subordinates who would likely relish the opportunity to lead the Polish First Army in battle. He replied, "General Pakla, if captured troops cannot be evacuated, then those leading the assaults will have to make the ultimate decision. The enemy absolutely cannot be allowed to gain advance knowledge of the capabilities of the Scythe Alpha and the Scythe Omega. Given that you are an experienced, professional soldier who enjoys much respect from the troops under his command, I am a little surprised I need to clarify this point of military doctrine."

Pakla's eyes dipped. He replied with the slightest hint of contrition, "Of course, field marshal."

Terry held the obvious rebuke on his tongue, not wishing to belittle Pakla, even though the Pole had asked for it. Terry said, "Very well. I would like to thank General Fox for his work. We have to be swift. It is now a quarter past the hour. On all of those points on our lines in the east and south, teams need to be selected and briefed. The counterattacks must commence before twenty-two hundred, and we need to have this unfortunate setback resolved before we can assess the rate of our retreat. That is all for now. Dismiss—"

"Field marshal?" said General Abrio of the French 2nd Dragoons. "If you don't mind to answer, when, exactly, will the improved Scythes be deployed?"

Terry replied, "In ten days. Until then, Operation Repulse is very much in the balance. Please impress this fact on your subordinates ahead of the counterattacks this evening. Dismissed."

Chapter 4

20.52 Monday 15 October 2063

C olour Sergeant Rory Moore looked down at the craggy, compact form of Sergent Jack Heaton. "Why?" he hissed, struggling to keep his anger in check.

Heaton's face stared back up at him locked in grim determination, as though carved from Yorkshire sandstone. He said, "We'll not have the same conversation again, my lad. If you've not been ordered to the briefing, it's because you're not going on whatever mission they've decided to—"

"Enough, grandad," Rory said with a wave of his arm, frustration triggering a headache behind the bone next to his left eye.

Around them, the fauna of the Spanish night carried on its languid business. A dark bat flapped overhead. Crickets chirruped close by. The warm breeze hinted at ancient olive trees kilometres away, without the scent of war.

Heaton added, "And I'll nay say any more, clear?"

"Yeah, all right."

"Dandy."

Rory watched Heaton trudge away. When the gloaming had swallowed the older man, Rory exhaled. He said, "Secure comms now. Colonel Doyle, 21st Royal Engineers."

Silence.

"Well?"

His Squitch said, "Colonel Doyle is currently unavailable. Would you like to w—"

"For Christ's sake, yes," Rory replied testily. He used the enforced pause to choke his anger down and to think clearly. Doyle would not appreciate a petulant show of emo—

"Yes, Colour Sergeant Moore?" barked the colonel in Rory's ear.

"Good evening, sir," Rory said, keeping his voice even, grateful that the communication was audio only.

"And what can I do for you? It's busy here, so I would—"

"Sir, something is happening on the line out here and I'm being kept out of it."

"And?"

Anger surged inside Rory again but he kept his focus. He said, "When I got back from Thunderclap, you told me that if I ever needed—"

"A favour? Yes, I recall. What is it?"

Rory shook his head in disbelief at having to make himself clear. "I want to be involved in whatever is happening here, sir. Op sec is preventing me from finding out."

"Wait."

Rory fell silent. Doyle had muted the call, so the colonel was either speaking to someone else about something entirely different, or getting permission for Rory to go on whatever the hell—

"Various missions are taking place tonight. They will involve local incursions back into what is now enemy-held territory. Your exemplary record means you have been placed on the reserve list and will only be briefed if required."

"I request to be put on the main—"

"You want to go on a rescue mission into enemy-held territory? There will be casualties."

"Sir, I've been six hundred klicks inside enemy territory. My experience would help the troops under my command."

There came a pause and Rory wondered if the colonel had heard him.

Doyle said, "Very well. Goodbye and good luck, Sergeant Moore."

The connection ended.

Rory muttered, "There, that wasn't so difficult, was it, sir?"

His Squitch announced: "Information: report for briefing now."

"Now?"

"Confirmed. Follow the directions in your lens."

In Rory's vision, an indicator flashed over one of the temporary staging barracks that a construction replicator had thrown up in the couple of hours since they'd retreated and paused in lower ground. Rory wondered what the point of it was—soon they'd have to withdraw further. He picked up his pace, swerving around others who were organising equipment or getting in position or following instructions. Autonomous air transports hissed behind him as the withdrawal went on while darkness continued to fall.

He arrived at the building; a bland, single-storey, windowless block constructed quickly from thin composite that would not last. He pushed the door open with care to enter as unobtrusively as possible. His view of the assembled troops became partially obscured as new data streams ran up either side of his vision. At the front of the room, a female colonel was speaking. When he looked at her, lettering resolved in the air next to her: 'Colonel Trudy Pearce, London Regiment, British First Corps'. Rory thought he recognised the name but struggled to place it.

She stood straight and looked her audience in the eye, martial professionalism suffusing her voice, "…and that's why timing will be critical. As you can see from the briefing map in your lens, the terrain is uneven. On the one hand, dead ground will likely assist us; on the other, there will be plenty of exposed positions on the way in and the way out. Squonk gives a range of two to four minutes to evac the captured troops once we reach them. However, this will vary depending on the assets we have in the air above us, how long they will last, and how many reinforcements we can get. Coordination among the teams is therefore also critical. We have several locations to attack at the same time."

Rory twitched his eye muscle to raise the map and zoomed and rotated it. He blew air through his teeth when he saw that the scattered routes to reach the captured troops all led through hilly terrain that offered steep climbs and deep gorges among the dry scrub.

Colonel Pearce went on, "In the hour and six minutes we have before the missions starts, you also need to review your in-action protocols. I don't want you relying solely on your Squitches to get you out of trouble if the enemy hits us with any surprises." She paused and stared around the room. "And that is an order. We've all been in challenging situations…"

Rory smothered a scoff given the clean, naïve young faces around him, staring in awe at the colonel.

"…and our Squitches are usually very reliable. But go back to your basic training and review what you were told then. We're going to be advancing into an environment many of you won't have been in before, outside training. We'll have hundreds of X–7s above us, and we'll advance with plenty of Falarete teams up front and flanking. But when the shooting starts, things can change very quickly. Any questions?"

From the other side of the crowded room, Rory heard Heaton's gruff voice ask with caution, "Aye, colonel. How can we be certain that these locations are where our troops actually are? That might just be where the rag–er, where the enemy has stored their gear."

Colonel Pearce nodded in consideration, "We won't know for sure until we get there."

"Grand," Heaton replied without enthusiasm.

"Anyone else?"

"Excuse me, ma'am?" asked a young voice from near the front. "When you say 'things can change very quickly', what do you mean exactly?"

Rory thought the colonel grimaced at the question, but couldn't be sure in the dim light.

She tossed her head back and replied, "The in-action protocols from your basic training use real-life examples of the enemy's tactics and behaviour since the war began. You should all therefore be aware that the enemy may still surprise us, for example with another new ACA that we haven't encountered yet. If that happens tonight, you need to be ready to take the kind of unorthodox evasive action that might save your life. In addition, what I said earlier bears repeating. If you've never been involved in close-quarters combat with the enemy, then be prepared for members of the elite corps in their ranks. Although their personal shielding can be defeated by Falaretes—and Squonk will in any case assign them target priority to the ACAs—they are likely to be driving the enemy's counterattack. We know that their primary role is to maintain discipline among the lower warrior ranks, often by driving them into battle. I'll be surprised if we don't encounter them at some point."

"Thank you, ma'am," came the response.

Rory wondered if his own experiences at the start of the war were now included in new recruits' basic training materials. The answer suggested itself.

Colonel Pearce's formidable gaze scanned her audience. After a few seconds' silence, she said, "Dismissed," and the attentive body of troops relaxed and began to melt away.

Rory stood aside to allow others to pass him and exit the barrack as he waited for Heaton. When the troops shuffled out and he glanced at individuals, his lens provided their details in the air next to them. Most were only two or three years younger than him, but he felt much older.

Heaton stood in front of Rory, his craggy face creased in an ironic smile. "It's good to see you're coming along on our little jaunt," he said.

"Looking at this lot," Rory answered with a nod to the exiting troops, "I feel as old as you, granddad."

Heaton tutted. "Come on," he replied, guiding Rory out of the building among the others.

When the troops had thinned and the night afforded them some privacy, Heaton asked, "Are you really sure you want to be on this mission, lad?"

Rory began to protest but Heaton stopped him with a wave of his hand and said, "Aye, I know you want to be treated the same as the rest of us, but this is different—"

"No, it's not, grandad," Rory broke in. "I'm sick of this bullshit 'celebrity'. I didn't intend to be Doyle's poodle and hate this... this..." Rory's frustration clouded his mind.

Heaton said flatly, "People are going to get hurt tonight. We are going to take casualties. Behind the lines."

Rory looked into the older man's eyes. He rejoined, "It won't be that bad. You remember when we were retreating back through Germany in June last year? No way can it be any worse than th—"

"Aye," Heaton broke in, "it damn well can, you Nancy southerner."

"Bollocks, grandad—"

"Did you nay think it a mite strange we've got that colonel here with us?" Heaton asked.

Rory's face creased, nonplussed. "No. Shit's going down everywhere and personnel are getting shunted all over the place. Should I care?"

"She's here because she's a loose cannon. She's popular with the ranks and Brass nay knows what to do with her."

A memory surfaced in Rory's mind. "I thought the name rang a bell. Is she the same colonel who shot those POWs back in Bli—"

"Aye," Heaton said. "And now she's here. Instead of Doyle."

"Why?"

Heaton glanced around but no other troops were nearby. He lowered his voice and said, "Brass needs an officer who will inspire the troops. You said so yoursel' how green this lot look. They've nay been in combat and tonight Brass is sending them to rescue captured troops."

"Yeah," Rory agreed, considering. "I s'pose too many have been captured for special forces to extract them all."

Heaton grunted and replied, "You think we've spare special ops guys to fix a problem like this?"

Rory said, "The ragheads were never going to let us just walk right over th—"

"Aye," the older man broke in. "And now, we're going in under a screen of ACAs he can blow out of the sky and a bunch of lads and lassies who've just finished their basic training."

Rory thought he saw something new in the sergeant's eyes: trepidation.

He opened his mouth to offer some reassurance, but Heaton spoke first, "See you at the start line."

Rory watched the older man's back as he walked away, heavy shoulders moving up and down. Rory turned in the opposite direction and strode further from the temporary barracks and into the clammy Spanish night. He shook his head in frustration at Heaton's cynicism. The movement became an odd tremor that spread out across his shoulder blades. He coughed and his upper body shuddered. This was a new and unfamiliar sensation. Since his deep clean at the Advanced Medical Research Establishment in August the previous year, he'd enjoyed almost perfect physical health.

His Squitch announced, "Caution: your heartrate and blood pressure are increasing."

Rory spun around, an irrational fear that someone was observing him fizzing his nerves. But he saw nothing save the deep blue night and warm black shadows of spindly branches close by, with the silhouettes of majestic mountains towering over them all in the distance.

The shudder ceased. He heaved in a laboured breath. Then, a shaking began in his left shoulder and moved down his left arm. A strange kind of panic grew inside him.

As if in confirmation, his Squitch said, "You are suffering symptoms consistent with post-traumatic stress disorder."

"No, I'm not," Rory insisted at once, knowing the super AI's diagnosis to be accurate.

"If symptoms persist, you will be relieved from combat duty."

"Don't even fucking say that," Rory hissed.

"Excessive profanity may be reported to your commanding—"

"Stop it," Rory demanded, hearing the note of panic in his voice. A calmer part of his brain told him that he would not win an argument against the super AI. He paused and regulated his breathing. He knew his objective and only had to take the required steps to meet it.

Minutes passed and he thought his heartrate had slowed.

"I'm fine now," he said in supplication more than insistence.

His Squitch replied, "Report to the nearest field hospital, as indicated in your lens. Diagnostic nanobots will evaluate your current level of combat effectiveness."

Rory shook his head in disbelief. He choked down his anger lest the super AI detect it and use that as another excuse to keep him away from the action. He would do as he'd been told. And if anyone tried to relieve him of combat duty, he would ignore them and go on the rescue mission anyway.

Chapter 5

21.12 Monday 15 October 2063

For the first time since she had fulfilled her destiny, confusion swamped Serena Rizzi. Cast adrift with her work complete, the alienness of the Caliphate's world terrified her. She should be dead now. The warrior's blade should've cut her throat and her spirit should've escaped with her blood until she arrived at the gates of heaven, to receive her reward for doing God's work on Earth.

But instead, she shivered uncontrollably as she lay on her side on the cold stone floor of the kitchen, where the warrior had thrown her and Tiphanie. Now, the broad, long room was empty except for the two women and a pair of dark, uniformed brutes who leered.

From the floor next to her, Tiphanie said, "I won't let them violate us again. We must fight them."

Serena stared back, every muscle trembling. "With what? Our nails?"

"If that is all we are left with—"

A sudden shriek from the other side of the door made both women look up. One of the guards turned as the door opened, scimitar raised, while the other's gaze remained locked on the two women.

The door creaked open and thick arms threw a small, pale body into the room. Serena recognised Liliana's waifish form at once and she assumed the younger woman must have been found and killed. But Liliana's reaction on hitting the floor told Serena that the youngest of their trio still lived, although the blood and dirt on her *abaya* betrayed her injuries.

The warrior in the doorway said, "We found that one hiding in a recess close to the grand hall."

The guard nodded in appreciation as Liliana crawled along the flagstones to join Serena and Tiphanie. He replied, "Good. Thank you, sir. Another one for the men to fuck."

The warrior in the doorway admonished, "You are not to touch them. The captain wants the fat one for himself. With the other two infidels, all warriors will take their turn. The captain will oversee the drawing of lots as to who will kill them when he finishes, as usual."

"But we will get on with this now, yes?"

"No," the warrior in the doorway replied. "First, the family of the house will be executed. Then, we shall burn this palace to the ground and throw the bodies of these murdering infidels into the furnace."

Serena sensed an almost workmanlike sentiment from the warrior. Although, despite their training and martial professionalism, the guards did not seem to benefit from any great level of basic intelligence.

With a nod to Serena and her sisters, the warrior in the doorway concluded with, "Look after our entertainment. Expect further orders when we have executed all members of the House of Badr Shakir al-Sayyab, shortly."

The guard closed the door to the kitchen when the warrior turned and left. He paced towards the three women and hissed, "Did you understand all that, you filthy infidel bitches? Can you understand our superior tongue? Do your implants translate what we say for you?" When the Europeans didn't reply, he turned back with a grunt of contempt.

As the three women wrapped their arms around each other, Serena felt the tremors running through Liliana's body. But the act of mutual contact seemed to calm all of them.

Tiphanie muttered to Serena, "Did that bastard say anything important that I missed?"

"No, sister," Serena replied. "Only that they will first kill Father and the family. Afterwards, we will be the 'entertainment'." She gently pulled Liliana's small body towards her and asked, "Where does it hurt?"

Liliana croaked, "Everywhere."

"Yes," Tiphanie said, urgency in her voice. "But where are you injured?"

"It is not so serious," Liliana replied in a whine that worried Serena. Liliana lifted her head and added, "Only I have also started menstruating."

Serena sighed, but Tiphanie's voice softened as she said, "That's normal, sister. It's from the stress."

Liliana shook her head and replied, "I heard what happened after they took you both away."

Serena said, "What?" in shock.

Liliana nodded and said, "I had hidden in the narrow staircase we use when we clean the upper floors, so we don't have to use the main staircase. You remember the small nooks there for storing cleaning equipment and such like?"

Serena and Tiphanie nodded.

Liliana continued, "It was not so easy to understand them. You know how I cannot cope with all of their phlegmy grunts and other noises, and in addition they were all very angry and emotional. But I tried."

Tiphanie said, "Tell us what you understood, sister."

Serena stole a glance at the guards by the door, but their eyes darted left and right, as though watching something relayed to them by their implants. She reasoned that perhaps the promised retribution on the House of Badr Shakir al-Sayyab had already begun. As if in confirmation, there came an urgent thump on the ceiling above them and distant, ghostly shrieks.

Liliana whispered, "The man who ordered you to die, sister," she began, looking at Serena. "He shouted things. He said no one must ever know what had happened this evening. He repeated that the Third Caliph's brothers knew what had occurred and then some things I did not understand fully. Although he did mention technology."

Serena said, "So, they really will hide his death."

Tiphanie insisted, "They cannot, sister."

"Of course they can," Serena replied. "With super AI and a cowed population, it would be very easy." Then she added, "But, it would mean that every single person here with knowledge of what has happened this evening would have to… die."

Liliana looked at each of them, let out a truncated sob and said, "We're going to be killed soon, are we not?"

Serena opened her mouth but the words caught in her throat when she realised she could offer the younger woman no comfort.

Tiphanie whispered, "Yes, we are, dear sister. Probably quite soon."

Serena stared at the other two. Her remaining strength deserted her. She had fulfilled her destiny and wanted only to join God. She said, "I think we should make the guards kill us before they all take turns violating us. But I have little energy left, my dearest sisters."

Liliana sobbed.

Tiphanie said, "They will not. Look at them. They will beat us even more than they have already, certainly. But they have been ordered to keep us alive."

"But," Liliana pleaded to Tiphanie, "you are strong, easily as strong as they are."

"Look at us," Tiphanie said. "We have nothing but our nails and teeth and now these animals know what we are capable of. We have only one future left."

A sudden realisation dawned on Serena. Irrefutable logic lent her exhausted limbs renewed strength, and she pulled herself to her feet. As she rose, the cotton of her *abaya* peeled off of her skin around her neck, torso and back, where the Third Caliph's blood had soaked in and dried while she'd lain on the flagstone floor.

The two guards saw her movement and at once readied their weapons. The taller, heavier-set one sneered and said, "What is it? Desperate for a fuck from proper men already?"

Serena stood upright, and sensed Tiphanie do the same to her right. She focused and spoke their tongue in her most imperious voice, like Father's wife. She said, "Do you honourable warriors not understand the full implications of what I and my infidel sisters have done this night?"

She paused, idly wondering if the brutes were sufficiently intelligent to be able to deduce the conclusion.

"Be silent, infidel. Whatever you may understand of our language and that conversation, the punishment for us for killing you now would not be great."

She decided they were not. She said, "Every single person who knows what has happened here on this night must die."

As if to support her statement, from elsewhere in the vast palace, more distant screams filtered through the doorway and windows and the ceiling. Serena felt a twinge of regret for Father and the children, but it withered quickly. They were from a different universe—a vast, poisonous pit of congealing hate that worked only to destroy the lives of other human beings. A pit into which she'd been flung against her own will, but to do God's important work.

She repeated, "Everyone here, in this palace, must die. Tonight. Do you not understand that the Third Caliph's brothers will have ordered more warriors to come here and to obey orders to kill everyone they find—even honourable, loyal warriors like you?"

"You lie, infidel," the smaller one said with a sneer.

Next to him, the taller guard took a step forward and said, "Do not think your witch's wiles will work on us."

Serena noted his decaying teeth for the first time. She said, "Why do you think I lie? What have I to gain? You will assuredly kill us no matter what we say or do. You are big and strong warriors; we are weak and pathetic infidels."

"Silence," the smaller one repeated, raising his voice.

Serena stopped talking. She only bowed her head in mock respect and took a step back.

The door burst open with an angry squeal from its dry, metallic hinge. In the doorway stood the commander, his expression betraying agitation. He ordered the two guards, "Bring those three bitches to the main courtyard now. The situation has changed. We might have to leave this place quickly. You may kill them at once if they cause trouble."

Serena stole a glance at Tiphanie, who had bent down and was helping Liliana to her feet. "Goodbye, dear sisters," she said. "Let us not show them any weakness, if we can." She turned and led her sisters towards the guards.

With practiced movements, both guards stepped back on either side of the three women, their stubby scimitars held at a defensive angle that would allow both thrust and slash. The taller warrior nodded to the other to go first. He gave

Serena an evil stare as he withdrew through the doorway with his body turned sideways.

Serena felt the previous calm of a few hours ago return. Her sisters shuffled behind her as they made their way out of the kitchen and along the broad corridor, Lilana sniffling but Tiphanie silent. Once outside the kitchen, the distant shrieks and shouts sounded closer; the unmistakable smell of burning wood, metal and fabric stung her nose.

The smaller guard in front of her strode ahead at an increased pace. Serena, Tiphanie and Liliana followed. They passed the vast doors that led into the great hall and Serena's mind drifted to consider what they might have done with the bodies and the mess in there.

The broad, dark, colonnaded corridor stretched ahead of them. Serena expected them to turn left at the stone archway as that would take them to—

"Kill the slaves," came a sudden cry from ahead of them. The figure of another warrior appeared at the far end, under the archway. He bellowed, "Kill them now and run for your lives. Spiders are coming for all of us and will destroy everything."

Serena's calm was shattered. The word 'Spider' brought back distant memories of Doctor Benini and the Santa Maria hospital and the ceiling falling down on her and smashing her legs.

The smaller guard in front of her ran ahead, towards the far archway. Serena turned around just as Lilana let out a truncated shriek. Her heart broke when she saw the other guard's scimitar half-buried in Liliana's neck, a look of grim satisfaction on the brute's face.

Rage flared inside Serena. Hearing but not noticing a click-clacking sound, she leapt to attack the warrior. Then, the world exploded.

Chapter 6

22.02 Monday 15 October 2063

Journalist Geoffrey Kenneth Morrow cursed whatever gods there might have been in the heavens for placing him in this location at this moment in time. The noises of military chaos leaked in through the windows and the door seals. Sergeant Savage had ordered him to stay in the makeshift field canteen for the duration of the recovery operation—alone. But the distant sounds of battle had been closing for the last few minutes, and the data to which the British Army allowed his lens access remained too limited to be of any reassurance that he wasn't about to get blown to kingdom come.

He glanced up at the ribbed ceiling struts—heavily shadowed in almost complete darkness—and wondered if a Spider or Lapwing were zooming in overhead to blast or burn him. While the limited data feeds in his lens reassured him that the flimsy building was not currently under attack, Geoff trusted the technology less as the violence closed in.

He muttered aloud, "What if a Siskin gets this far? What then? It'd be over pretty quickly." He shook his head and stared at his hands, clasped around a cold, empty mug that, fifteen minutes earlier, had contained hot tea. "And what kind of name is 'Siskin' for such a weapon anyway, for Christ's sake? Siskins are tiny, sweet little birds—"

A comms indicator flashed in his view. He cursed and raised it.

"Update, Geoff," his boss, Alan, demanded without ceremony.

"Yeah, I'm fine, thanks for asking," Geoff answered with sarcasm. "Hope the weather's nice over there in London." He continued when Alan ignored him. "Savage has told me to stay at the temporary barracks, in this grotty little canteen while they go on their 'rescue mission'."

"Oh? How bad is this new weapon of the enemy's, exactly? We've got conflicting reports here and even my contact inside the MOD is stalling, which tells me it might be worse than it seems."

"Savage only says it is, quote, 'a load of old bollocks', unquote. He's not the most expressive guy—"

"You're a journalist. You know the ropes. You've been embedded with those Royal Marines for months now. Why can't you get him on side? He should be confiding in you like you're best buds. Other outlets are leading with all kinds of unattributed titbits that they can only be getting from troops close to the front li—"

"Because the guy's a fucking animal," Geoff protested. "They all are. And they still treat me like I'm either as bad as the enemy or like I'm some kind of pet, albeit there to be abused."

"Get back to the point, Geoff. How bad is this 'Siskin'? How much better is it than our weapons?"

Geoff sighed before answering, his thoughts driven by a positivity bias he knew well from his work. He replied, "No, I honestly don't think it's as bad as people make—" Geoff broke off when the noise of air and ground vehicles surged outside. "Look, Alan, I've been in enough shit in this war to know when to make what the army would call a tactical withdrawal, and if I'm honest—"

"That'd be a first—"

"Not now, Alan. If I'm honest, I think we—meaning all of us—are getting slack with overconfidence. Repulse has gone too well so far."

"It's been a long way from perfect, Geoff... Geoff?"

Geoff had paused, the increasing commotion distracting him. Memories of the monorail incident in Spain eighteen months earlier resurfaced as though his subconscious was trying to warn him of a similar, mortal danger. As if in confirmation, something heavy crashed into the ground outside. For a moment, the field kitchen juddered as though an earthquake were beginning. Geoff decided he didn't want to be paralysed from the neck down again.

"Gotta move," Geoff muttered, ending the connection with London. He let go of the mug and made for the door. At the same time, the evacuation protocol activated in his lens, telling him to follow directions to the location of a British Army autonomous air transport outside that would take him away from the approaching danger.

He opened the door and a wall of heat hit him. On the rocky ground lay the misshapen remains of a downed ACA, the erratic flashes of flames it emitted causing shadows from the small shrubs close by to dance. Figures hurried past, in military uniform and carrying weapons, but running with the urgency of imminent threat.

Geoff leapt outside and turned north to follow the directions in his lens. Flashes of light from above made him glance skywards. Bright lines of white and yellow lit the night sky and hisses both near and far split the air. Geoff ran in the direction indicated. The rocky ground of the low Carpathians forced him to concentrate in the darkness to make way. An ache in his chest reminded him how unfit he had become.

At length, he approached the evacuation site. He slowed to a fast walk, his lungs heaving in the warm air that carried a tang of burnt thyme. He became aware of others converging at the same location, and realised the troops would all be following orders given by their Squitches. Again, he cursed his lack of access; on the other hand, he told himself, perhaps when the soldiers saw he was an embedded journalist instead of a freelance, they might help him, for example by letting him board the evacuation AAT more quickly.

His hope would soon be put to the test. He slowed to walk when the land flattened, further away from the rocky outcrops that marked the Polish/Czech border. His journalistic sense prickled when he noticed similarities among the orderly lines of troops around him. Now he was closer to them, he saw that many laboured with heavier loads than he'd witnessed the Royal Marines carrying when everything had been going to plan. But more than that, the faces were creased in anger. He hadn't seen NATO troops looking this pissed off since the start of Repulse, because, as in the previous year, the enemy was once again forcing them into reverse.

A voice in front of him yelled, "Come on, leg it."

An abrupt hiss announced the arrival of a large, bulbous autonomous air transport. The ugly Boeing 818 touched down and doors on the fuselage either side of the starboard wing slid up. At once, the troops at the heads of the lines hurried forwards. Geoff joined one of the lines but, without instructions, he decided he'd just have to blag his way—

"Morrow?" a sudden voice sounded in his ear.

He spun his head left and right but could not see who'd addressed him.

The voice spoke again, "Get to the AAT in front of you. Don't worry about the queues. You're slated to go out on this one."

"Okay," Geoff answered, the speaker's nonchalance irrationally unnerving him further. He exited the line and strode to the Boeing's entrance. "There's no way all of the troops are going to fit in this thing," he said to the fresh-faced squaddie he chose to push in front of. Belligerence creased the girl's pale skin before, Geoff assumed, her Squitch must have told her who he was.

She answered in a Scottish brogue that Geoff barely understood, "Dinnae fash yirsel. Thare wull be anither in a minute."

Geoff just nodded like he agreed and stepped up onto the retractable footplate. Inside, the aircraft smelled of stale sweat and hard metal. He sat in a pull-down seat near the front of the fuselage and strapped himself in.

When he looked at the other soldiers on the opposite side of the aircraft, he noticed for the first time how young they all were. Savage and his fellow Royal Marines had tended to be career soldiers in their early twenties to mid-thirties, but this AAT looked to be full of teens. Geoff suddenly felt old.

The troops began talking to each other, young men and women with accents ranging from Scotland to the north of England.

"Ah, did ye see that?"

"Aye, the mechies are gonna be toast."

"This is the same shit what happened this morning at the border."

"Yup."

"The mechies dinnae get clear in time."

"Weren't no time to get cl—"

"Shit."

"Those wee fucking nasties are coming in too quickly."

A sterner voice yelled, "Brace, brace."

The inside of the aircraft lit up with a burst of bright orange light. Geoff felt the fuselage tip over. Panic gripped him until he realised the Boeing had in fact lifted off.

The sterner voice boomed out, "Everyone shut the fuck up now and stand by in case we have to emergency evac. Listen to your Squitches. We're going on a picnic."

Geoff closed his eyes and kept his head down. His heart hammered in his chest and questions swirled in his head: where was Savage and the other Royal Marines? He'd only been left in the field canteen for fifteen minutes—the time it had taken him to drink his mug of tea—and now he was being withdrawn with a bunch of kids in uniform. Was Savage even still alive?

Flashes of light from the sky outside lit the troops' faces, and Geoff saw anger and frustration on them. He turned to the soldier on his right, an intense young woman with impossibly well-plucked eyebrows. "What's happening?" he half-shouted above the noise of rushing air.

She spied him with a frown before her features relaxed and she answered at a similar volume, "They're pulling us back."

"No shit?"

"You dinnae ken, but if what I can see is the same shit all along the lines, then we are totally fu—" she broke off and then muttered, "Aye, sarge. Sorry, sarge," and gave Geoff a shrug as if to say she'd said too much.

Geoff lowered his head and sifted through the data feeds to which he did have access. He could only confirm his location to within one kilometre and that they were already descending. "And where the hell am I supposed to go next?" he muttered to himself.

The AAT came to earth with a soft bump. The youngsters around Geoff followed well-practised training, unclipping their straps and retrieving their weapons. He remained seated until the majority of troops had shuffled out of the hatchways.

The same voice that had told him to get on the aircraft a few minutes earlier now told him to get off and go to the rear to find land transport away from the front. Geoff did not wish to argue. Out in the open with his feet back on solid if sandy ground, the horizon in the direction from which they'd come glowed orange. He stomped away from the AAT and, as he expected, the aircraft rose high enough to fly over the spindly trees and sped back towards the distant, shimmering inferno.

He reached a decision and twitched his eye.

Alan's voice sounded in his ear. "You on your way out, right?"

"Yes," Geoff replied, fists on hips as he stomped towards the rear area.

"Good. I want you to—"

"I've had enough, Alan," Geoff said, trying not to wonder how the hell he'd survive in London without a regular income. "I've been thinking about it the last few days and I'm done in."

"Shut up and let me finish," Alan replied, irritation in his voice.

"Whatever," Geoff said with a sigh.

"I want you to go to Paris. The army has asked all outlets to withdraw or otherwise sideline their embeds 'during the current situation', so you're not going to be any use there now anyway."

Geoff stopped walking. "Why Paris?" he queried.

"Something important is going to happen there in a few days, and I thought you'd appreciate a little downtime."

Geoff's journalistic instincts came back refreshed. "If it's important, you'd send a more senior hack than me."

Alan chuckled and replied, "Of course. The city will be heaving with hacks as well as VIPs, and there'll be lots to do for all of you."

Geoff didn't expect an answer, but he asked the question anyway, "So what's it all about, then?"

"Can't say, but it should be safe enough for the likes of you. I've made sure the army knows where you need to go, so get there. Got it?"

Geoff stared into the darkness, outlines becoming clearer as his eyes adjusted. An indicator flashed in his view to show where he had to go to continue his journey. He replied, "Sure. Assuming those bloody Siskins don't drive us all the way back to the English Channel in the next few days, I'll be there."

Chapter 7

22.17 Monday 15 October 2063

Rory Moore descended through the shrubs and trees, relieved to be leading his troops down into dead ground after the stress of crossing the ridgeline behind them. His boots gripped the sandy ground; his Pickup, cradled in his arms, provided comfort; his Squitch laid all the relevant data out for him in his vision. His relief at being on an active combat operation carried an irony, given that now, advancing through enemy-held territory, his physical stats could be off the charts and the Squitch would regard that as acceptable.

Unlike Operation Thunderclap and the necessity then to wage war as though he'd been fighting in the stone age, now he went to work with everything a modern soldier needed. He didn't have to communicate with stupid hand signals, and his subordinates didn't have to adhere to arcane analogue routines to ensure they didn't get killed.

He paced on, moonlight that his Squitch used to enhance his vision hueing the terrain a greyish-yellow. He paid equal attention to the data streams in his display and his footing. He led a platoon of twenty troops, including a four-person mobile Falarete team who followed behind his own unit of four. All five units advanced at distances that ensured a sudden enemy attack would cost the fewest possible casualties.

Fifty metres on his right, Sergeant Jack Heaton led a similar platoon. On Rory's left, a sergeant he'd never met before, a woman called Parker, also led a platoon in support. This three-pronged advance—with Rory in the vanguard—intended to recover a group of US Marines who had been overwhelmed the day before on the introduction of the Siskin to the battlefield.

His Squitch advised, "Caution: uneven terrain ahead. Follow directions. Increase your pace to match the anticipated arrival of assets in the battlespace."

Rory trod on a large stone and let out a grunt when it shifted under his weight. He slid a metre to a patch of flat ground and stumbled but kept his balance.

"You have reached the perimeter. Release Pathfinders and stand by," his Squitch instructed.

Rory crouched down and waited, placing one hand on the dirt, his Pickup leaning into his opposite shoulder, barrel pointing skywards. From behind him came an almost imperceptible shuffling as the responsible troops in the platoon released the small countermeasures. In his enhanced vision, he watched eight of the devices trot off ahead to attempt to trigger any dormant Spiders the enemy might have placed to defend its newly retaken territory.

His Squitch spoke again, delivering news that made Rory's heartbeat accelerate, "Probability of enemy detection at one hundred percent."

"Still no attempts to jam the battlespace?" he asked in a whisper.

"Negative. Any such attempt would offer no tactical benefit."

"Hmm," he murmured. Although all NATO troops knew about the new SkyMasters and their improved SHF burners' ability to prevent enemy jamming over the battlespace, Rory expected the Caliphate to deploy a countermeasure to it, sooner or later. He twitched an eye muscle to contact Heaton and said, "All okay with you, grandad?"

"Aye. Do you really need to ask?"

"They know we're here."

"That's nay the point."

"If the ragh—" Rory broke off when a silent, orange glare erupted in his vision. It curled into a ball and rose into the sky. A boom followed and the ground juddered. "Game on," he muttered.

His Squitch announced, "Prepare to advance."

Heaton's voice sounded in Rory's ear, "Ready for a wee jog, laddie?"

"Not a problem for—"

"Follow the countdown displayed now and advance in the indicated direction," his Squitch broke in.

The countdown on the right of his vision decreased to zero. He leapt ahead, trusting that the ground under his boots—lit only by the digital enhancement his lens offered—would not deliver any more surprises. On his right, to the southeast, another vast flash pierced the night sky less than one klick away. At the same time, the air over him came to life with the hiss of the first waves of Scythes entering the battlespace. Adrenalin heightened the clarity of sounds and the scent of the warm, still night air.

He descended further into the ravine, hoping to reach the bottom quickly. He had to devote his full attention to his feet lest he stumble again and suffer an injury. He sensed movement and urgency from the other troops following him. More tongues of orange and yellow flashed overhead when the

Scythes met the new enemy machines. Seconds later, the air split with the shrieks of the ACA clashes.

He had to leap to avoid a furrow in front of him and landed with crunch on a gravel path. He paused, beathing hard. In the left of his view, a number blinked, denoting how many seconds he and his troops were from direct attack. The digits changed at random, not chronologically, depending on the current conditions. Fifty-two seconds abruptly became four minutes and eleven seconds.

He trotted along the path, praying that no debris from the ACA battle overhead would fall and squash him before his Squitch could warn him.

His Squitch said, "Accelerate your pace. Detonation of sentry Spiders has alerted the defending enemy to your presence. The risk to captured personnel has increased."

Rory cursed between breaths. His display led him off the mountain path and downhill again. Finally, he reached the bottom of the ravine, where trickled the remains of a river. The impression came to him that getting back out of the danger area was going to involve some hard climbing. He silently hoped that some of the marines would be injured and require a medical evac, as that would force the super AI to bring autonomous aircraft in to lift them out. If the prisoners were by some miracle unharmed, it would be the hard way out.

He slipped again, this time on the stump of a withered shrub, but still kept his balance. A downed ACA whined and smashed into rocks on his right with a hard, dull thud. The flash revealed the broad, stony bank of the river.

His Squitch instructed, "Wait and prepare to advance."

Grateful for the respite, Rory enhanced the data feeds in his view as his troops arrived on the stones behind him. Heaton's platoon were forming up fifty metres to the east, on Rory's right, while Sergeant Parker's platoon formed up to the west.

Rory opened comms to his platoon and said, "Any issues?"

A Private Ravenhill replied, "Sorry sir, but I've hurt my foot a bit."

Rory frowned in confusion. "What did your Squitch tell you to do?"

"Withdraw, sir."

"So why didn't you?" Rory asked, dismayed he even had to ask.

"Didn't want to be thought a coward, sir."

"Jesus." Rory fought back the flash of anger. Basic training for all troops drilled them on understanding that there was nothing heroic about continuing with a minor injury that would likely worsen in battle conditions. He sucked in a calming breath and replied, "Withdraw now if you can do so safely, roger?"

There came an apologetic, "Yes, sir. Sorry, sir."

Rory said, "The same goes for any of us who pick up an injury. Do what your Squitch tells you. All biometric data is recorded so, post-action, there'll be no doubt if your withdrawal was justified."

New indicators flashed to confirm that Heaton's and Parker's platoons were in position. His Squitch told him to advance. Rory walked towards the trickle of water, trying to identify any hidden pools among the stones and dead branches that might swallow up his boot and leg. There came a lull in the air battle overhead and he heard the steps of his troops crunching behind him. He leapt forwards and his boots splashed towards the objective. Halfway across the stream, he came to a large tree trunk and thanked whatever gods existed for giving him long enough legs to surmount it in a single stride.

"Caution," his Squitch announced, "enemy warriors are anticipated to be waiting in ambush at the indicated location."

"Shit," Rory cursed, immediately crouching next to a large boulder. A red icon blinked in his view to denote the warriors' hiding place. He said, "So, when will a Scythe clear them?"

"Due to the density of the rock and the probable location of captured personnel, that is impossible."

"But a Scythe will flush them out, right?" Rory asked, appalled at the prospect of having to engage enemy warriors with no ACA backup.

"Affirmative. However, prolonged ACA support is currently unavailable."

As if to confirm the super AI's statement, the narrow, inverted triangle of sky visible to Rory from his location at the bottom of the ravine flashed white and orange when the remains of another ACA twisted and whirled to destruction.

"Standby to advance and engage the enemy," his Squitch announced.

Rory tensed and drew in a deep breath to steel himself. He thought of all the young troops in the ravine around him, all receiving precise, individual instructions from their own Squitches. The sounds of boots splashing through the trickling stream behind him echoed on the dry rockface.

The air hissed with the sudden arrival of a single Scythe. It halted high and off to Rory's left. The rock formation in front of it immediately cracked and popped under the intense heat from the invisible laser pulses. Its supporting fire delivered, it sped into the sky and disappeared.

"Advance where indicated, now," his Squitch said.

Rory forced his legs forwards. He held his Pickup ready. A digital line guided him onto a path that wended between two sides of jagged rock. The stench of brackish steam and burned foliage invaded his senses.

"Aim and fire where indicated."

Without conscious thought, he fired short bursts up at a black void in the darkness. Over the sound of his own weapon, he heard other NATO troops firing, which reassured him.

His Squitch instructed, "Cease fire and advance where indicated."

He hurried further along the path and turned right, the digital indicator leading him onto rocks from which steam still wafted. Rory cursed at realising he'd have to climb. He slung his Pickup over his shoulder and gingerly trotted up the uneven path cut into the rock, in places only a few centimetres wide. The surroundings lit up with more explosions overhead.

Heaton suddenly spoke in Rory's ear, "We're closing on your position."

"Thanks, grandad. Sergeant Parker?"

Parker's laconic voice replied, "Western flank is secure, so far."

Volleys of gunfire flashed from below, where Rory had been seconds earlier, directed at the same location. The rapid punches into the rock ahead and above him made a shudder run through his limbs. The body of a warrior slid with a wet scrape over the edge and flopped down onto an outcrop below, motionless.

Rory advanced towards the foreboding darkness. He focused on the objective, trying to blot out the screeching ACAs in the sky above him and the platoon's worsening tactical situation as relayed to him by the numbers in his display. He steadied himself with one hand but withdrew it before the hot rock could blister his palm.

"Fire now where indicated," his Squitch said.

"Shit," he repeated, struggling to keep his balance while he unslung his Pickup.

The troops below opened fire once more.

"You must advance now," his Squitch insisted.

"I know," Rory replied in frustration. He trod with caution towards the black entrance where at least one member of the enemy's elite cadre resided. He fired and chunks of rock split and broke and flew out into the air.

A new hiss seared the air when one of the mobile Falarete teams fired. A flash of bright light streaked past Rory and into the cave entrance, followed by a piercing human shriek.

Rory's Squitch said, "Advance where indicated and deploy an FT-23 to secure the cave entrance."

He hurried along the treacherous ledge of uneven rock. With his free hand, he reached into his webbing and extracted a small Footie. An indicator in his view flashed red to confirm that his Squitch had armed the bomblet. An overwhelming urge of self-preservation made him stop short of the entrance and toss the Footie sideways with a flick of his wrist.

He backed off and sensed rather than heard the other soldiers who had come up behind him. There came a deadening thump and a small cloud of smoke wafted from the entrance.

"Do not move," his Squitch instructed.

Gunshots rang out from the opposite side of the ravine. Rory heaved a sigh of relief, realising that the super AI must've placed some of Parker's troops there for this eventuality.

When the firing ceased, his Squitch said, "Stand by to advance."

From behind Rory, a Pathfinder trotted ahead on its four metallic legs and entered the cave.

Rory waited to see if it would trigger a dormant Spider. He hoped not: this close, he could imagine a detonating Spider lifting the entire rockface skywards, and all of them along with it. The time-to-attack figure also concerned him. It had remained steady at plus or minus two minutes. Now it fluctuated from as little as twenty seconds to nearly five minutes. Whatever was happening in the wider battlespace, it had to be costing a lot of Scythes to allow this extraction.

"Enter the cave and fire at the highlighted targets."

Rory did so, ignoring the unpleasant sensation of his sweat stained uniform sliding over his skin. He turned and entered the darkness. His Squitch lit one target crouching to Rory's right. He fired a short burst and the warrior slumped to the rocky floor.

"The battlespace is secure," his Squitch announced. "Advance to the last known location of the captured personnel."

"What about boobytraps?" Rory asked as he moved deeper inside the cave.

"None detected at this time."

"One dormant Spider in here and I'm mincemeat."

"The Pathfinder did not trigger any such munitions."

"Gee," Rory said in a voice thick with sarcasm, "I hope the enemy hasn't introduced a newer version yet."

"The probability is less than three percent."

Rory opened comms. He said, "Moving towards the last known location of the hostages."

"Roger," Heaton replied. "Western perimeter secure out here."

Rory reached the warrior he'd shot and glanced at the crumpled form. He said, "Dead raghead at this location, although I think he might've already been dead before I got to him."

Parker said, "Eastern perimeter is getting hot. Squitch says we're good for two minutes but to the south there's a lot of ACA activity."

Rory's Squitch announced, "Captured personnel detected, three metres ahead."

Rory arrived in a dank cavern. Several bodies of US Marines lay scattered.

"One member of the captured personnel remains alive," his Squitch said.

Rory lowered his Pickup as two soldiers overtook him and hurried to the injured marine.

"It's a mess in here, people," he said by way of an update.

Heaton answered, "It's nay a picnic out here, either, laddie."

Rory watched while one of the soldiers placed a battlefield GenoFluid pack on the head of a marine. "Confirm the remaining hostages are dead."

His Squitch replied, "Confirmed."

Rory said nothing but a ball of anger began to spin in his stomach. Of course, they had to attempt a rescue; every soldier had to know that if the tide of this war turned against NATO and they too ended up captured, they could expect a rescue attempt. But the super AI's forecast of success had remained low. The only way to increase the probability of getting at least some of the captured troops back alive was to mount the operation as soon as possible. That meant there would be no time or facility to collect and return the bodies of NATO troops. Such recovery would have to wait until the ground was recaptured—if it ever was.

"Status?" Rory asked the troops in front of him.

A young man's eyes looked back at him with professionalism that failed to conceal their owners' fear. "She needs to be air-evac'd, sir," he said.

"Can you move her?"

"I think so. She's lost a lot of blood due to bladed injuries but the bots can keep her brain oxygenated for up to twenty minutes."

"Okay, that's good. No problem," Rory said, trying to sound as though the situation were still under control. "Get her on a stretcher and let's move."

The soldier who hadn't spoken laid his Pickup on the floor. He unzipped the front of his tunic and slid out two linked rods, each fifty centimetres long. Laid perpendicular to the casualty, the rods extended lengthways, the linkages extended between the rods, and a gossamer-thin pale material unrolled from the rods.

Rory turned back and strode for the entrance, dismayed that a mission that had sought to rescue eleven captured marines would return with only one—if they could get her to proper help in time. Many of the troops in the three platoons also carried battlefield stretchers that were now no longer required.

"Caution," his Squitch announced. "A Lockheed BFX–6 is inbound and will land in approximately forty-four seconds."

Rory yelled behind him to urge the soldiers carrying the injured marine, even though their own Squitches would be impressing on them the importance of getting the casualty out.

Heaton's voice sounded in Rory's ear, "Step on it, laddie."

Then his Squitch said, "Danger. The strategic situation is deteriorating. You must withdraw as quickly as possible."

Rory said nothing. He trod down the rough-hewn path, checking the stretcher-bearers as they followed him and offering cautions and advice on where they should place their boots on the treacherous rocks. The required caution to get the casualty down ate up precious moments.

They arrived in safety at the stony stream. A gentle but deep hiss split the air as, in complete darkness, the small Lockheed descended and set down on the stones with a crunch. The BFX–6 was less than half the size of the more common BFX–12, little more than a small shuttle that could carry four people, two of them prone with injuries. Rory realised he would be obliged to climb his way out.

The stretcher party arrived at the transport, breathing heavily.

Rory gave them a smile and said, "It's your lucky day, troops. Get in there and get out of here."

In a fluid movement, they carried the casualty through the oblong hatchway that had opened to receive them. It closed and the aircraft increased power.

Rory opened comms to all troops in the three platoons. "Let's get back to our lines, now, people. It's only a couple of klicks, a short jog. Move as your Squitches tell you. Falarete teams keep sharp."

Parker then contacted only Heaton and Rory. She cautioned, "We've got movement on the high ground above us."

Before he could reply, Rory's Squitch said, "Danger: enemy combatants are closing on your position."

Rory said, "So bring in a Scythe to deal with them."

But his Squitch replied, "That option is unavailable at this time."

"Why?" Rory demanded, although he could guess the answer.

"All airborne assets in the battlespace are employed defending your positions from enemy ACA attack. Note that this defence is time-limited. You must retreat now."

The Lockheed lifted off the stony riverbed and rose into the night sky, only a grey outline visible as the AAT flew without lights. A flash of envy inside Rory vanished when a volley of shots thudded into it. The aircraft's shielding held and one of its small, underwing engines spun. The machine turned north and accelerated away before any material damage could be inflicted on it.

Rory trod over the wet stones without slipping and reached the other side of the ravine. More gunshots rang out above him. Parker's curt voice sounded in his ear, "We're in a contact. The warriors above us are from the elite cadre."

Rory swore. They didn't have time for this. He opened comms to Heaton and Parker. "We've got two minutes to get through them before we lose aircover."

"Aye, lad," Heaton replied. "That's the job of the warriors up there: to keep us from escaping till a wee Siskin can toast us."

Parker interjected, "That's not a certainty, sergeant. Both sides are bringing reserves up. This sector is the centre of the action across the entire front."

Rory ended the communication when a wave of nausea swept over him. He knew at once what it signalled, so he caught his breath and tensed every muscle in his body. "Not now," he hissed, his head lowered. He fought to control the surge of trembling that began at the top of his spine and ran out to his arms. Then, it vanished when his Squitch said, "Aim and fire now where indicated."

.

Chapter 8

22.34 Monday 15 October 2063

Serena returned to consciousness surrounded by heat, flames and an overwhelming sense of chaos. Confusion swamped her spirit: how had she arrived in hell? She'd served God as he'd guided her. After months of pious patience, He had provided her with the opportunity to avenge the Devil's brutal attack on her beloved Italy.

How then could she now find herself in the Evil One's foul domain?

Confusion gave way to pain. Stinging, aching, burning pain. Serena clung to the belief that this was her punishment for some unknown act that must have upset God, but as the seconds passed, a more grounded common sense told her that she still lingered in the corporeal world. Therefore, she deduced, her work remained incomplete.

She pushed herself up and opened her eyes. Dry from the heat, she blinked and moisture eased the irritation. In front of her, Liliana's burnt remains lay slumped over a damaged wall like a broken doll. Serena could only be sure the charred body belonged to her sister because she recognised the width of the hem of her *abaya*, and recalled the previous week when they'd repaired it together, restitching the garment to make it shorter.

Serena rose to her hands and knees, her senses returning and informing her of congealed blood on her legs, back and shoulders. She turned to take in the burning palace and her muscles and joints protested. Glancing at her surroundings, incredulity grew that she could've survived the Spider's destruction. In turn, this served to reinforce her hardening conviction that she still lived for a reason.

"Sister?"

She turned her head on hearing the faint, strangled plea over the crackling flames and distant thuds of collapsing rubble.

"Sister?"

Serena saw Tiphanie lying some way among the debris. She stood and went to her. As she moved, she gathered the shreds of her *abaya* around her lower legs. She reached Tiphanie and said, "Let me help you."

Serena crouched, moved splintered wood and swept dust from Tiphanie.

"Does it hurt?"

"Yes," Tiphanie croaked, "but that does not matter now. Is Liliana truly dead?"

"Yes," Serena said. "She is with Him now, enjoying His mercy."

Tiphanie grunted and struggled to sit up. She said, "I do not wish to complain, sister, for you look to be worse than I, but my skin stings all over my body."

Serena grasped Tiphanie's hand and replied, "Mine as well. Do not move if it hurts you so."

Tiphanie shook her head, "We must go from here."

The thought had not entered Serena's head. She said, "Where can we go? We still have the implants, remember?"

But Tiphanie said, "Father restricted their use against us, so only he had the power of life and death over us. You told me so yourself."

"Yes, but that cannot apply now, can it? Father and the entire family must be dead."

Tiphanie sighed and replied, "I do not know. But if we can, we should leave here."

"Let me help you stand." Serena put her arms under Tiphanie's and pulled. She felt the woman's body stiffen and Tiphanie groaned. Serena's own injuries pained her as well, but, in each other's arms, they rose to their feet.

Tiphanie held on to Serena's slighter frame. The Frenchwoman sobbed.

Serena repeated, unsure, "Where can we go? We are thousands of kilometres—"

Tiphanie pulled back from the embrace and Serena saw the familiar twinkle in the woman's eye. She said, "Do not think about that now. We must take one step at a time. For now, we should get away from here. The city lies to the southwest. We can try to reach it under cover of dark—"

"You there! You slaves."

Serena turned with care not to aggravate her injuries. Her spirit fell on seeing Ahmed striding towards them. Tiphanie pulled away and began limping towards the mangled and burnt body of one of the guards close by. Serena thought Tiphanie would attempt to escape, but then realised she was trying to retrieve a scimitar.

Ahmed was not alone. He strode at the head of a formation of eight warriors.

A familiar sensation resolved inside Serena. Just a few hours earlier, she had ended the Third Caliph's presence on Earth and sent him to the Underworld. There was nothing this minion of the barbarians could do to her now.

Tiphanie returned to Serena's side gripping a short scimitar behind her back. She said, "I had hoped we might have a chance."

Serena replied, "I have achieved everything I set out to, dear sister."

Tiphanie grunted again and replied, "I have not. They have killed poor Liliana. They will probably violate us. I think they have to pay a price, hmm?"

Serena shrugged. "We may try, sister."

When Ahmed drew closer, he pointed a bony finger at the women and yelled, "Computer, kill these slaves at once," in echo of the fat man who had said the same thing earlier in the evening.

A rivulet of blood ran down Ahmed's face, but his sneer of revenge meant nothing to Serena. She closed her eyes and prayed that now, finally, she would be freed to join the one true God.

As before, nothing happened.

Ahmed turned to the warriors behind him. He said, "Kill these two infidels, now."

The warriors lumbered towards Serena and Tiphanie. Serena closed her eyes, relieved only that she and her sister would not have to endure any more violations before they died.

Tiphanie yelled with an anger tinged with physical pain. Serena heard a truncated gasp and the sound of a body collapsing to the ground. She decided to open her eyes to confirm that her sister had been killed. But when she did so, Tiphanie stood alone and unmolested, holding the scimitar in a defensive posture, as though waiting to be attacked.

In front of Serena, the warriors' eyes bulged from their sockets and their weapons dropped from their hands as they reached for their throats. A look of horror spread across Ahmed's face. He pointed an accusing finger at Serena and spat, "You. You caused this. You killed…" His words faded and he sank to his knees. As the warriors around him collapsed in paralysed agony caused by nanobots shredding their hearts, Ahmed stared at the women, eyes also bulging, throat gagging to draw air into his lungs.

Serena, recalling the moment of her abduction in Rome, when she'd first witnessed the Caliphate's ability to kill its subjects at its pleasure, understood that now, forces greater than those Ahmed could marshal had been unleashed against him and the House of Badr Shakir al-Sayyab.

Ahmed, his heart stopped forever, fell forwards and his head slapped with a dull thud onto the stone path.

Serena stared in silence. A gentle breeze blew embers and dust through the warm night air. It lifted and flapped at the tunics of the warriors, but the bodies in the clothes remained quite still.

Tiphanie returned to Serena's side and spat, "That was a better death than any of those barbarians deserved."

"But how are we still alive?" Serena said, speaking her thoughts aloud. "I remember when they captured me and first put the implant in me. I recall that I and many others were waiting. A woman tried to escape and they killed her, just like that. So why do they not kill us now?"

Tiphanie turned and gripped Serena's shoulders. She said, "I do not know why, sister. Our implants were put in nearly two years ago. How long ago were theirs?" she asked, nodding back to Ahmed and the warriors. "There could be so many reasons. We do not know even what is happening in this awful land. You told us, months ago, that there are all kinds of factions and intrigue and subterfuge. Tonight, there is a fight among the Council of Elders. I don't know why we still live while everyone else is dead. But I do know we must flee and hide. Now."

Tiphanie's words cut through Serena's confusion. "Of course, you are right."

Tiphanie lifted her bloodstained arm and indicated the destruction all around them. "In all of this chaos, they have missed us. Let us go towards the stables."

Serena hurried and noticed that Tiphanie was limping as badly as her. She said, "The animals will be terrified, if they have been left alive."

Tiphanie replied, "Let us get there first, sister, and take shelter from this inferno. One step at a time."

Chapter 9

22.43 Monday 15 October 2063

Colonel Trudy Pearce couldn't decide if she felt sick because of the twists and turns her mobile command vehicle made, or because the overview of the rescue missions the screens gave her insisted that NATO soldiers had to die this night. After briefing the troops involved earlier in the evening, she'd decided to keep close to the front lines, not only to assist if required or necessary, but also to be able to kill any wounded enemy if the opportunity arose.

From the tactical map on the main screen in front of her, she saw which rescue platoons were in greatest danger. She ordered Squonk, "Move to shadow enemy deployments at Hill 673."

"Not recommended due to the probability of enemy ACA attack in that battlespace."

"Can't you reassign more Scythes to protect the Royal Engineers there?"

"Negative. To do so would lead to a greater number of NATO casualties in Sector Tango 43."

Trudy peered at the broader, strategic map to the left of the tactical map. "You're assuming the enemy's overall strategy is to push us back around Huesca, yes?"

"Confirmed. That objective has the highest probability."

"Based on the assumption that the enemy intends to use the Siskin to roll our forces all the way back across Europe."

"Affirmative."

As usual, Trudy distrusted the super AI's logic and wondered if the enemy had considered and estimated the probability of NATO also introducing improved ACAs. If that transpired to be the case, then the Siskin's use would be much more tactical than strategic, with the aim of punishing NATO forces rather than defeating them. "So," she asked, "the troops on that particular rescue mission are going to be killed, yes?"

Squonk replied, "Negative. The troops withdrawing from Hill 673 have been notified of the need to engage enemy warriors. Available ACA assets are defending larger concentrations of NATO troops engaged in rescue missions."

"Take me there," she repeated.

"Not recommended. If the troops withdrawing from Hill 673 do not break through the advancing enemy warriors in less than two minutes, they will likely come under enemy ACA attack."

"Take me to Hill 673, now. Don't argue."

"Confirmed."

The mobile command vehicle spun around and Trudy gasped when it seemed to fall down an almost vertical incline.

"Warnings, please," she hissed through clenched teeth.

The vehicle came level and accelerated.

"Caution: this vehicle will continue to traverse uneven terrain."

Trudy gripped the shoulder straps and tensed. She closed her eyes and wondered when she would be together again with her beloved Dan. Since finding his final resting place at the destroyed chateaux in France two months previously, she'd continually pushed the limits of her command. The field marshal's threatened court martial at Crowhurst Barracks, after she'd killed warriors during the enemy's attempted invasion of England, only carried weight as long as Operation Repulse proceeded according to plan.

Of course, her superiors would fire ranks at hers and above in the event of gross negligence, but this was almost impossible given that super AI made the majority of tactical and strategic decisions. She presumed that bad publicity might change TT's considerations, but what journalist would dare to criticise the war effort by publicising the intentional execution of wounded warriors? Especially when so many ordinary citizens had joined their country's armed forces driven by a desire for revenge?

However, despite Operation Repulse's initial success, now the enemy had struck back. She recalled the popular sentiment after the enemy's failed invasion attempt at Hastings, and how a majority of the general public favoured retribution—

She gasped when the vehicle began a climb that steepened until she thought it must tip over backwards. It crested a ridge and pitched forwards for a few seconds before rolling to a stop.

Squonk announced, "Danger: an active fire zone is ahead. Protection of senior ranks prevents this vehicle from closing—"

"Override that, by my order, Colonel Trudy Pearce."
"Confirmed."

Trudy straightened herself in her seat and peered at the main screen. She swore aloud when she saw that the three platoons had engaged enemy that included elite-cadre warriors.

"Danger: this command vehicle is certain to be targeted within two minutes. Tactical withdrawal is highly recommended."

Squonk's phrasing provoked a double-entendre of the kind Dan always enjoyed. She muttered, "As the nun said to the vicar."

"Please clarify."

"Nothing."

"You should withdraw from the battlespace."

Trudy drew in an expansive breath and said, "Nope. And stop issuing tactical cautions." She tapped a location on the screen in front of her and said, "Move this vehicle to this position."

"Your personal security cannot be guarant—"

"Shut up and do it," Trudy said, irritated that the super AI insisted on restating that of which she was already aware. "Those troops are running out of time."

The vehicle bumped and dipped over the uneven terrain. Again, she clung to her shoulder straps, frustration growing as the density of foliage caused a diversion that added precious seconds to the relocation. The vehicle stopped on the crest of a ridge, the most exposed location in the battlespace.

Her Squitch announced, "This vehicle will be destroyed in less than forty seconds."

Trudy unclipped the restraints and said, "Open the door and activate my Squitch." She leaned behind her and grabbed her Pickup from its secure mounting in the floor. She slapped a panel next to it that opened to reveal magazines of ammunition. She scooped up as many as she could with a single hand and stuffed them into her smock.

The warm night air that greeted her exit triggered more buried memories.

Her Squitch said, "Danger: you are in an active battlespace. Seek cover immediately."

Trudy clipped a magazine into her Pickup. She slapped a panel on the curved rear of the mobile command vehicle. It slid open. With her free hand, she grasped the tube of a Falarete.

She paused, a recollection suddenly removing her senses from the urgency of impending battle. The dry Spanish air smelled like a vacation she and Dan had once enjoyed. Images of vodka and tonics, the laughter, the flirting, the lovemaking surged into her mind's eye. She remembered lying in Dan's arms and his promises of how their military careers would ensure financial security for the beautiful family they would raise...

A loud crack from overhead brought her back to the moment. The data feeds in her lens guided her downhill, towards a lower ridge. She skipped and hopped over withered scrub as irregular staccato bursts of gunfire echoed below her. On the other side of the deep valley, the black ridgeline of the mountain opposite obscured more of the blue night sky, in which ACAs from both sides streaked and pitched and hissed and sought out the slightest advantage. In the distance, Trudy thought she could see a cube of fixed lights undulating high and low. But abrupt, stinging flares of white light from destroyed ACAs made her look away.

In the valley in front of her, muzzle flashes lit up the scrub and spindly branches of mostly dead trees. The battlespace was alive with mortal threats and evil screeches in the sky, but the scent of the air made all the chaos of war feel so alien and wrong.

What had Dan said? He'd promised her that they would have at least one son and one daughter. Dan loved football and wanted to have their son as soon as possible to be able to—

A jarring explosion made the ground fall away from her and sucked the air from her lungs. She rolled into the sandy dirt and fronds, seeing behind her the whole world light up with a gout of orange flame.

Her Squitch said, "Your mobile command vehicle has been destroyed. Seek cover immediately and wait for friendly forces to retake the battlespace."

She rolled onto her front. Sharp pain stabbed from her left leg, but instinct told her that the injury was not serious. She asked, "Where's the ACA that did that now?"

"Likely diverted to respond to a more urgent threat."

"How long will Squonk be able to keep the enemy ACAs off me and the troops down there?"

"Between sixty and ninety seconds."

From below came yells and shouts. She got to her feet and ordered, "Put me in their comms, now."

At once, a cacophony of voices invaded Trudy's ears in tones of urgency and frustration. As the voices spoke, their owners' names resolved in Trudy's vision:

Sergeant Parker said, "Moving up on the right fla—"

Sergeant Heaton broke in, "Is your flank clear?"

Parker replied, "My Squitch says 'yes' but I do not believe all of the enemy are accounted for."

Sergeant Moore asked, "We're pinned down in the centre. Do you have any Falaretes left?"

Parker replied, "Negative."

Heaton said, "They're trying to flood the area with jamming; my team's Squitches are getting interference."

Parker replied, "Our SHF burners must be under the same kind of pressure as the Scythes."

Moore urged, "We don't have time for this. We must break through."

While she listened to this exchange, Trudy hurried towards the line of contact. She forced memories of the life she and Dan should've shared and the children they might've raised away as the martial urgency of the situation intensified.

Her Squitch said, "Danger: you are approaching enemy combatants who are certain to be alerted to your presence. You should withdr—"

"Shut up and give me only visual warnings, no audio." With a twitch of her eye, Trudy opened comms to the three platoons further down in the valley. She said, "I'm closing on the enemy from the east. I'm about thirty metres out. When I engage them, use the confusion to get going."

Sergeant Moore replied, "Roger that. Welcome to the party, colonel."

Above her, the battle in the sky seemed to intensify. From the chaos, a plume of orange flame flickered and flashed as the ACA from which it billowed tumbled through the air. The machine hit the rock formation on the other side of the ravine. The light helped Trudy jog in irregular hops and leaps further down through the flora and rocks. She slung her Pickup over her shoulder and popped open the Falarete tube with a deft flick of her wrist.

She spoke in a lowered voice, "Select the Falarete to go for the most critical target, and I want all my Pickup mags to fire explosive shells."

She recalled briefings on the enemy's elite cadre, understood from the brain scans of injured warriors to be divided into several battalion-size units and assigned to ensure discipline among the warrior armies, in addition to serving in specialised roles. Their personal shielding was generated by small cryo-magnets located at the base of their equipment backpacks.

Indicators and warnings flashed red in her view. The temporal proximity of lethal threats narrowed until it became clear only seconds remained to her.

Trudy hoped it wouldn't hurt too much or for too long. An emptiness deep in her throat made breathing difficult. Christ, she missed Dan.

She shouldered her Falarete. Another series of bright flashes again lit the descending terrain ahead like a drunk strobe light. The sharp popping of gunshots followed.

She came down to a gravel path and stood upright with her feet on even ground. Her Squitch lit targets in front of her and just a few metres below the path—a squad of six enemy warriors crouched among the Spanish scrub shooting at the rescue party below them.

Her Squitch targeted a warrior and Trudy fired her Falarete, immediately discarding the empty tube. The projectile sped into the target and the net disabled the shielding with a green flash.

She shrugged her Pickup from her shoulder and aimed at the target the Falarete's net had hit. With the enemy warriors' attention now on her, she hoped the troops in the rescue platoons would have the wit to prosecute the advantage she'd intended to afford them.

Her display confirmed that the targeted warrior was defenceless. She fired the first burst at him, grim satisfaction frowning her face as the man leapt from the ground and tumbled over, his limbs flapping like a rag doll. She scattered the rest of the magazine among his surprised comrades. White flashes hued green threw the warriors off their feet before they could return fire, but Trudy knew there'd been less than a fraction of a second in it.

The instant the magazine emptied, she dropped to one knee, ejected the empty, withdrew a replacement, and snapped it into her Pickup. At the same time, the NATO troops below attacked.

She rose upright to more red warning indicators in her view than she could ever remember seeing before. She fired, again scattering three-shot bursts at all of the warriors she had in her sights. White flashes gave way to balls of orange flame all along their positions. But green flashes proved that, although the sheer physical power of the shells might have knocked them over, they were certain to get back up.

She repeated the manoeuvre of crouching to reload. She heard the rescue platoons she herself fought to rescue attack the warriors again, who were now caught in a pincer, and wondered if she and the platoons below might have enough time to finish them. She stood and her display told her that the remaining warriors were forming into a defensive square.

Trudy thought it quaint as she shot another magazine of explosive shells into the group, scattering the individuals once more. Additionally, her rate of fire prevented the enemy from responding effectively because everything around them that could burn was now on fire.

She crouched and reloaded, her confidence growing. But when she stood back up, a piercing, searing white light erupted all around her. There came a moment's break in her consciousness; she only blinked, but when she looked again, everything had changed. She lay on her back. The ground around her burned and her mouth was filled with the taste of dry, smoked carbon. Pain that she'd never felt before surged through her entire body and, in her agony, part of her mind wondered how she could tolerate it and yet remain aware.

A base, animal urge made her turn onto her front and try to crawl away from this place of danger. But her fingers would not function. The dirt close to her face burned her skin.

Her whole body shuddered and she couldn't draw in a breath for the agony that seized her muscles.

Suddenly, an external force pulled her over onto her back again. Part of her hoped it would be help, but a dark, masculine face peered at her with a sneer of satisfaction. She wanted to recoil or react in some way, but she still could not move or breathe. She smelled his fetid breath and recognised the hatred in his eyes—the same as the hatred that had burned inside her for so long. He held a short scimitar in front of her face, raised it, and brought it down on her neck.

Trudy's last thought was of comfort, knowing that she would be with her beloved Dan very soon.

Chapter 10

23.51 Monday 15 October 2063

Rory's limbs ached with exertion as he heaved his body up through the burning scrub with what remained of the platoon. He glanced at the back of the soldier in front of him and wondered how these new recruits were coping with the night's engagement. If he, a veteran of this war with more injuries and close calls than he cared to remember, were at the end of his tether, what might these green soldiers be feeling?

His Squitch urged, "Increase your pace. You must exit the battlespace as soon as possible."

Given that he laboured uphill in light kit, Rory lacked the breath to respond to this inanity. He concentrated on the numbers in his display and an irrational optimism began inside him that they might yet reach safety.

Like a summer thunderstorm that drifted away, the massed ACA battle in the sky lessened in intensity. It had been at least a full minute since a smashed-up Scythe had come crashing to earth. The urgency had not gone, but since

Colonel Pearce had interceded and brought them valuable seconds, time had been on their side.

Parker's laconic voice spoke in his ear, "We have reached the ridge. All opposing enemy are dead, although we've lost people as well. Conditions clear and we have a descent into dead ground ahead of us."

In a voice that suggested he was struggling, Heaton replied, "We've got one wounded who needs evacuation. Computer says 'no'."

Parker answered, "Get the casualty higher up and we'll rotate carriers."

Heaton observed, "If we could get even a small AAT in, it would help. My boys and girls nay have much experience of carrying wounded under fire."

"I assume the casualty is not critical?" Parker asked.

"Aye, otherwise the super AI might give more of a shit. The GenoFluid pack is keeping him stable but our progress is slow."

"Okay, stay quiet for now. We are not entirely in the clear yet."

Rory trudged on, his limbs becoming heavier as the adrenalin subsided, caused by a notification that German Leopard tanks had been released from the neighbouring sector to give additional cover. The time-to-attack figure increased to over five minutes and then, finally, vanished as it lost relevance.

The night air in Rory's throat took on a cooler edge and the sweat on his exposed skin became chilled. Laborious minutes passed. Finally, he and his squad reached the ridge. With the young troops around him panting, hands on hips, he said, "I need two volunteers. We've got Charlie three-zero a hundred metres that way and they need support carrying a casualty."

Two privates raised their arms and Rory led them along the broad road of rocky chips that crunched under their boots. They descended again into the scrub where Heaton's squad laboured upwards, two members carrying the casualty. Rory's squad members relieved Heaton's and together they brought the casualty to the relative safety of the road to await extraction. The sky had quietened, the massed ACA battle seemingly spent.

Five minutes later, Rory sat back in the seat of an autonomous troop transport. He looked at Heaton next to him and said, "Christ sweet Jesus. We lost three people to get one marine out of that stinking cave. What the actual fuck for?"

"Ah, laddie. You still nay get it, do you?"

"Don't give me that one-for-all and all-for-one bollocks, again. Most of those marines were dead the minute the poxy Siskin turned up on the battlefield. I don't even reckon that the one we got out will live till the morning—"

"She will."

"The whole platoon was seconds from being fried when the colonel who gave the briefing rocked up. If it hadn't been for her, we'd've—"

"Quit ye bleatin'," Heaton broke in. "You're alive, nay? Or do you wish you'd taken up Doyle's offer to be his poodle? Remember, laddie, you nay have to be here. It's your choice."

"Christ," Rory repeated, frowning, "don't remind me. I wish I could have a drink about now."

"You'll have to wait a while yet."

"Oh yeah? Why?"

"Check your Squitch."

Rory did so. He read the latest battalion orders and said to Heaton, "We're pulling back another thirty klicks?"

"Aye, back to the Pyrenees."

Rory blew air through his teeth and replied, "Wow. What if this bloody Siskin can push us all the way back to Blighty?"

"Brass will have to pull something out of the bag a mite sharpish."

Chapter 11

05.55 Tuesday 16 October 2023

Serena awoke with a start, an odd sense of having had a nightmare meshing with the return to a reality that had become all too nightmarish. Broken sleep on the fetid sand in the stables aggravated her wounds. In front of her, in the half-light of the predawn, Tiphanie's round, blue eyes stared back into hers, carrying a warning.

"Sister, wake up," Tiphanie said.

"What is it?" she asked.

Tiphanie moved aside to reveal two individuals standing in the doorway, covered with *abayas* and headdresses.

The Frenchwoman said, "I could not understand what they want, only that they want to know something."

Serena swallowed to try to get some moisture into her dry throat. She looked at the figures and croaked, "Who are you?"

One of them stepped forwards and pulled a hood back to reveal a dark, round and deeply lined female face. The woman said, "It is remarkable that an infidel can speak our tongue. Do you truly understand me?"

Serena felt an irrational fear of the woman despite her advanced years. Serena pushed herself to her feet and replied, "I do. So, with respect, honoured madam, I ask again: who are you?"

The old woman shuffled inside the stable, her taller, slimmer colleague following. She said, "I am the mother of Aziz. He was an apprentice cook in the House of Badr Shakir al-Sayyab. However, the palace lies there now in ruins that smoulder. Are you a slave from that palace? Did you see Aziz?"

Serena opened her mouth but Tiphanie prodded her in the side and hissed, "What is she saying?"

Serena replied in English, "She is looking for Aziz, the young cook. I do not think we are yet in danger."

Tiphanie's responding grunt told Serena the Frenchwoman disagreed.

Serena addressed the old woman, "I am sorry for your situation, but I do not know what became of Aziz."

"But you knew him, yes? You were indeed a slave in the House of Badr Shakir al-Sayyab, yes?"

Serena replied with a cautious affirmative, concern growing.

The old woman asked in an accusatory tone, "So why do you still live, slave? The palace lies in ruins. They are certainly all dead there. In the town we are forbidden even to mention the name of the House, for to do so will also bring death. So, how can it be that two infidels remain alive when all else is destroyed?"

The taller figure standing next to the old woman threw back her headdress to reveal a younger female, likely the daughter, Serena surmised, given the similar foreheads and narrow, dark eyes.

Serena wondered where the men might be. Two females could not be travelling alone before dawn, and certainly not in an area that had recently seen such violence. Serena glanced at Tiphanie to convey her anxiety. She looked back at the two Persian women and replied, "I do not know. But I spoke with your son just yesterday, as I did every day. He was a good man; honourable and decent. I am sorry for your loss."

Serena bowed to show her feigned respect for this hag, her would-be rapist son, and her foul culture. The stinging in her throat grated until she could hardly breathe. The certainty came back to her that her work on this Earth was complete. Why had God given her this extra vexation when she neither required nor desired it?

As if in answer, Tiphanie prodded her again and said, "Let us use them. Beg them for help; show them meekness. We are finished if we do not escape this place. And I do not want to die here. Not after what we have gone through to get this far, sister."

Serena looked at the two local women and began to frame her thoughts into language that might convince them to help. But before she could articulate those thoughts, the hag spoke: "Will you tell me about my beloved Aziz? Will you tell me about his last days before he went to Allah's comfort?"

Despite her injuries and the stress of the situation, Serena sensed something else from the hag: a mother's eternal love for a lost son. Serena looked at the younger woman and felt certain that she was Aziz's sister. She replied, "Yes, I will tell you. Do you have some water, please?"

The disdain that crossed the hag's face in response to Serena's request confirmed the woman's sense of innate superiority over the infidels. She sniffed and answered, "Very well. I will give you water. Come, both of you."

Serena glanced at Tiphanie, ready to relay the message, but Tiphanie nodded to confirm that she'd understood enough of the conversation. Serena turned back to the women and asked, "Where are your men? How can you be travelling without them?"

At once, the hag's face flashed in anger and her voice took on a bitter edge. "Because they are dead," she hissed. "My son in that place; my husband in the town last night. My daughter and I are not the only women seeking their menfolk on this morning, infidel. Now, will you tell me of the last days of my son, or will you continue to ask questions that are above your station?"

Serena again bowed and apologised in the most formal language she knew.

Tiphanie urged, "Let us go with them now, sister."

Serena said nothing as the two Persian women exited the stable. She weighed the pros and cons of following them. She had to accept that, in truth, they had no choice. With a sudden, strange foreboding, she turned to Tiphanie and croaked through her barren throat, "Perhaps we should say farewell now, sister?"

Tiphanie shook her head, "There is no need. We must still be here for a reason. Perhaps you are right and your work is not yet finished?"

Serena felt Tiphanie's hand squeeze her own as the two European women left the stable. Outside, the clear sky glowed orange and yellow as sunrise approached. The Persian women waited for them. The hag offered Serena a metal flask. Serena took it and enjoyed a sip of stale but clean water. She handed it to Tiphanie with an unspoken wish that they should not, between them, take too much. Tiphanie drank, returned the flask, and thanked the woman.

The hag placed the flask inside her *abaya* and said with a wave of her arm at the horizon, "The town is in that direction. But before we go, I must know how it can be that you both still live. Do you not have the implants?"

The woman's small black eyes bored into Serena. She decided to be honest, and given that both she and Tiphanic would otherwise be lost without these two women, it would not be wise to lie in any case. "I do not know, for certain."

"Oh?" the old woman queried.

"The Father of the House," Serena said, "ordered the computer that only he had the authority to…" Serena chose the word with care, "discipline us. I do not know how this remains the case."

The younger woman spoke, her voice light but guarded, "I have heard such things are possible, but only with certain designs of implants."

Serena asked, "Are they not all the same?"

"No," the younger woman replied. "There are many kinds."

The old woman said, "But you infidels have greater problems than that. If you were part of the House of Badr Shakir al-Sayyab like my dear Aziz…" she trailed off, letting out a sigh.

Before Serena could say anything, Tiphanie spoke, struggling to pronounce the words, "If some person would know we still lived, we would be killed at once."

"Of course," the old woman replied with a shrug. Then she stopped walking. "But you will tell me about my Aziz. And as long as there are people alive who remember him, then he is not really dead, is he?"

Serena sensed the old woman's guarded offer, but wondered how much weight it really carried. The sun's rays crested the distant horizon and the bright, fresh blue of a new day spread out above them.

Chapter 12

14.44 Tuesday 16 October 2063

Field Marshal Sir Terry Tidbury read the names on the latest casualty lists, heaved a sigh, and said, "So, Colonel Pearce, you even saved me the disagreeable task of having to court martial you."

The door to his office clicked open and Simms moved smartly through to deliver a fresh cup of tea. Simms said, "Number Ten has been in touch, sir."

Terry stifled a groan and asked, "What's happened now?"

Simms's thin eyebrows came together in a frown. He reported, "The American president is concerned, once again, that Operation Repulse is being pushed back."

"She is not alone in that feeling… Damn."

"What is it, sir?" Simms asked.

Terry pointed at the list of names on the screen in front of him and explained, "We lost Donnie Bell yesterday. I did my basic training with him." There came a pause, then Terry added, "He was too bloody old for combat, but he always liked being close to the action."

"Shall I schedule some time for you to give your condolences to his next of kin?"

Terry shook his head, "No, on the few occasions we met, his wife seemed to have a problem with me. But I want to be at his funeral, although try to keep my presence as lowkey as possible."

"Very good, sir."

"Squonk? Contact General Stud Stevens, US Airforce. If he's available, put him on my personal screen here." Terry ran his hand over his bald head. He glanced at Simms and said, "Go back out there and start contacting the section leaders, beginning with AGE, then South."

Simms nodded and left Terry's office.

Before the door had closed, Suds' face resolved on Terry's screen.

The American airman leaned back in his chair, held up a large, white porcelain mug and said, "Good morning, field marshal. Can't say there's anyone else I'd rather spend having my morning cup of Joe with."

Terry smiled, "I hope that doesn't include Mrs. Stevens."

"What she doesn't know won't hurt her," Suds replied with a wink.

Terry lifted his own mug and said, "On this side of the pond we're already on to afternoon tea."

"It's good to see you, Earl. I guess you calling now ain't just for social reasons, right?"

"Right," Terry confirmed. "Got any other 'guesses'?"

Suds frowned and the scar above his right eye deepened. "Only that I still don't want your job. How are you getting along with Torres and Roberts?" he asked, naming the two most senior US Army generals in theatre.

"Fine," Terry replied with a shrug. "They're dependable and competent commanders, just as I'd expect from the US military."

"But?"

"But I don't think they have a great deal of knowledge regarding our political masters' trials and tribulations, and they're over here, in Europe, not over there. Like you are."

Suds nodded in understanding and took another pull of coffee. He swallowed and said, "When did we last talk, Earl, you and I?"

"A week ago."

"A lot's changed since then."

"What's the mood in Washington, Suds? Your president can't seem to help but rile up everyone here. I've no time for Coll's and Napier's problems, but as I've said before, it's important her belligerence doesn't filter down to the ranks."

"I was at a function on Saturday—a fundraiser for victims of 10/13 on the first anniversary. Can you believe it's already been a year since those floods? Anyways, I was sitting next to the chief of staff—"

"Ava King?"

"Yup. I wasn't too keen on talking shop, to be honest. You know, we were there to honour the victims and praise the efforts of the first responders. She made a comment after Coll finished her speech. It was kind of arch—I don't know how well you know King, but she doesn't suffer fools too gladly. She made it clear most of the military folks in Washington are pushing back on suggestions that the rest of NATO isn't doing enough. On the other hand, the loss of so many marines—"

"That's no one's fault," Terry broke in. "And the introduction of the Siskin has cost everyone a great deal, Suds. I've had generals from almost every NATO member army talking to me about the troops they've lost in the last few days. Have you seen how far we've had to pull back?"

Suds shook his head.

Terry went on, "There are towns and villages we liberated and then suddenly we're withdrawing again. Of course, the US Marines have taken a pounding, but that was by accident, not by design."

Suds raised his free hand and patted the air as if trying to calm Terry. He said, "Earl, the point here is that you don't need to worry about anything changing in Washington anytime soon, at least as far as I know. Let our political bosses keep going at it all they want. Our job—well, your job—is to make sure the enemy doesn't push Operation Repulse any more off track."

Terry eyed Stevens and replied, "It's not really in my hands though, is it? The enemy's introduction of the Sis—"

"You're doing it again, Earl," Stevens broke in with a shake of his head. "Giving the initiative to the enemy. What about reacting to this setback? Hell, when was the last time you kicked some lower-ranking ass over our next-gen ACAs?"

Terry considered Suds' point but shook his head and replied, "Testing can't go any faster. We've got to be certain the new Scythes are sufficient to deal with the Siskin. If it were only a question of discipline, that would be solvable. You think I don't spend a portion of my time wondering what the hell hit us forty-eight hours ago?"

Suds frowned, "I don't wanna be talking out of turn here, Earl, but you need to get over that shock real fast."

Terry chuckled, enjoying sparring with probably the only NATO soldier who spoke to him on equal terms. "It's not the shock; it's managing the fallout. I've been certain since Repulse kicked off that he'd come back at us with something better. But his timing is atrocious. If he'd waited just a few more days… In any case, speaking of managing the fallout, I need to consult my field generals."

"Sure."

"Are you due to come over here anytime soon?"

Suds shook his head, "Nope. We're working on some high-spec sub-orbital countermeasures here. You've had them in your nightly sitreps, for sure, but you might've missed them."

"We'll catch up with that later. Thanks for the inside track on your side of the water."

"Anytime, Earl. Good luck over there."

Terry grunted as the American's face vanished. He grabbed his tea and strode out of his office and into the main area. Simms stood at the central console, a green map of central Europe rising high above him. Terry took in the scattered items of information and other data dotted around the jagged line of contact, which zigzagged from the Baltic Sea at Szczecin in Poland all the way down to the low, western end of the Carpathians in the Czech Republic.

"Squonk," Terry instructed, "overlay ground lost since the enemy introduced the Siskin."

"Confirmed."

Terry gulped tea down as tiny areas on the map changed from green to red. "Zoom in on the Baltic coast and track down. Add in casualty figures for last night's counterattack ops."

The image enlarged and more details resolved. Terry read it and appreciated the actual size of the territory lost and the number of personnel who had been captured, and then either recovered or lost. As the view moved south, Terry's concern centred on his troops' morale. He could well imagine the dispiriting sensation of suddenly coming under withering enemy fire, when many soldiers' commanding officers had assured them that NATO finally had the advantage.

Simms spoke, the edge of diplomacy in his voice unwavering, "Sir, General Fox is overseeing First Corps' operations. He filed an update half an hour ago noting that brigades of Germans, Poles and Czechs have taken notable losses." Simms indicated the map with a wave of his arm, "North of Staven, a salient collapsed and buried two counterattacking platoons. All of the captured troops were also lost."

"Damn. And the enemy killed them?"

"We can't be sure how they were killed. We'll conduct an investigation if and when we recover the territory."

"No one said bad luck stops for a war."

"Indeed. Further south, there was better news. The French recovered over fifty percent of a Dutch regiment that had been cut off since yesterday morning."

Terry said, "Very well. Schedule calls with the sector commanders and let the generals on those parts of the line know I will be giving some of their subordinates a peptalk."

"Very good, sir."

"Squonk? Let's see Attack Group South's contact line."

The huge map withdrew to its original size and shifted downwards and to the left. Southern France and northern Spain came into view, with a similar set of indicators and other data resolving around a contact line equally as jagged as that in central Europe.

"Zoom to show the locations of US Marine casualties."

The area of northern Spain enlarged and new flashes of light told Terry where the most marines had been captured and either recovered or lost. He nodded and said, "I recall being in that part of the world on exercises a few years ago. The terrain is a challenge."

Simms pointed out, "The highest casualties were in the three sectors north of Pamplona."

"I had better speak to the sector commanders there as well, then. Squonk, what are the totals regarding last night's counterattacks, and those totals compared to forecasts?"

Squonk replied, "Thirty-one percent of known personnel captured since the introduction of the enemy's new autonomous combat aircraft were recovered alive. Fifty-eight percent were confirmed deceased. The locations and conditions of the remaining eleven percent remain unknown. The counterattacking units suffered twenty-two percent casualties. These figures are broadly in line with worst-case scenario forecasts. Do you require a more detailed breakd—"

"No, I do not," Terry broke in testily. "What is the probability that the enemy has gained operational details of the new Scythe ACAs?"

Squonk answered, "Less than four percent."

Terry stared in silence at the display and shook his head.

Simms cleared his throat and spoke in a lowered voice, "Sir, if I might say so, I believe this was the correct course of action."

Terry held on to his temper. "Oh, really?"

"As you said yourself, in order to fight well, our troops must know that if they are captured, a rescue attempt will be made, irrespective of any classified information they might have."

"Perhaps I should eat my words a little more often?"

Simms replied diplomatically, "The tactic remains sound, sir."

Terry turned back to the display. "Forecast required withdrawals from now until we can deploy the new Scythes, first Attack Group South, then East."

The view withdrew once more until the entire Attack Group South contact line juddered across northern Spain. The line moved back to the Pyrenees. Squonk said, "The mountainous region of the Franco/Spanish border offers a number of scenarios where the NATO forces' retreat may be either slowed or accelerated. Do you wish to—"

"No, I do not. Why should that even be the case? The enemy has weapons superior to ours. Again. Why would we not be obliged to fall back in the same manner as during the battle for Europe last year?"

Squonk answered, "By maximising production lines and related facilities, sufficient quantities of Scythe X–7 and X–9 autonomous combat aircraft can be deployed to delay the enemy's advance in a manner not available earlier in the conflict."

Terry muttered, "Ask a stupid question. Now display the same scenario for Attack Group East."

The view withdrew once again and recentred on eastern Europe. Projections of the enemy's advance and NATO's corresponding retreat were more pronounced on terrain with varied elevation.

Simms observed, "One thing in our favour this time are these geographical features we will be able to exploit to slow the enemy's progress."

"It won't slow progress enough. Damn it, Squonk, when can I expect my Scythe Omega to be ready?" Terry asked. Even though he knew the answer, a part of him hoped there might have been some kind of acceleration.

But Squonk replied, "As scheduled, providing all projected operational tests are completed as anticipated."

"Which means," Terry noted ruefully, "that there might yet be further delays."

Squonk said, "The probability is less than five percent."

"And what is the probability of the enemy releasing the ACAs he has on his border with India, and what will happen to our campaign if he does?"

The super AI replied, "The probability ranges from thirty to sixty percent, but is subject to variables for which there is limited data."

Terry tutted.

The super AI continued, "However, according to available information, if the enemy were to utilise the entirety of its autonomous combat aircraft, supported by warriors, Operation Repulse would have a ninety-one percent probability of failure, being permanently reversed within four to eleven days."

"Then why doesn't he?" Terry asked in frustration.

"Insufficient data."

"So speculate, damn you," Terry almost shouted.

Squonk replied, "The New Persian Caliphate's general predisposition towards belligerence and its rigid hierarchical command structure tend to delay or prevent appropriate, timely responses to dynamic military developments."

"I think," Simms suggested, "that the computer means that given our enemy's history of violent internal struggles, those in charge may have, shall we say, been obliged to take their eye off the ball."

"You're suggesting they simply have too much going on elsewhere to fully appreciate the advantage that deploying the Siskin has given them?"

Simms replied, "We know from the brain scans of wounded warriors that there are regular attempted coups and uprisings in areas of his territory that have significant minorities from sects who are not represented on the Council of Elders. Perhaps something is happening inside the Caliphate which demands the Third Caliph's undivided attention?"

Terry looked up at Simms and replied, "Yes, if he's had another challenge to his power—perhaps some members of the Council of Elders aren't keen on a nuclear confrontation with India?—he might tell his super AI to maintain the status quo for as long as he needs to purge them and their supporters."

Simms said, "Let us hope it takes him some time to sort out."

Terry returned his gaze to the digital map above the main console. He said, "Squonk, take all steps necessary to maximise the production of Scythe X–7s and X–9s. Prioritise their manufacture and deployment over all other tactical priorities. And override all current civilian requirements."

"Confirmed."

"Further, in cooperation with the Americans, run full diagnostics on all SkyMaster units and supporting satellites to ensure they are functioning at optimum efficiency. We will need to know the instant the enemy brings more ACAs to the battle."

"Confirmed."

Terry glanced from the main console to the individual stations with their diligent operatives. Again, the irrational yet irritating sense of redundancy came back to him; that the humans were simply no longer required at the organisational level of this war. The orders he'd just issued were little more than common sense given the urgency of the situation, and the computer hardly needed him to tell them what was required to hold the lines until NATO could respond with its own improved weapons.

Terry looked at Simms and said, "I've had enough of this damn computer. Let me talk to the generals who actually have to ensure that Operation Repulse doesn't fail."

Chapter 13

16.45 Tuesday 16 October 2063

Captain Pip Clarke returned to consciousness.

"Well, hello there," a cheerful voice called.

Pip lay flat in a bed staring at a white ceiling, and could not be sure that the salutation had been addressed to her. She swallowed and her throat had moisture in it. She flexed some of the muscles in her back and legs and her skin rubbed against soft material that felt like cotton. She tilted her head and the walls of the hospital ward appeared solid. She deduced she'd been transferred back from the front line. A slim doctor approached her. She expected his name to resolve in the air next to him, but it did not.

He reached her bed and said, "Good to see you awake, captain and hero of the hour. Well, that hour being a couple of days ago, but no matter. My name is Doctor Raymond. How are you feeling?" The doctor's demeanour unnerved Pip. His pointed nose bent to the right and gave his otherwise friendly smile an element of falsity.

"I don't know," she replied. "Still alive, I suppose. Although I didn't expect to be."

"Don't worry, sweetie-pie," he said without patronisation. "The bots in that GenoFluid pack have been busy little bees for the last forty-eight hours, seeing to your burns."

"Where is my lens?"

"Just there, in the drawer in your bedside cabinet. But you might want to wait until you're feeling a little better before you put it back in."

"Why? What's happened?"

Doctor Raymond's eyes rose in apparent surprise. "The bots tell me there is nothing wrong with your cognitive abilities. Do you remember your last contact?"

"Yes," she replied. Her memory replayed the last few minutes of the confrontation. She saw again Sergeant MacManus's shapeless, burning body. She recalled looking through the sights of her Pickup at the tiny black dot in the sky that should've burned her to a crisp. She felt once more the overbearing heat and the sweat on her skin as the Lapwing came on. She shuddered, not understanding how she could've survived. "Yes," she repeated. "I'd had enough. I'd reached—"

"Indeed, you had," the doctor exclaimed. "And that is why you are being hailed a hero."

A sick feeling began inside Pip's empty stomach. She said, "You're not making sense."

"Ah, sorry. According to the report from your CO, you attempted to take on an enemy Lapwing singlehandedly to give your troops enough time to get to cover. However, you were fortunate that one member of your squad came back for you."

"No," Pip said. "You're still not making sense. Who came back for me?"

"A fellow called Hines. He's in the next ward. Although it has to be said that nature did not bless him with the most chiselled jaw. But don't fret about that now. The most important thing is that you rest and get your strength back. I usually recommend to casualties like you to avoid putting your lens in for at least forty-eight hours after you regain consciousness. And given the way things are going right now, I really recommend it for you."

Confusion swirled inside Pip, even as her faculties returned. She recalled the last time she'd been injured, during the battle for Europe, and how quickly the bots in the GenoFluid pack seemed to return her to better health. An urge to regain some kind of grip on this new situation asserted itself as recollections of the utter despair she'd felt on losing MacManus receded.

"Why?" she repeated. "Are 'things' very bad?"

Doctor Reymond harrumphed and said, "Rumour has it that we might all be packing up soon and heading back to Blighty. But, as I said, don't concern yourself. For you, the war is most assuredly over."

"What?"

"According to your record, you've now endured such a number of combat injuries that you qualify to be assigned to a non-combat role."

Something in the back of Pip's mind concerning army regulations confirmed what the doctor said.

He added, "And the way things are starting to look, if I were you, I would not mind a bit about getting back to Blighty ahead of the rest of us."

Pip eyed the man and replied, "I don't believe it's as bad as you're making out. I fought my way out of Spain last year, Doctor Raymond, and our ACAs now are a hundred times better than they were then."

The man pouted and said, "I don't make the rules, sweetie-pie. I just try to get you poor squaddies back on your feet, if you've still got them when you get here, natch. You've got at least three days here before your burns will be sufficiently healed. Then, you will need some physio to get fully mobile again. In the meantime, let me or one of my colleagues know if you need anything. Ta-ta." With an exaggerated flick of his head, he turned and strode to the bed opposite Pip.

His voice, with the same tone and cadence, carried back to her, but she could not make out what he said. She glanced at the bedside table, yearning to reach into it and reinsert her lens. But she decided not to.

Pip laid back in the bed and rested. She recalled when she first met Barny Hines during the initial assault on the first day of Operation Repulse. She thought then that she'd have to keep an eye on him. And it turned out the lumpen private with kleptomaniac tendencies had kept an eye on her.

But where did she go from here?

After eighteen months, the war had taken everything from her. And when she'd decided to give it the last thing that remained—her life—fate had interceded in the form of Hines to seal off that final escape.

She shifted her legs and lower back in the bed. The cotton material caressed and massaged her skin and reminded her that there existed feelings and senses and pleasures for which she'd had too little time.

Where did she go from here?

She searched her memory to identify something or someone that might give her an answer; or, if not an answer, then at least some clue how to cope, to engender a recovery from the abyss of hopelessness, to help light some path back from the brink, to somehow continue living a life she thought was over, in the midst of a war that had left a drained soul in a body that GenoFluid bots would soon return to physical fitness.

The name of the one person whom she knew this war had punished more than her, yet who had kept fighting and coping and moving forwards, leapt to the front of her mind. Pip realised she had to contact him as soon as possible. She glanced again at the bedside cabinet that held her lens. A cautionary voice sounded in her mind. It told her to rest, to recover. First get her body healed, then get to work on her spirit.

Chapter 14

17.23 Tuesday 16 October 2063

Serena Rizzi walked along the seemingly endless rock and shale terrain, struggling to cope with thirst that made her throat feel like sandpaper. The older woman, called Aafreen, had explained the need for them to travel to a smaller town further away from the palace. Some time after setting off—Tiphanie insisted it was less an hour—they'd reached a shallow lake and drank some of the metallic water. Thereafter, their route had wended through low, rocky hills with mountains to the north. Aafreen had warned them that there would be no more lakes or streams, and now Serena regretted not husbanding her canteen of water better.

As promised, Serena had told Aafreen and her daughter everything she could recall about Aziz the apprentice cook. She described how hard Aziz had worked for Father and that Aafreen should be proud at having raised such a conscientious son. Serena omitted how badly he'd treated the slaves in the house and how, when not preparing food, he was a loutish, boorish thug with neither talent nor compassion, although she considered Aafreen would likely see such behaviour in a positive light.

But the talking during their journey through the valleys in the heat had dried her throat. Her mind reverted to her previous life to cope with the debilitating pain of her injuries the previous night. She recalled being a trainee nurse and how she'd only ever wanted to help people get better. An image of her little brother, Max, resurfaced, followed by a deep sadness engendered by the certainty that he must have been killed, probably a long time ago.

A flash of orange light caught her eye as the sun dipped below the furthest barren hill. Serena came back to the moment. The straight lines of low buildings came into view, and her spirit rose a little at the thought they finally approached journey's end.

Serena glanced at Tiphanie to see determination etched on the Frenchwoman's face. She croaked, "Do you have blisters, sister?"

Tiphanie replied without looking, "Not yet. I have had these shoes for a while and they are comfortable. Do you think that is our destination, finally?" she asked, indicating the town that emerged in front of them.

"Night will fall soon, so it must be. I think we can trust this Aafreen," Serena replied with a nod to the two women walking a few metres ahead of them.

Tiphanie's voice dropped, "I am not so sure. Aafreen seems bitter from what has happened these last twenty-four hours."

"She is having to cope with pain and uncertainty, like us. Which is why I think we can trust them."

"And her daughter; what was her name?"

"Fariba."

"She is hiding something, I am sure."

Serena glanced at Tiphanie, trying again to get some moisture into her throat so she could talk more easily. "What could that be? We are fugitives now, sister. The only reason we still live is because every person who witnessed what we did last night is dead."

"But why do we need to walk so far? What is this journey for?"

Serena said, "Is it not obvious?"

"I know what the old hag said about it being too dangerous for us to return to her local town, but I think she was lying."

Serena sighed and said, "As you wish." To Serena, nothing mattered anymore. Her work on Earth was done, and she could not fathom what reason the one true God might have for leaving her here. If they were to have a future, the most they could expect would be to be sold into slavery again, and Serena doubted in the extreme that their new owner would be as munificent as Father had been.

They came into the town. Aafreen told Serena and Tiphanie not to speak or meet the eyes of any man they saw. They proceeded along streets first affluent and then mean. And on all of them, Serena felt the fear. It oozed out from the conduits in the roads that guided the autonomous vehicles; it hung like an invisible mist over the palm-fringed boulevards they crossed; it choked the narrow backroads lined with homes and shops shuttered against the dusty, oppressive heat.

At length, they arrived at a nondescript apartment block four storeys high. When they entered, Tiphanie whispered that she was tired. This struck Serena as unusual because Tiphanie seldom complained. But Serena's own legs and feet ached from the distance they'd covered. Serena eyed Aafreen and thought the old hag was bent over a little more than when they'd begun their journey.

Serena and Tiphanie followed Aafreen and Fariba up two flights of narrow concrete stairs. On the landing, Aafreen tapped on a heavy looking metal door. It opened. Aafreen ushered the Serena and Tiphanie through the door with haste.

Once inside the narrow corridor, the door closed and Serena turned to see another woman, similar in age to Aafreen.

Fariba said, "This is my aunt, Minoo."

A fragile woman who exuded timidity, Minoo held her hands together as though offering a prayer and welcomed the European slaves. She shuffled past them and insisted, "Come, come. You will eat now."

Serena stared but Minoo did not meet her eyes. They all removed their footwear and went through the narrow hall and into the apartment's living area. The scent of stale saffron seemed to suffuse the walls and dated wooden furniture. Serena swapped a glance with Tiphanie, whose reaction reflected Serena's own shock at being in such a modest abode.

Aafreen indicated chairs around a dining table from which the plastic veneer peeled with age. "Sit, please," she urged.

Serena said, "Thank you for your hospitality."

Fariba, her voice light and young, said, "We will eat *Abgoosht*."

Tiphanie said to Serena, "Something is wrong. I can sense it."

Serena replied, "You are overreacting, sister."

Aafreen turned to Serena and said, "I hear from the tone of your voices that you worry, yes?"

Serena said, "Please, madam, we are only a little tired after our journey."

Aafreen sniffed and gave a flick of her head. She sat at the other end of the table.

Minoo emerged from the kitchen carrying a large, ornate casserole dish. Fariba followed with her hands clasped around a stack of wide, shallow bowls. Minoo ladled the food out without speaking. Serena's stomach reacted to the rich aroma of boiled beans, onions and potatoes from which whisps of steam floated into the still air.

Aafreen said, "My sister's hospitality is to offer our thanks to you for sharing your recollections of Aziz."

A silence fell over the table and Serena wondered what point Aafreen wanted to make.

As if reading Serena's mind, Aafreen said, "Have you thought about where you will go next?"

Serena answered, "No. Could we find some kind of work in this town?"

Aafreen shovelled a spoonful of *Abgoosht* into her mouth and shook her head. She spoke while eating, "You can see that few people in this town are wealthy enough to own slaves. And, of course, you could never get any kind of work as free women. You must have an owner."

Serena hid her disgust at the hag's table manners. She stirred her bent spoon around her bowl of *Abgoosht* but her appetite had suddenly vanished. Homesickness overwhelmed her. She fought to keep the feeling from her face by casting her head downwards. She wanted to speak Italian, to enjoy a meal with people who appreciated good food and who had decent manners. She wanted to go home.

"However," Aafreen said through another mouthful of food, "I think one thing we might do is get your implants removed."

Serena came back to the moment. "You can do that?" she asked in shock.

Tiphanie said to Serena in English, "What is it about the implants? I did not understand."

Serena repeated Aafreen's offer and Tiphanie's mouth dropped open.

The hag explained, "Not I, oh no. But two streets along there is a technical shop. You know, in a town like this there are people who prefer not to be known. And if you slaves do not have an implant, you will be a little safer."

"Of course. Thank you for your kind offer," Serena replied. She turned to Tiphanie and explained what Aafreen had said.

Tiphanie's voice remained even, but Serena sensed concern. Tiphanie said, "I do not believe her. How can an implant be removed without anyone in authority knowing? For example, how can people do anything in this hell without their implant confirming their identity? In addition, now, the implants will only kill us if we leave these foul lands—"

Serena said, "Be calm, sister. We are in God's hands, and He has made it clear He still has work for us in this land of the devil."

Tiphanie took in a deep breath and replied, "I was able to listen to you when we were comparatively safe, but now we are not safe. Not at all. We must make a plan. We must try to find a way to survive without being slaves." Tiphanie paused and her face brightened. She offered, "Perhaps, if this woman is not lying and we can get the implants removed, we might escape the Caliphate altogether and return home?"

Serena, loving Tiphanie a little more for still being able to find a positive, despite everything they'd been through, replied, "You are right, dear sister. We shall find a way forward." Serena turned to Aafreen and spoke in the old woman's language, "We thank you again, madam. And we agree to your suggestion."

Aafreen's eyes narrowed and she said, "Very well. Let us finish our food and we shall go there."

Serena said, "It is already after sundown. Will this technical shop still be open?"

"Yes," Aafreen replied. "They are always busy and work late into the evening."

Silence fell over the table as all five women finished their food. A large screen on the wall to Serena's left chimed and came to life with the circular crest of the Third Caliph superimposed on the background of a vast mosque.

At once, Aafreen stood and said, "Let us go. Now."

"Why?" Serena asked, her curiosity aroused at the hag's sudden reaction.

The old woman replied, "This may be an announcement of another curfew. If you want us to help you, we must go this minute." She stood and made for the corridor, followed by her daughter. Minoo remained at the table, head cast down at her plate.

Serena and Tiphanie stood. She thanked Minno again for the meal and proceeded to leave.

On the screen appeared the image of a handsome, dark-skinned young man who announced, "His Excellency the Third Caliph of the New Persian Caliphate hereby addresses all of his subjects. Listen and take heed."

Serena stopped and stared at the screen as an image of the same man she had stabbed in the neck less than twenty-four hours earlier resolved, standing proud and confident at a lectern with a vaster image of his crest on the backdrop behind him.

He said, "Subjects of our beloved Caliphate. Now our daily prayers are finished, I command you all to go peacefully to your homes and care for your wives and children. I further command that there shall be no more disturbances in the northern provinces, nor anywhere else. I have taken robust steps to crush the usurpers who allied themselves with our new enemies to the east…"

Tiphanie prodded Serena and demanded to know what the Third Caliph said.

Serena gave her a summary and then added, "I cannot believe he still lives."

Tiphanie replied with a sneer, "He does not, sister. That is a performance manufactured by their computers. Whoever controls this hell wants everyone to think that what we did last night did not happen."

Serena glanced back at Tiphanie, "So, you mean that was the reason for all of the violence?"

Tiphanie nodded, "Exactly. And that is why we still live. Because all those who knew who we are, have been killed."

Aafreen and Fariba waited at the open door, their shoes already on their feet. Serena went to join them, now believing that her and Tiphanie's longer-term safety lay in the chance to have their implants removed. As she put her shoes on in the corridor, the voice of the announcer carried from the main room, "...and remember that there are substantial bounties for handing over any fleeing enemies to the authorities."

Serena joined Aafreen and Fariba outside the apartment in the stairwell. When Tiphanie reached her, she and the Frenchwoman followed the two Persian women out of the building. The air in the dark street hung heavy and Serena wondered how much the quietness had to do with the Third Caliph's address. Her thoughts returned to her previous life. She tried to imagine what Rome looked like now, but could not. Deep inside her, a strange regret formed. When the opportunity to do God's work arrived, she'd never dreamed she would live to see the repercussions. Unanswerable questions flitted around her regret like fruit flies darting to and fro above a rotting apple. Had she really assassinated the Third Caliph? Why did whoever was in power unleash such destruction in response?

Aafreen suddenly stopped and said, "We have arrived."

The dim streetlights revealed the frontage of a shop that carried no indication of what lay within.

Tiphanie said, "I do not like this, sister."

Her own spirit rising, Serena turned and urged, "Have faith. Soon we will have more control over our future." Serena turned to Aafreen. "What is this place? There is nothing to indicate its purpose," she asked with a nod to the frontage.

The old woman shook her head, "People who offer such illicit services would be unwise to advertise them, no?"

Tiphanie spoke directly to Aafreen, struggling with her limited command of their language, "How much it cost? Where money have we, or you?"

A half-smile played on Aafreen's mouth. She replied, "You knew my Aziz. And now he is gone, forever. Perhaps, if I help you, Allah will bless Aziz and provide for his comfort in *Jannah*? Come, let us enter. If we delay, eyes in other windows around us will watch and wonder." She turned to Fariba and instructed, "Wait here, daughter."

The younger woman nodded and stepped backwards.

Aafreen pushed the door open and went in. Serena stood back to let Tiphanie enter. The Frenchwoman threw Serena a nervous glance as she did so. Serena followed.

The dimly lit interior was bare save for a worn couch on the right. At the back there was a serving counter with empty shelves behind it, and a closed doorway off to one side that, Serena presumed, led to the rear. The place smelled of diluted antiseptic. Aafreen shut the door behind them and called out a word that sounded like the name of an animal.

Serena sensed the trap an instant before it was sprung. She lunged for the door to escape, but when she pulled on the vertical handle, another arm on the outside—Fariba's—held the door fast. Serena's ears registered a noise behind her and Tiphanie yelled a foul curse in French. Serena turned and saw a huge, dark man in military fatigues lumbering up to her. An electrifying bolt of power shot out from the small of her back and she lost her breath and all feeling in her limbs. Rough arms manhandled her onto the couch. Another brute dragged Tiphanie and deposited her next to Serena.

The only part of her body over which Serena had control were her eyes. She looked at Aafreen, standing by the door, a half-smile on the hag's face. At once, the thought came to her that the hag might not be Aziz's mother at all. An old, sad mother would be the perfect disguise for a bounty hunter.

Serena fought to move her arms. Her brain insisted she held them out in front of her horizontally, but when she cast her eyes down, her arms hung limp and useless by her side. She lolled her head to her right to see Tiphanie looking as helpless as she. The Frenchwoman's eyes pleaded with Serena's, but for now there seemed to be little either of them could do.

The hag called out, "Well? Do you see where these two infidels are from? How much are they worth to His Highness?"

"Wait," came a gruff reply, from somewhere out of Serena's sight.

The hag who called herself 'Aafreen' came into Serena's view and addressed her, "You did well to learn my language, infidel. I had not expected that when I found you in the stables this morning. I thought I might have to cajole both of you with simple words and hand signs."

One of the men stomped back into the room. He said, "Yes, they belonged the House of Badr Shakir al-Sayyab."

"Excellent," she said. "It has been a most fruitful day's work." The hag turned away from Serena and addressed the soldier, "And my bounty?"

"Wait," he repeated.

The hag went to the front door and delivered a sequence of gentle taps on it.

In response, 'Fariba' pushed the door open and entered. "Is everything in order?" she asked her 'mother'.

The hag nodded towards Serena and said, "Oh, yes," with satisfaction.

A tingling sensation began in the tips of Serena's arms and legs. Whatever they had done to her, she hoped this indicated that the effect was starting to wear off.

The silence lengthened. The hag and the younger woman swapped a glance. More time passed. Serena struggled and regained movement in her shoulders. Feeling returned to her face in a haze of tingling on her skin.

"Sister, what have we done?" Tiphanie croaked.

Serena saw the tears in Tiphanie's eyes. She said, "We must—"

The door broke open and the two men stormed back into the room. They darted through a gap in the serving counter and pounced on the bounty hunters.

The hag exclaimed, "What are you?—" when the first man jabbed a small, handheld device into the folds of her *abaya*. She let out a gasp of stunned surprise and fell backwards.

The younger woman leapt for the door. She got one hand to it when the second soldier paralysed her. Each man dragged his quarry through the back door.

Serena burned with frustration. The effects of the paralysis were wearing off with agonising slowness. She looked through the open doorway into the rear of the building, but saw only darkness.

There came the clanging of a metal door then a muffled pop, like a gunshot. Then a scream. Then another gunshot.

115

Serena looked aghast at Tiphanie, whose tearstained face refocused into anger and hatred.

Serena's breathing slowed in realisation.

The men returned. The heavier-set one complained, "It is annoying when the blood splashes back like that. Now I will have to make my wife wash my uniform tonight."

The second one also moaned, "The worst is we cannot fuck them first. I do not like it when we can only have fun with them when they are dead."

The first one grabbed Tiphanie by her paralysed arm and dragged her off the couch with a grunt. He asked his comrade, "Javeed, the regional commander made it clear: every single person who has had contact with the House of Badr Shakir al-Sayyab is to be liquidated at once, without mercy. Besides which, did you not have enough fun in Europe?"

The second one grabbed Serena by an arm she also could not control, saying, "Yes, I suppose so. I understand. If we do not kill them now, we might be next." He added, "It was clever of these infidels' owner to block their implants like he did."

"It means we have to do things the old-fashioned way, like with those stupid bitches," the other replied.

Serena felt no pain, only increased tingling as the man dragged her over the cold floor.

Tiphanie cried out and swore at the men.

They reached the execution chamber. As far as Serena could see, lumpy, bloodstained sand covered the floor and spats of dried brown blood flecked the opposite wall like a poor imitation of modern art. In the corner lay the crumpled bodies of the two women whom Serena had met that morning.

The one called Javeed said, "I will do this one, then you can do yours. If you must, Mahbod, you can fuck them afterwards. And you should enjoy yourself. Next week, we are scheduled for duty in Europe."

"I know. I cannot wait."

"Why?"

"More infidels like these to fuck."

"You think there will be any good ones left? All the best were taken long ago."

Out of the corner of her eye, Serena watched as the first soldier sat Tiphanie on a rickety wooden chair, with her facing the opposite wall. Tiphanie whimpered, the noise from her throat a manifestation of impotent rage and despair. He held her there with one hand gripped around the back of her neck. With his other hand, he withdrew a pistol and shot Tiphanie through the back of her head. The Frenchwoman slumped off the chair. Her body did not move and made no sound.

Without speaking, the second soldier hefted Serena onto the same chair.

She could hardly feel his hand gripping the back of her neck.

So, the one true God no longer had work for her on Earth, after all.

She sensed the cold, hard steel of the pistol centimetres from the back of her head.

Serena Rizzi did not hear the shot that killed her.

Chapter 15

07.00 Thursday 18 October 2063

Pip Clarke did as Doctor Raymond advised her, deciding to wait not only the forty-eight hours he recommended before putting her lens back in, but also another night. She'd found it strangely comforting to have no distractions whatsoever, simply sleeping as much as she wanted and staring at the walls. The glimpse of a simpler life that she'd only ever heard about at school appealed to her. Perhaps, if she survived the war, she might seek somewhere far away to escape to—

"Good morning, sweetie-pies," called Doctor Raymond from the entrance to the ward.

Her thoughts broken, Pip managed to return the greeting while noting that none of the patients in the three other beds did so.

Raymond strode towards Pip's bed with a young orderly in tow pulling a small trolley. He said, "Let's start with our lovely captain." He pulled back the sheet covering Pip's legs and looked at the control panel on the GenoFluid pack. "Hmm, good," he murmured. He glanced at the orderly and said, "Let's get this off as soon as the bots have exited the patient." He turned to Pip, "And how are you this morning, Captain Clarke?"

Pip said, "Feeling better now, thank you. I think I will put my lens back in."

"Of course," Raymond replied.

The orderly lifted the GenoFluid pack from Pip's lower body and placed it on the trolley.

Raymond rolled her gown up and said, "Your legs are looking very good on the outside. Would you like to stand?"

Pip swung her legs off the bed and stood. A slight wave of dizziness came and went.

"Anything feeling a tad not-quite-right?"

Pip shook her head.

"Good. Let either me or Orderly Davis here know if you feel a bit wobbly. Get some walking in but don't overdo it just yet, okey-doke?"

Pip mumbled her confirmation and sat back down on the bed.

Raymond and the orderly moved on to one of the beds opposite, the doctor calling out a loud 'good morning' presumably to ensure the patient woke up.

Pip opened the drawer of the small cabinet and extracted the clasp that held her lens. She pushed the tiny latch and the lid sprung up. She heaved in a breath and threw her head back. Pulling the lids of her right eye apart, she upended the open clasp and felt the lens drop onto her eyeball. She lowered her head, blinked until the eye welled, and closed the clasp.

At once, data splayed out in her view. She needed a few practice blinks and twitches to get used to controlling the feeds again. "Oh no," she said with a sigh as she enlarged maps and saw how far the line of contact had been reversed since the enemy deployed the Siskin. She zoomed and rotated sectors and noted in dismay the casualty lists.

She refocused her vision to the ward. "What is the current location of Private Barny Hines, 33 Armoured Engineer Squadron?"

Her Squitch replied, "Private Hines is in the men's ward adjoining your current location. Do you require visual directions?"

Pip stood and stretched. "Don't be asinine," she replied. She reached for a hospital dressing gown folded on top of the bedside cabinet and undid the knot in the belt. A pair of cheap slippers slid out when she opened it. She put the clothes on. She paced out of her ward, along a narrow corridor, and into the men's. Hines was sitting in the second bed on the right, his head moving in small jerks as, Pip assumed, he read something in his lens.

She approached him and said, "Good morning, Private Hines."

His eyes focused on her. "Good morning, captain. You won't mind if I don't get up and salute, only I've got—"

"At ease, private," she said, her hand outstretched. "I just dropped by to thank you."

Hines shrugged his heavy shoulders. "It weren't nothin', really, ma'am."

"What made you do it?"

Hines's grin revealed uneven teeth. "I dunno. I had a feeling. You know, when the shooting starts, I have an 'abit of getting right angry. I don't like missing out, you know?"

Pip smiled.

Hines went on, "When I come up there and saw what them bastards did to Mac, I got right upset. I weren't gonna let them do that to you as well, ma'am. And it was a brave thing you did, taking on a Lapwing on your jack jones like that."

Pip's smile fell away at the mention of Sergeant MacManus's name. She glanced at Hines and said, "I didn't do anything brave, private."

Hines shrugged again. "I reckon you did, but whatever you say, captain."

Pip said, "Thank you, Private Hines. I owe you one."

Hines's square face perked up at Pip's casual offer. "Really?" he said.

Pip realised that the man might have misconstrued her meaning. She decided to put his name forward for a mention in dispatches, at the very least. "Yes," she confirmed.

Hines lowered his voice and glanced at the other patients in the room, presumably to ensure they would not hear. "Er, well, if I might speak freely, ma'am?"

Pip steeled herself for whatever medal or other commendation he would ask for. "Of course," she said.

"Look, if it should happen that you see me helping myself to the spoils of war, or if I should get into any kind of trouble—not saying that I will, mind you—for whatever a military policeman should find in my kitbag that shouldn't really be in my kitbag... Well, I'd be grateful if you could, you know, vouch for my honesty and general good character."

Pip shoulders relaxed and she laughed for the first time in longer than she could remember.

"What's so funny?" Hines asked, his face creased in confusion.

"Nothing. Nothing at all," she said, becoming professional in appearance and feigning a more martial posture. "I would be delighted to accede to your request."

Hines replied, "Do you mean 'yes'?"

Pip nodded. "Get well soon, private. See you back at barracks."

"Right you are, ma'am."

Pip left the men's ward. She walked further along the corridor and steadied herself when another wave of dizziness came over her. Outside, a gentle rain fell on the autumnal leaves and on the shrubs in the garden. Through the window,

Pip could almost feel the baked earth gasping with relief at the water.

She glanced around to make sure no one was within earshot. She said, "Contact Colour Sergeant Rory Moore, 21 Engineer Regiment, Royal Engineers."

She waited, and then came a somnolent, "Ah, hello, mate."

"I can call you back later, if you li—"

"No, no, that's fine," Rory replied. "But, er, maybe audio only for now."

"Sure. Where are you?"

"Probably can't say, although there's plenty of paella about if you like that kind of thing."

Pip smiled. "Listen," she began, "have you got a minute?"

"Yeah, sure. Just let me get out of our digs."

She waited, listening to Rory's movements and wondering how much drama he had. She knew better than to ask, as the Squitch would block any information it deemed sensitive to op-sec.

"Yeah, okay. In the clear now. It's good to hear from you. Are you okay?"

Pip bit her lip and said, "I had another close one a couple of days ago."

"Occupational hazard."

"How do you cope, Rory? How do you manage when so many troops don't make it?" Pip heard an edge of desperation in her voice and regretted it. In addition, she realised she called Rory by his name, which she couldn't remember doing before and didn't know why she had now.

"It's called 'survivor's guilt', mate," he said, the tone of his voice changing.

"I know that. And I've read up on it. But I'm asking you. You've been through more shit than me—"

"I'd say we're about equal on that score," he broke in.

"And I could really do with hearing your take on it."

There came a pause and Pip wondered what he was thinking. He said, "Look, it's not a conversation we can have first thing in the morning when I've got the brown stuff flying into the fan from ten different directions."

"Sure."

"If you want it in a nutshell, it's just about keeping going on, moving forward. Don't stop to think. Keep busy and push on. But, one: I think you're smart enough you've already worked that out; and two, it's not as simple as that."

Pip said, "One good thing is that I've been injured so many times, I can be transferred off combat ops."

Rory's reaction surprised her. He exclaimed, "And you want that, do you?"

Nonplussed, Pip stammered, "Er, well, if I've done my bit for the war effort."

"Yeah, but the war is still on. And we're right back in the shit with this poxy Siskin."

"Yes, but—"

"And another thing," Rory broke in, his voice taking on a harder edge, "when I got back from—ah, can't tell you—Doyle offered that I could be his poodle—"

"Poodle?"

"Yeah, like his batman, his adjutant. Sauntering around in safety like regular Brass—"

"Okay, take it easy—"

"You need to know this, mate. He offered me to do speaking tours in the US and tedious shit like that to make sure the bloody yanks keep on side."

Pip didn't say anything, wanting to give Rory the space to calm down.

He said, "Listen mate, we're on the move here soon, pulling back all along the line. You need to just keep pushing on. Got that?"

"Yes, I've got that. Thanks."

"And don't let Doyle grab you for his poodle, right?"

"Right," Pip confirmed.

"And seeing as you outrank me, why don't you use your captaincy to try to get us at least in the same bloody theatre? That way, maybe we can chat. Okay, gotta run."

"Thanks again," Pip said, but Rory had already ended the connection.

Chapter 16

07.12 Sunday 21 October 2063

Field Surgeon Maria Phillips watched as her new orderly, Igbe Kalu, stepped out of the small Airbus autonomous air transport.

The young woman had her kitbag slung over a shoulder and jogged up to Maria. She saluted with her free hand and said, "Orderly Kalu reporting for duty, ma'am."

Maria returned the salute and replied, "Welcome to Casualty Clearing Station Sierra Zero-Four, orderly. At ease." Maria stuck her hand out and Kalu shook it. The smooth skin of her face, a soft brown like English oak, reminded Maria of her dead friend, Nabou. "Come along," Maria said, turning to go. Behind them, the AAT rose into the dry morning air. Maria strode towards the collection of single-storey sheds and huts that made up the station. Despite camouflage colouring, the fact the station sat in open, barren fields, made Maria feel as though the whole place were a sitting duck.

Maria said, "First things first, orderly."

"Yes, ma'am," came a breathless response full of anticipation.

Maria smiled; Kalu was just six months younger than her, but Maria felt much older. "We tend to call each other by our first names, but don't feel obliged if you'd prefer not to. Ranni is my head orderly. I'll introduce you to him and the other orderlies once I've shown you to your quarters, where you can drop your kitbag."

"Roger that, ma'am."

"Next, things have been more hectic than usual since the enemy's new ACA arrived—which is one of the reasons you're here."

"Right."

"Although your Squitch will guide you in your work, you need to keep in mind a couple of things." Maria waved her arm at a long, narrow casualty ward on their left. "That shed is where injured enemy are kept before they are transferred. Take care when you're in there. Most of them, if they're still alive, are in a pretty bad way. We usually keep them in induced comas until they get evac'd out. On the off-chance a lightly injured warrior comes in, we put them into an induced coma as well, so they can't cause us any trouble."

"Right."

"On that side of the field," Maria went on, indicating more buildings on their right, "is where our boys and girls are kept. Seeing as this is your first posting, you best try to prepare yourself."

"In what way, exactly, ma'am?"

Maria stopped walking and looked into Igbe's blemishless face. "Casualties will die on you. You will not be able to save all of the troops who arrive here. Some may beg you; some may plead. It can be… draining, sometimes."

"But others do recover, yes? We—well, you—do save lives, yes?"

"Yes," Maria replied. She resumed walking towards the staff billet. "Any questions?"

"How frequently do we receive casualties?"

"Depends on a lot of things, although I'm tempted just to say 'too often'. But the enemy's tactics have been off, lately."

"How so, ma'am?"

Maria shrugged and said, "With this new ACA, they've got the advantage, but they don't seem to be pushing it as much as they could. Like today, if they don't kick off before sunrise, then the morning is usually quiet. The worst is when we get casualties at night."

Maria turned right between two of the long sheds and opened the nearest door. "In here, Igbe." She entered first and led the young woman to the orderly's single room billet. "That's a nice name. Does it mean anything?"

Igbe threw her kitbag in the room and turned around, replying, "I have Nigerian ancestry. My family arrived in England over half a century ago, and giving us kids the old country's names is a kind of tradition."

Maria's memory noted the contrast and the similarities: Nabou's family had originated in Senegal, similar but so different, in traces of culture, of—

"Caution," her Squitch announced, breaking into her thoughts, "an enemy attack is underway in the sectors shown in your map now."

Maria smothered a curse and raised the map. She said, "Send out a general alert to the others and notify Doctor Miller."

Igbe asked, "Is Doctor Miller nearby?"

Maria shook her head, "No. He has to manage five of these stations and is often away for days at a time. Come on." Maria strode towards a different shed.

"That attack looks quite close," Igbe observed.

"That's normal," Maria said.

The air pressure changed around them in a manner Maria recognised.

Igbe's face creased in uncertainty. "What on Earth—?"

The hissing passage of wings of Scythe X–9s split the air above them, the lowest less than fifty metres over their heads. Maria couldn't help but stop and stare at the sky. Countless Scythes flew at altitudes ranging up to thousands of metres in disciplined arrowhead formations.

Maria glanced at Igbe, "There must be thousands of them. Reassuring, isn't it?"

"Er, yes, ma'am. I suppose so. Maybe a little nerve-wracking, too?"

Maria's attention came back to the ground. "Right, let's get on with it." She resumed striding and came to the door of the command office. She pulled it open and called, "Ranni?"

"Yes?" came a voice.

"Get ready," she instructed, entering the small office. "It looks like we'll be getting more casualties if flesh-and-blood troops become involved."

"Roger that. Unusual time for an assault."

"Here's our new orderly, Igbe."

Ranni's narrow, bald head spun away from the screen in front of him. He gave Igbe a friendly, gap-toothed smile and said, "Hi. You've picked an interesting time to arrive."

"Yes, I see," came Igbe's measured response.

Ranni looked at Maria, "I have not woken Lyla or Grayson yet. Lyla just went off shift, less than ninety minutes ago. She had a tough night and is sure to be sound asleep."

Maria recognised Ranni's coded message that he suspected Lyla had used sleeping drugs which might've knocked her out. She said, "So leave both of them for now, until we know for sure we going to receive casualties."

"And we have our new addition to the team to help," Ranni said with a toothy grin.

Igbe beamed, "Yes, you do."

Maria smiled, "Okay, that's great, Igbe. Let's have a brew while we wait. Ranni?"

Ranni didn't answer. The screen in front of him lit up with red warning indicators.

Maria stepped over to him, looked at the data feeds in the screen, and said, "I really don't like it when the probability figures start changing like that."

Ranni scratched behind an ear and opined, "The Siskin is a known quantity now. Squonk should be able to tell us what to exp—"

"Last year," Maria broke in, "when they were easily rolling us back off the continent and attacking England, their weapons were far better than ours. Now, it's more complicated."

With his eyes fixed on the screen, Ranni said, "Yeah? How?"

"They are not so much more advanced. Plus, we've got lots more than we used to have. I don't think it's going to be quite so easy for them this ti—"

"Danger," her Squitch said in her ear. "This casualty clearing station will come under enemy attack in three minutes. Evacuation procedure begins now. Prepare to embark autonomous air transports that will arrive in Alpha LZ in one minute."

Maria saw from the looks on the others' faces that they'd received the same warning.

Ranni said in frustration, "This is nuts. There's no need whatsoever for this kind of drama. If the super AI has got its shit together, we should have—"

"Ranni," Maria said, "the super AI isn't in control of the battle; the enemy is."

Igbe stammered as she said, "Er, what do we do now, if we have to evac?"

Ranni spoke, "Not much apart from get the hell out of here."

Igbe's eyes widened, "You've had to evac before?"

Ranni looked at her, "Nope. But there's always a first time for everything."

Maria said, "We need to get as many casualties as possible out, hopefully to a proper field hospital."

Ranni said, "Nearest one of those is forty klicks behind us."

"Do we know what kind of AATs we've got coming to get us?" Maria asked.

Ranni squinted at the screen, "Half a dozen Airbuses."

"Damn," Maria said. "Right, Igbe: go to the NATO sheds and make sure the walking wounded are okay. Then start wheeling the worst cases outside." Maria left unspoken the obvious doubt over whether there would be time to load the stretcher cases into the AATs.

Igbe acknowledged the instructions and disappeared outside.

Maria put her hand on Ranni's bony shoulder and said, "Come on, let' get Lyla and Grayson and then help Igbe with the gurneys."

Her Squitch announced, "Proceed to Alpha LZ for evacuation."

"You bet," Ranni said. "I'll set the burn up for three minutes."

"Okay."

Ranni stood, dabbed at panels on the screen, and confirmed, "Burn up in three minutes. Mark."

Maria exited the command office. In the sky to the south, distant puffs of smoke appeared. Her concern rose. She hurried towards the sheds for NATO troops. Walking wounded were filing out, some holding the smaller battlefield GenoFluid packs on their injuries.

Her Squitch repeated, "Proceed to Alpha LZ for ev—"

"What about the stretcher cases?"

"There is insufficient time to evacuate them."

"What?" Maria nearly shrieked. "What's happened?"

"Orderly Kalu is reprogramming the GenoFluid packs to sedate the seriously wounded."

Dismay swept over Maria. Indicators blinked in her view to denote the approaching AATs that would evacuate them. She repeated, "What's happened?"

Her Squitch replied, "The enemy's tactics have changed."

Maria hurried to the AATs, trotting backwards away from the casualty clearing station. Injured NATO troops strode towards the landing zone as the friendly aircraft arrived, sweeping down from the sky like ungainly, overweight gulls and settling in designated locations.

Panting with exertion, Maria identified Ranni, Igbe, the lanky Grayson and athletic Lyla hurrying away from the sheds. She silently urged them to run faster. She reached the nearest AAT and helped the last walking wounded, a young man clasping a GenoFluid pack to the side of his head. Little needed to be said: the troops' Squitches issued precise instructions, including which aircraft they should board.

She hurried to the next aircraft, twenty metres away. She entered it and helped a young woman who held a pack against her chest. When Maria looked at the casualty, the list of injuries resolved in the air close by and included internal bleeding. Maria helped lower the casualty down and then pulled the restraining belts around her and clipped her in. Maria made sure the other seven occupants were also secured before leaving.

Her own Squitch spoke, "Board the furthest aircraft within fifteen seconds, as indicated."

Maria had to run to cover the distance. She said in frustration, "Can't we save the stretcher cases?"

Her Squitch did not answer. The noise of the first AAT taking off whined through the air and she realised the enemy attack had to be nearly on them. She reached her designated aircraft at the same time as Igbe. Gasping, she pushed the orderly through the dark, rectangular opening in the AAT's fat body before ducking in herself. The fuselage smelled of warm steel and cold fear. She sat down next to Igbe in the last two available seats.

Her Squitch said, "Secure yourself as the journey will involve mild turbulence."

The hatchway snapped shut and the aircraft rose. From her seat, Maria watched the oncoming attack through a porthole in the opposite side. The enemy machines were formed into a vast cube in the sky. Around it, tiny flashes of orange flame and puffs of smoke described the end of tens of NATO Scythes. As more friendly ACAs attacked to cover the retreat of wounded and medical personnel, the cube undulated and elongated in a dazzling geometric display. The scene quickly shrank as the aircraft accelerated, but the impression came to Maria that they faced a repeat of the previous year; that, once again, the enemy had got the upper hand. She pushed herself back into the unyielding seat and closed her eyes, her memory replaying the battle she'd just witnessed. But while her heart broke for the casualties they'd had to leave behind, at least she'd escaped with her team intact.

Chapter 17

09.34 Wednesday 24 October 2063

English Prime Minister Dahra Napier watched the last of her ministers of state exit the main cabinet room. The permanent private secretary waited with his hand on the door. She gave him a slight nod and he closed it behind him, leaving her alone with her director of communications, Crispin Webb.

"What is the latest?" she asked.

He replied, "Checking now."

She tucked a strand of hair behind her ear as he twitched his eye to find out how badly her government leaked.

He shook his head and said, "No, boss. Up to now, we're in the clear."

"No, Crispin," she admonished. "The fourth estate is 'in the clear'."

"Sure. They all know we'll slap an R-Notice on them, so I'd say the probability of the you-know-what leaking is still remote."

Dahra turned away from her aide and sauntered around the huge table to the windows that looked out over the stone terrace and the garden, the slabs there having been bleached by decades of hot sun. She said, "You know what's funny?"

"No, boss."

"Now the fighting is firmly on the continent once more, I can't quite believe how tedious all the minutiae of governance is."

As she expected, Crispin didn't say anything. That's what she appreciated most about him: he knew when to shut up. She went on, "Did you see the looks on some of those faces? Did you see how earnest people like Joanne, Wendy, Linda and Trevor were when we discussed resource allocations for their portfolios?"

"Didn't seem to be anything unusual to me, boss," Crispin said.

She turned to face him. "All of those blasted cowards now behave as though nothing had happened. They ran away when it looked like England was finished. And now the war has moved back into Europe, they return and start swanning about like… like I don't know what."

"All of them have young families, boss," Crispin said in his placating voice. "You yourself sent your family to the states for safe—"

"Yes, that's right," Dahra broke in. "My family—not me. I remained where the public expected me to be. I did not—despite my husband and children pleading with me—skedaddle off to evade the grim fate we thought we would not be able to stop."

"I think they see it that because England didn't fall, what they did carries a bit less—"

"Stop justifying them, Crispin," she said. "For now, the war is still on, and given recent developments, we might yet end up the losers in this debacle."

"Yes, boss."

"In any case," Dahra said, walking towards the large oak doors, "my point is that I find myself asking whether those cowards deserve a place at the highest table in England."

"Is this a good time for a reshuffle?" Crispin asked, his eyes tracking her movement.

She considered his point. "Perhaps not yet. But there needs to be a reckoning. Otherwise, the public might think I'm overly tolerant of my ministers running away in a crisis and then behaving as if nothing had happened when it's over."

She paused to allow Crispin to open the door for her, then reconsidered. "I did encourage them to go though, didn't I?"

Crispin said, "The situation was slightly on the dire side, boss."

"Well, that was then and this is now. Come on." She strode out of the cabinet office and stopped at the desk of her PPE. "I've got a notification that the Economic Forum might overrun this afternoon. I want to stay for the duration, so take care of rescheduling other government business for the rest of the day."

The young man nodded with enthusiasm, "Yes, PM. Right away."

Crispin said to her, "You've also got the hospital opening in your constituency at midday, so we need to leave by—"

"Yes, that has priority but it's party business, not government." She strode off along the corridor that led further into the warren of rooms that made up Ten Downing Street.

"Do you want me to see if I can get them to postpone the opening?" Crispin offered.

"No, absolutely not. I need some good press now it's got bleaker in Europe."

"Yes, boss."

They arrived at the lift and entered. The doors closed.

Crispin, his eye twitching, asked, "Have you got your lens in, boss?"

"Yes, but it's deactivated. I find it fills up with many things I don't really care for. And this meeting is important."

"Okay, only—" he broke off as the lift doors opened, "—a group of councils in Humber have just issued a joint press release saying that construction replicators promised several weeks ago have still not arrived, and they're struggling with failing flood defences."

Dahra tutted, "Timed to coincide with my opening a hospital in my constituency rebuilt with one of said construction replicators, yes?"

"I'd have to research the details, but if that's what they're claiming, it probably is."

They arrived at the PM's personal flat. Dahra stood back once again to let Crispin push the door open for her. She thanked him and they entered.

She said, "Let's not worry about that now. I'm sure you'll think of something to minimise any negative publicity."

"Of course, boss," came the reply.

She stopped outside the door to the living room and turned back to Crispin. "Are they already in there?"

Crispin nodded.

"Good. See that we're not disturbed."

"Yes, boss. You're sure you don't want me to sit in?"

Dahra replied, "Quite sure. It's just a chat among friends. And if either of my most valued ministers gets any... ideas? Then, the reshuffle might come sooner rather than later."

"Okay. I'll come back in an hour for the trip to open the hospital."

Dahra watched Crispin go. She turned and entered the spacious living room. Defence Secretary Liam Burton and

Foreign Secretary Charles Blackwood stood by the elegant fireplace accepting hot drinks from Monica. Her PA smiled and said, "I took the liberty of fetching you a latte, ma'am."

"Thank you," Dahra replied. She took the proffered coffee and watched Monica leave the room. The door clicked shut behind her.

After exchanging pleasantries with her ministers, Dahra sat in the two-seater couch opposite the fireplace. The young defence minister lowered himself into one corner of the three-seater couch to her left. He sat leaning forward with his forearms on his thighs, exuding energy. Charles Blackwood sat on Dahra's right in the armchair, back straight, one hand brushing imaginary fluff from the crease of his pressed trousers.

"Gentlemen," she began, "I wanted to have a chat, just the three of us, now that things in the country are beginning a return to some kind of normality. Liam, how are things going on the continent?"

Burton nodded in consideration and said, "Pretty bleak, actually. This new weapon the enemy have hit us with is pushing the lines back quite successfully."

"Damn," Dahra said. "That might negate the reason for me asking you here. Where do you see things going in the next couple of weeks?"

Liam scrunched his face dismissively and replied, "They've only got the advantage until our Omegas and Alphas come to the party. Those beauties will give us the edge back, no doubt about it."

Charles Blackwood didn't seem impressed with the defence minister's bravado. He said, "Still, it's a bit rough on the troops having to face these things now, isn't it?"

"Well, yes. Of course," Burton conceded.

"I've seen reports that we've taken more casualties in the last ten days than since the first two weeks of Repulse, in August."

"My point," Dahra said, "is this: do both of you think that the November conference will go ahead as currently planned?"

"Undoubtedly," Laim answered at once. "We will have the initiative entirely back with our forces by then." He waved an index finger as though instructing a child, "Our super AI forecasts for when those new machines reach the enemy are fantastic."

"The really odd thing is," Charles said, "why the enemy keeps up this antagonism with India. It must be tying up, what, half his total forces? If he were serious about defeating us a second time, he'd sort that out."

"Gentlemen," Dahra said, "we have to discuss our strategy for the November conference. If the enemy continues to drive our forces back, then we shall end up where we were a year ago. But if, as you Liam seem convinced, our forces will regain the advantage, what then?"

Liam's face creased in confusion. "Sorry, PM?"

Dahra sipped some warm coffee from under the silky-smooth foam. "To make my question clear: how does this war end?"

Liam shrugged his shoulders and said, "I'm pretty sure 'not yet' is the answer there, PM. Once we have evicted the ragheads from Europe and got our lands back, then we take the fight to them. We've got to go for unconditional surrender, like in World War Two. Isn't it obvious?"

Charles's face took on a pained expression. He said, "I'm not altogether sure it is obvious, old chap."

"What do you propose instead, then?" Liam asked him with a flash of confrontation.

Charles shook his head, "I'm no military expert, but the New Persian Caliphate does cover quite a substantial landmass. Are you suggesting NATO forces could really invade and subjugate it?"

"What choice do we have?"

Dahra said, "I don't know that we have many choices at all. As you both might've guessed, I personally just want this awful war to end. We have all suffered grievously, and while I don't want to sound as if I just wished it would go away, I tend to agree with Charles that invading the Caliphate would be quite out of the question."

"Okay," Liam said, putting his hand out flat. "Then what you're saying is that we expel the enemy from Europe and just let him be, yes? You understand what that means, don't you? That for the foreseeable future—certainly long after all of us have left office and gone into retirement or whatever—we are going to leave a mortal enemy intact on Europe's southern border for those who follow us. That is what you're proposing."

Dahra said, "No one is proposing anything right at this minute, Liam. This is why I wanted this discussion. In a couple of weeks—assuming the tide does in fact turn again in our favour as you insist—there is going to be a conference at which the leaders of all the members of NATO, all subjugated European countries, and the Americans, will have to agree on some kind of post-war strategy. I intend that my government should lead it with a clear and reasonable plan."

"Er," Charles said, "have you spoken to the field marshal about this, PM?"

Dahra shook her head, "No. I will, of course, but in any case, his job is to follow orders." She saw Charles's eyebrows rise in surprise.

Liam said, "I don't want us to start going round in circles, but I cannot for the life of me see how it could be acceptable to eject the enemy from Europe and leave him unmolested in his home territory."

Charles said, his voice thick with irony, "We could always try and nuke them like Israel did."

"There's no need to be facetious, Dahra said. "Gentlemen, please. For now, let's keep this between ourselves. I want us to at least have the bones of a plan for the conference before I put it to the full cabinet."

"As you wish," Charles said with a hint of imperiousness. "But I tend to agree with you, PM. If and when we ever recover the main European landmass, the military will at least need to pause and rearm. And there'll be an entire continent's worth of damage and destruction to clean up."

Dahra stood and said, "Thank you, both."

The men also rose. There came a tap at the door.

"Come," Dahra said.

Monica poked her head into the room and said, "Defence Minister, your car has arrived and is waiting in the garage."

"Yes, thanks," Liam said. "I received the notification." He looked at Dahra and said, "Right, I have to get to my constituency. I've got some nice new flood defences to inaugurate. At least things are getting better here, eh?"

"I suppose they are," Dahra replied in neutral tone.

When the door had closed behind Burton, Charles said, "He's very popular among the grassroots membership, you know."

"Is he?" Dahra said, still staring at the door. "Are you trying to tell me something, minister?"

"Not at all, PM."

"Good. Successful ministers make for a successful government." She turned to face him, "Unless you think it's something I should worry about."

Charles smiled, his blue eyes flashing openness, "You've all-but-seen England through its worst crisis easily since Churchill a hundred and twenty years ago. Your position in the party and the country is unassailable."

She said nothing. She'd known Charles for many years and liked to think they enjoyed a grain of trust in an occupation where any seldom existed.

Charles seemed to sense her thoughts and said, "He's still quite young, in any case. I'll be on my way."

"Thank you for coming."

She watched him leave the room and said aloud, "Really, how can all the tedious drudgery of this blasted job return so quickly?" With a twitch of her eye, she told Crispin to send her Liam Burton's security file, reasoning that she couldn't be too careful.

Chapter 18

10.29 Friday 26 October 2063

Terry Tidbury sat in his personal office in the War Room, a pair of VR glasses on his face. These placed him inside an entirely virtual auditorium at the morning's situation report for Attack Group East, the NATO spearhead driving for Poland's eastern border, and down towards Bulgaria and Romania.

In normal circumstances, Terry would not attend such a sitrep—he invariably didn't have the time, and the most important developments would be relayed to him by his generals or Squonk—but this morning he wanted to see for himself the extent of the problems that the enemy's new ACA was causing.

Rows of digital seats fanned out in front of him, with equally digital attendees. At the front stood a thin, tall soldier with his hands behind his back and legs slightly apart in the standard at-ease pose. When Terry peered at him, the man's details resolved in the air close by: Lieutenant-Colonel Paul Wainwright, 4th Special Airbourne Warfare Regiment.

Terry sipped from his mug of tea as he glanced around the auditorium, noting the names and ranks and regiments and nationalities of the other attendees. A part of him still marvelled that so many men and women from all of the broad range of European cultures could come together and fight in unison when faced with a merciless enemy.

"Hi, everyone," Wainwright began in a businesslike north American accent, reminding Terry that the US played a not insignificant role. "And welcome to the forty-third sitrep for Attack Group East. First, this briefing will give you a description of the enemy's latest massed ACA tactics. Second, there will be an overview of battlefield movements in the last twenty-four hours. And after that, Group Commander General Sir Patrick Fox will be, er, available to take any questions."

Terry sat back and relaxed, appreciating Wainwright's easy delivery yet professional mannerisms.

Wainwright disappeared when a graphic display enlarged over him and the auditorium. On it resolved the image of an enemy Siskin, slender and more elongated than the Blackswan, with two continuous recesses around its body and a smattering of stabilisation fins. Wainwright said, "Now we've had the opportunity to analyse the Siskin in a little more detail, we better understand its performance parameters—which, by the way, far exceed those of our current Scythes—and our super AI has been able to mitigate a fraction of its battlefield superiority."

The Siskin withdrew to a far less threatening distance, only for tens and then hundreds more to appear. Wainwright went on, "However, yesterday, on all contact points on the frontline, the enemy began arranging his ACAs into what we have dubbed 'the cube'. It's actually called that because, as you can see in the top-right of the view now, this is the first footage we got yesterday."

In a new rectangle in Terry's view, blurred and juddering video depicted a vast panorama of rolling hills and brown fields, over which hung hundreds of Siskins arranged in a cube that stretched at least a hundred metres on each edge.

Wainwright continued, describing the action, "Up to now, the super AIs on both sides have fought in waves, oftentimes ranging from a few metres' altitude all the way up to more than 50 kilometres, using open space to seek any advantage. What we saw yesterday is this: as Scythe X-7s attempted to engage the enemy, the cube changes shape to defend itself. As you can see in this footage, it will, er, undulate to any three-dimensional geometric shape required for its primary objectives. These are twofold: one, the protection of as many of its ACAs as possible; and two: the destruction of the selected ground targets."

Terry considered that he was watching the evillest murmuration ever to have been seen in the sky. The cube changed shape with grace and subtlety to counteract attacks by wings of Scythes. It didn't seem to matter from where in the sky the NATO machines attacked, the cube or globe or cone or whatever shape it took could maintain its cohesion while those Siskins at the base retained the relative freedom to use their lasers with deadly effect on the ground targets beneath them.

The image withdrew and Wainwright stood in the auditorium. "Even before today, we knew the number of Scythes needed to bring down a single one of the enemy's new ACAs had been slowly creeping up, but in yesterday's contacts, it exceeded eight-to-one for the first time. Given the length of the front and the number of enemy ACAs currently deployed, despite a record number of Scythes we can use, a controlled withdrawal of our forces remains the only tactical option in all sectors."

Terry swore under his breath.

"Okay," Wainwright resumed, "now let's take a closer look at losses sector by sector. Beginning with the French Fusiliers battlegroup in northern sector Charlie Alpha—"

Terry pulled the VR glasses off and left the sitrep. He let out a heavy sigh. He stood, took his tea, left his office, and went out into the central area. The hum of activity around the various stations felt familiar yet alien. An irrational sense of isolation rolled over his shoulders like the cold air from an aircon unit in the ceiling above him. He tensed away a shudder when he considered the questions that General Fox would have to field; questions that would likely come to Terry when they next consulted each other later in the day.

Terry put his mug on the console and said, "Squonk? Map of the Caliphate now."

A green outline describing the enemy's borders resolved in the air above the console.

Terry said, "Zoom to the border with India. Display estimates of ACA deployments on both sides of the border."

The righthand section of the image enlarged. Flashes of simple geometric shapes appeared along either side of the jagged line that separated the Caliphate and India: red for the enemy; blue for the West's sometime ally.

Terry asked, "According to latest intel, how many and what kind of armaments has the enemy deployed there?"

Squonk replied, "Approximately five to eight million autonomous combat aircraft, estimated to comprise forty percent Siskin, thirty percent Blackswan, and thirty percent Lapwing. In addition, up to two million warriors are estimated to be either in position for an invasion or in reserve."

"But why?" Terry whispered.

"Please clarify the question."

"Withdraw. Zoom in on Europe."

The map withdrew at once and the image rolled downwards and to the left to bring Europe into view.

"Show me all current contact lines with enemy deployments."

To the south, on the Spanish/Franco border, more simple shapes flashed into life. On Terry's right, in the east, there resolved a similar scattering.

"Speculate and run a simulation," Terry ordered with some trepidation. "What would happen if the enemy moved all or a substantial portion of his assets on his border with India and deployed them to defend his gains in Europe and push us back? Include the maximum possible NATO reactions, such as arms' production increases and deployments of reserves. Advance projections at one hour per second. Begin with the assumption that the enemy commences his redeployment now."

"Confirmed."

The date and time resolved on the righthand side of the image: 11.00 Friday 26 October 2063. With each second, the time advance by one hour. For the first twenty seconds, Terry struggled to notice anything change. Then, more shapes flashed into existence on the enemy's side of the contact line, which began an inexorable shift westwards, driving NATO forces into retreat. There were some additions to the defences, but Terry accepted at once that they could never be sufficient to arrest the enemy's advance.

Terry's eyes flitted from the contact lines as more and more enemy forces joined the battle, to the time indicator as the simulation ran into the third day. Both Attack Group South and Attack Group East were driven relentlessly back, to meet and combine in central France. When the simulation reached five days, it stopped.

"Well?" Terry asked. "Is that it?"
"Affirmative," Squonk answered.
"Explain."

"At five days, the forecasts become unreliable due to the anticipated collapse of NATO lines."

"You mean a rout?" Terry said, trying to keep the shock from his voice. "You estimate that we would be routed within five days if those forces were brought to bear?"

"Affirmative."

Terry shook his head in disbelief. He grasped his mug and drank the cold tea in it. From the corner of his eye, he saw the backs of the operators at their stations and wondered if they'd been listening. No matter; they'd all been properly vetted.

"Well, Squonk, that begs a very obvious and simple question: why does the enemy not do this?"

The super AI didn't miss a beat, "In order of probability: one, it would be too great a risk for the Third Caliph to lessen his defences against India. His projected strategy is to attempt to conquer the entire Eurasian landmass. The leadership of India is aware of this—"

"No, no," Terry broke in. "That is not correct. The enemy is the belligerent in that theatre. India is simply responding to the threat he created, taking the necessary steps to defend itself. What is the probability of India attacking the enemy, even pre-emptively, in any scenario?"

"Less than ten percent across all scenarios; less than four percent if the Caliphate offers no provocation."

"Right," Terry said with a click of his fingers. "Then, in theory, he could redeploy those forces to Europe and India would be more likely to breathe a collective sigh of relief than to attack him, yes?"

"Affirmative," the computer replied with no hint of contrition.

"So, what's the next probable reason he hasn't?"

"A lack of urgency."

"Meaning?"

150

"The initiative is with the enemy's forces. Only the high production volumes of the current Scythe variants are preventing the enemy from advancing more quickly."

"So," Terry said, drawing the conclusion, "he sees no need to rush. He's got us on the back foot." Terry thought for a moment before asking, "But his computers must be telling him that it's likely we're also producing new and better weapons, yes?"

"Affirmative."

"Then why does he not take that into account and pursue his current advantage to the maximum?"

"Insufficient data."

"Again, speculate."

"The most probable reason is related to internal dynamics."

"Expand."

"There is likely to be internal political upheaval. The Third Caliph may be facing challenges to his authority and may be occupied with reasserting that authority, to the detriment of utilising the advantage conferred by his current battlefield superiority."

"Speculate causes," Terry said, without a great deal of hope that the super AI would be able to offer any significant insights.

"Given the range and histories of the cultures that the New Persian Caliphate has subsumed since its creation in 2042, and further given the technological and societal advancements the subject populations have benefited from in the twenty-two years since, there are approximately eighty-seven potential causes for dislocation or upheaval that could generate such disruption that the current strategic advantage in Europe has been overlooked by those in positions of military authority."

Terry said nothing, considering it fruitless to explore any further the reasons why Europe's mortal enemy was not taking advantage of this current battlefield superiority. He stared at the results of the simulation and tried to imagine the ramifications of his forces being routed in five days so that they would be driven all the way back to central France.

He asked Squonk a question to which he already knew the answer, "When will the new Scythes be deployed to the battlefield?"

"In seven days' time."

"Can this timetable be accelerated in any way?"

"Negative. Final testing, manufacture, and deployment are already on the fastest possible track."

"Seven days," Terry whispered. "Whatever problems are going on in the enemy's lands, may they last another seven days."

Chapter 19

07.34 Sunday 28 October 2063

Pip awoke with a jolt when the bulkhead against which her head rested seemed to hit her. The cold, hard surface acted as a reminder that the field hospital lay far behind her now.

Her Squitch announced, "You are arriving at staging post Zulu One-Four. Prepare to disembark for transport to your battalion."

She blinked and struggled to stretch in the confines of her seat. The changing air pressure rippled in her inner ears as the aircraft descended. She glanced at the other occupants but none seemed troubled in a similar manner. Through the portholes opposite, the morning sky glimmered blue with the promise of another warm autumn day.

The Airbus descended the last few metres and settled on the ground. The hatchway slid up at the far end of the fuselage and Pip sensed the air in the craft warm at once. She unclipped her harness and freed her Pickup from its stowage behind her seat. As she shuffled her way out following three others, she prepared herself mentally for a return to combat she'd never expected she would live to see. Lost in thought, she grabbed her Bergen and stepped off the AAT.

"Good morning, Captain Clarke. Do you need a lift to your billet?"

Pip's eyes widened when she heard Rory's voice. She said, "Well, if it isn't the notorious Colour Sergeant Moore, the regiment's lucky charm?" Pip paused, saw something in Rory's eyes that betrayed her own feelings at finally meeting again after so long, and decided to keep the situation light. She said, "You know, I think you've grown even taller since I last saw you. And anyway, I thought we were going to meet later on, once I'd got to my billet?"

Rory shrugged and said, "Decided to surprise you. Hope you don't mind," he said, casting his eyes down.

"Of course not," she said, not at all sure she was telling the truth.

He looked back up at her. "Great. Look, I managed to snag a mobile command vehicle to take you to the camp."

"Nice," she replied. "So, being so well-known does have its pluses."

He shrugged again and said, "And your rank, captain. An officer can't really be expected to travel with the great unwashed. Can I take your Bergen?"

"No, thanks, I can manage, mate," she replied, intentionally limiting his bravado.

"Sure," he replied, seemingly unbothered. "The transport's over here." He strode away from the landing zone and Pip followed, a light breeze making strands of hair swish across her face.

Ahead of them, barren fields descended into a patchwork of brown interspersed with occasional green. Above it all rose the majestic Pyrenees, angular and indomitable, shimmering in the bright blue morning.

Rory glanced back at her and said, "You know, there are still US Marines in those mountains making a real fight of it."

She drew level with him. "I read the latest sitreps. According to intel, the only thing making this an even-remotely well-managed withdrawal is the fact that Scythe production has never been higher."

Rory scoffed, "The X–7s and the X–9s are no match for these bloody Siskins, mate."

"Yeah, I also know that," Pip replied.

They arrived at the mobile command vehicle. Pip tossed her Bergen in the stowage bin in the rear.

Once seated and secured, Rory told the vehicle, "Windows, normal configuration. Return to forward operational base." He nodded again at the mountains and said, "The week before last, we were going in there on rescue missions that Brass insisted on calling 'counterattacks'."

The vehicle trundled away from the landing zone.

Pip said, "I saw the sitreps for those, too. Didn't look like much of a picnic."

"There's some real macho bullshit going on there. A tactical withdrawal makes a lot of sense now."

Pip didn't want to talk about the current situation. She said, "You were right about Colonel Doyle."

"Ha, knew it. Did he offer you the same bullshit he offered me?"

Rory's combative attitude unnerved Pip. She replied, "Yes, he did. But I don't get why you think that was so bad. I told him I'd think about it. He seemed genuinely keen for me to agree to a non-combat role. There's a lot of experience I— we—could pass on to new recruits."

Rory shook his head and said, "It's still a bullshit posting, mate. There was no way he—"

"Anyway," she broke in, "I did him the courtesy of waiting a couple of days before declining."

Rory glanced at the scenery. "I'm glad you did. So, how come you're here? Did you wangle that, too?"

Pip smiled, "Nope. Reorientation at corps level."

"See? Us non-coms don't get told shit, while you officers—"

"Give over," Pip said light-heartedly. "Most deployment decisions at battalion level and above are need-to-know—"

"Still quite a slog, though, isn't it? Why start sending officers from one attack group to the other?"

Pip shrugged, "Not sure. At an educated guess, I'd say we're getting loads more recruits in the ranks now, so maybe that's got something to do with it?"

The vehicle turned right onto a wide dirt track with ruts that evidenced much recent use.

Rory said, "Strange when you think how few of us there are left; since before the war, I mean."

Pip didn't reply. Talking to her old commanding officer reminded her of all the reasons she'd joined up two years earlier. She said, "I remember doing my basic training and first-time live firing a Pickup on the range. We all said then we'd never see action, but it was fun to learn how to shoot."

Rory said, "Me too. Back then, if you wanted to see real action, you'd have to get yourself into the SAS or one of the other special ops regiments." He sighed and added, "Yeah, that was when the British Army was a good career choice that paid a decent pension at the end."

Pip smiled and said in black humour, "Still does, only for some of us, pension is compensation and goes to our next of kin."

"Don't tempt fate."

"I'm not. Do you remember spending our days fixing flood defences on the Humber?"

"Like yesterday." He looked at her and asked, "Who could've foreseen what the Terror of Tehran was about to do to Europe?"

"Not many," Pip agreed. "And he's still doing it." She looked ahead and saw low buildings and military vehicles. With their destination approaching, she asked, "Where do you think it's going to end this time? Can the enemy push us all the way back to England again, like they did last year?"

The mobile command vehicle rolled to a stop, the next in line in a row of similar vehicles.

"I reckon you probably know better than me," Rory replied.

"Yeah, how so?"

"Every base is a bloody rumour mill. There's a load of chatter that we've got better weapons on the way."

Pip shrugged and unclipped her restraints, "I've heard similar things, but you know what Brass is like with op-sec, and I don't blame them."

The doors opened. She got out of the vehicle and collected her Bergen from the rear.

Rory stretched and said, "You want to grab some breakfast before you meet the base commander? We've been spoilt with a new replicator that can turn out a half-decent black pudding in its fry-up."

"Thanks, but my Squitch is telling me Colonel Addison is waiting to welcome me. Maybe later?"

"Sure, I'll walk with you."

"What's Addison like, anyway?"

"I've heard he's all right for an Ox and Bucks."

"Okay, thanks." She stopped outside a temporary single storey building. "What's your schedule today, assuming the raghead decides to have a Sunday off?"

Rory scoffed and replied, "The usual. I need to make sure my squad are all kitted out and happy bunnies. Then, I need to brief some bereavement liaison officers back in Blighty. There's no shortage of bad news to deliver to next of kin."

"Yeah, been there," Pip sympathised. "Maybe see you later, then?"

Rory nodded, turned to go but stopped and said, "Good to see you again."

Pip smiled and watched Rory walk away, convinced he really was even taller than when she'd last seen him.

She walked up to the building and tapped smartly on the plain grey door her Squitch indicated. A gruff, "Come," sounded from the other side. She entered.

A well-built man with a wide face and muttonchop whiskers stood and stomped towards her with furrowed brow, "Ah, Captain Clarke. Welcome to Attack Group South. Good to have you here."

Pip stood her Bergen against the wall, turned, saluted. "Thank you, colonel," she answered.

Addison made a half-hearted attempt to return the salute, sighed, and said, "As you were, captain." He stuck out a hand that looked like a slab of concrete and Pip shook it. He said, "I have a lot of time for you Royal Engineers. And, I must say, your record is most impressive: escaping from behind the lines; defeating a Spider in combat; playing a role in saving England last year; and then taking on a Lapwing on your own. Your CO must be must be quite proud of you."

Pip tensed her muscles so that Addison would not see her shudder. He appeared old—at least forty, possibly older—and she wanted him to sense the respect she had for him. She glanced down at her boots and replied, "Thank you, sir. I'm just trying to do my duty."

"I rather think you've done a bit more than that. In any case, let's get back to business. Now, elements of your battalion will begin to arrive tonight and into tomorrow. I can't impress upon you enough how subject to events all of this is. For now, those American marines are doing a sterling job of holding the enemy up in the mountains, and we need to support them. But if, and it is quite a big 'if', the enemy is able to find a way to turn the marines' flanks, we will have to be ready to respond in a lively manner."

"Yes, sir," Pip answered. "I am familiar with current deployments and the enemy's attempts to drive us back."

"Good," Addison said. "In the meantime, I would ask you to make yourself known around this base. We have many new recruits who, a couple of weeks ago, were training on simulations in England. Now, they're faced with a resurgent enemy who might very well steamroller right over us if we're unlucky. I worry some of my green recruits are fretting that they shall be burned to a crisp before they can even fire a single shot. I'm relying on battle-expert, experienced soldiers like you to help me to help them resist this unpleasant turn of events. Can I, in fact, rely on you, Captain Clarke?"

The breath evaporated from Pip's chest. Feelings welled inside and seemed to concentrate in her chin, pulling her lower lip down as though she would weep. The tidal wave of emotion she'd felt when she'd decided to end her life by facing down a Lapwing alone now coalesced in this perfectly reasonable question from a commander who, like her, was fighting to do his best. She sniffed loudly to smother any distortion in her voice. "Yes, sir," she squeaked.

"Excellent," Addison replied. "Right, if there's anything you need help with, let me know. Dinner in the officers' mess at six would be an opportunity to introduce you to the, er, other officers, so I expect you to attend. Any questions?"

"No, sir."

"Very good. Dismissed."

Pip saluted, collected her kitbag, and left the colonel's office. Outside, the sun had climbed higher and warmed the dusty ground. Squaddies strode along alone or in pairs, autonomous vehicles loaded with stores and munitions rolled, turned, and parked at their designated delivery points. Above this activity, brilliant-white cotton-wool clouds hung motionless, and Pip's imagination placed thousands of enemy ACAs among them.

Her Squitch showed her the way to her billet. She deposited her Bergen and went for a brew. The business of the day occupied her until an hour before dinner, when she met Rory again. They went for a walk to the perimeter of the base and deactivated their Squitches. Rory told her about Operation Thunderclap. Pip had a hundred questions that had to wait because she needed to return for dinner in the officers' mess. In the evening, elements of her battalion arrived, including the platoon with the redoubtable Private Barny Hines.

The following day, she met Rory again and they discussed all that had happened in the time they'd been apart. Afterwards, when each had to return to their duties, Pip realised that it was possible to go on, to continue no matter the odds, no matter the risks. Like Rory, she knew the enemy was far from finished and her personal war likely still had some distance to run. But slowly, she could begin to accept this.

As the days passed and the Americans fought valiantly to stop the enemy pushing NATO further back, Pip's inner strength returned. She felt less like she maintained a veneer of martial professionalism, and more like a captain in the British Army. Whatever else this war might throw at her, she regained the courage to face it. She resolved that never again would she try to throw her life away.

While fulfilling her admin duties late one evening that week, she officially proposed Private John "Barny" Hines, 33 Armoured Engineer Squadron, to be awarded the Military Cross for bravery.

Chapter 20

16.57 Thursday 1 November 2063

Geoff Morrow threw his backpack on the bed and resisted the urge to do the same with himself. The Paris hotel room was ridiculously small, like the worst London had to offer: a little over two metres wide and perhaps six deep. At the far end, the bed ran the full width of the room, under the window, while to his right, the so-called bathroom reminded him of a luxury outdoor portable toilet.

"And Alan expects me to go out and get more content, does he?" he muttered aloud. "So, they put me in this dump to make sure it's the last place I'd want to stay. Makes sense."

His lens linked to the hotel's super AI and Geoff twitched an eye muscle to select the menu of room functions in his view, from which he lowered the blind to hide the forest of construction replicators rebuilding this part of the city. His thoughts returned to the book he would write when this bloody war finally finished. He had an idea for the title, something fitting but not overly morbid or too grandiose. What he needed—

A flashing comms signal broke into his thoughts, from the one person he couldn't reject. He raised it and said, "Hi, Alan."

"You're finally in Paris, then?"

"Just checked in to the hotel. Glad to see *The Gnm* is still as tightfisted as ever."

"The piece you sent in yesterday has just gone live."

"The orphans stealing the aid in Vernon? Great, but why did it take so long?"

"The emergency mayor's office stalled on their rebuttal."

"That's a load of shit, Alan. You can't—"

"Don't tell me how to run my newspaper, Geoff," Alan replied, using the outdated word for media outlet. "I'm still giving a right of rebuttal in situations like that. You just keep getting me copy and I'll keep paying. Sound reasonable?"

"Yeah, yeah," Geoff mumbled.

"Speaking of which, I want you to hook up with a journo from the *WSJ*."

Geoff mouthed a curse but kept his voice light, "Oh, really? Why's that?"

"We've made an ad-hoc deal to pool copy. A lot of the other players are doing it, mainly to benefit from cross-contacts. You've got contacts in the British Army and English politics; this guy's got the same in the US."

Geoff shook his head as he reached for the door handle. He exited the room as he spoke, "But that's bound to be a better deal for us than for them, right? Why does the *WSJ* need us?"

Alan's voice took on a familiar sarcastic edge, "Because I convinced them with my extensive journalistic acumen, that's why. So, if you don't mind, please haul your sorry arse to the Hôtel Providence and meet him. His name's Daniel Buckley."

"And he gets to stay at the Providence while I'm stuck slumming it in the Rue Cler."

"You can always lose your job instead."

Geoff trotted down the stairs instead of waiting for a lift. "Yeah, yeah. I've heard of him. Wasn't he in Chile during the Cyber Wars?"

"I don't know. Just meet him, then get out and about around the city and get me something worth publishing."

Geoff reached the moody, ill-lit lobby and strode for the main doors. "Sure. Do you have any update on when what we think will happen, will happen?"

"Not yet. And like I told you last time, you don't need to ask. You're in Paris for the duration, Geoff."

With that, Alan terminated the connection. Now out on the narrow street, Geoff muttered in sarcasm, "Yeah, it was a pleasure chatting. Thanks, Alan. You take care, too. Bye for now… Wanker."

Geoff raised the map in his view and found the location of the Providence. The Metro in this part of the tenth arrondissement had not yet been reopened, so he walked, enjoying the cooler air now darkness had fallen. Many high, bright lights lit the streets, often from construction replicators.

His thoughts returned to the book he would write. He had grown comfortable—at least, less daunted—at his determination to record every victim of the war. He kept telling himself that, as a modern-day journalist, he had access to supporting tech that the poor hacks who covered previous wars could only dream of, and thus his book would be unmatched in its depth and detail.

Geoff tried to call Buckley, but an automated message came back that Geoff would be able to find him in the terrace lounge of the Hôtel Providence. As he turned the last corner and entered the Rue René Boulanger, Geoff appreciated how much progress the authorities had made in reconstructing the city. Although most of its main monuments remained either piles of rubble or were hidden behind hoardings to keep out curious eyes, many amenities appeared to be in good shape.

The glass entrance to the Hôtel Providence shone clear and clean in hues of white and yellow, reflecting the glare from the surrounding city lights. He twitched an eye muscle to send a localised ID burst. In response, the concierge nodded him through the lobby. As he went, his lens indicated the direction of the terrace lounge.

At its entrance, however, a waitress held a barring hand up while her face shone with a welcoming smile. "*Monsieur a-t-il une reservation?*" she asked.

Geoff kept his annoyance in check. He replied, "I have a meeting here with one of your guests, a Mr Buckley. I did send out a pulse, you know?"

The young lady's perfect eyebrows came together in an apologetic expression. She replied in English with a soft accent of liquid gold, "But, of course. Please forgive me, Mr Morrow. We have limiters in this lounge as many of our guests prefer to enjoy some privacy."

"Fine," Geoff replied, his irritation vanishing at the gorgeous sound of her English. "In that case, where can I find Mr Buckley?"

"I will show you to him." She led Geoff deep into the lounge, past wing-backed chairs, the majority of which were empty. They arrived and she held out an elegant hand to indicate Buckley.

The American journalist looked up and said, "Hey, Geoff. Good to meet you. Sit down. Scotch?"

"Fine with me, thanks," Geoff answered.

Buckley asked the waitress for another glass.

Geoff sat in a luxurious chair opposite the American. "Good to see the *WSJ* looks after its staff this well."

Buckley looked at Geoff with narrow, penetrating eyes that unnerved Geoff. But when he spoke, his soft voice invited trust. He said, "It ain't such a big deal. There's a ton of money coming out of Washington to help with the rebuilding, so media outlets like mine get 'special rates', if you know what I mean?"

"Good for you," Geoff replied without rancour.

The waitress arrived and deposited a second tumbler on the table and offered to pour from the elegant decanter. Geoff declined. She left and Geoff poured for himself, saying, "I read a lot of your stuff from the Cyber Wars a few years back. That must've taken some bottle. Refill?"

Buckley nodded and held out his glass. "'Bottle'?" he queried.

Geoff poured for him and said, "Yeah, you know—balls, courage."

"Sure," came the laconic reply.

Geoff held his glass up, "Cheers."

"Bottoms up."

When he drank, Geoff savoured the flavour and waited to see if and how Buckley would try to take control of the 'relationship'. In reaction to the scotch, he said, "I'm no expert, but that's pretty rich."

"Sure is. Anyways, Chile was very much a team effort."

"I suppose we could say that about a lot of big stories."

"But afterwards, the Pulitzer I got for it let me sweet-talk them into giving me Europe. Never thought stuff would happen here that could be worse than Chile, though."

Geoff gave a mirthless chuckle. "And it's not over yet."

Buckley contemplated the whiskey in his glass, a golden honey shot through with rays of amber. "I'm tending to think it is."

Geoff said, "You sound certain," despite Buckley's lazy delivery.

"Tehran is picking the wrong fight with India," the American said. "That risks having nukes going off right next door to China, and Beijing is not gonna like that one little bit."

"I think the last two years have proved the Chinese president doesn't have anything like the hold over the Chief Raghead everyone thought he did when the war started."

"Either way, that's where the attention is now, not here."

"Agreed," Geoff said, "but I've not long been back from the front lines, and the new Siskin is driving NATO into reverse. Not as bad as the original invasion two years ago, but bad enough. The Caliphate's not done here yet." Then a thought occurred to Geoff. He asked, "Where have you been for the last while, anyway?"

Buckley gave Geoff a tight smile and replied, "Stateside."

Geoff realised at once that the super-amazing *WSJ* journalist must've chickened out and run away last year when England looked finished. However, Geoff couldn't afford confrontation. Alan didn't buddy them up for nothing. But it didn't hurt to know that Pulitzer-prize-winner Daniel Buckley was a bloody coward. Geoff answered, "Sure," in neutral imitation of Buckley's preferred affirmative.

"How rough is it at the front?" the American asked.

"I was an embed with the Royal Marines when the Siskins turned up. All of them got wiped out. I only escaped because it was the evening and I was in the mess."

"Too bad."

"So, my editor took some pity on me and gave me a less dangerous assignment. And here we are."

"Well," Buckley said, lifting the decanter and refilling both glasses, "I got a suggestion for you. Have you ever been to the Louvre?"

Geoff picked the glass up and swirled the liquid in it. "Nope."

"Wanna go?"

"How?" Geoff exclaimed, looking back up. "The authorities have got that place totally locked down."

"By getting the right authorisations," Buckley said, a half-smile playing on his shadowed face. "Look, it's a huge museum and it took a beating when Paris was occupied—hell, they're still figuring out what's left in the vaults, what can be saved, what can't. We'll go there and each cover different areas. We can put together a special feature. Then both our editors will be happy."

Geoff nodded in appreciation. "Sounds like a plan. Cheers."

Chapter 21

23.45 Thursday 1 November 2063

Officer Mark Phillips of 3rd Airspace Defence reclined in his usual pod, headset on, and monitored his assigned sector. This night, Lieutenant Rose Cho had given him the same sector in which his sister Maria was stationed, but this was not by accident. A few weeks previously, he'd taken advantage of the regiment's bereavement service. As he had now lost his parents to an enemy Spider, and his brother Martin in action, the regiment ensured he would always be put in charge of monitoring the sector of the front that included his sister Maria's current location.

Tonight, enemy activity was extensive, as though the new month had brought new intentions. However, up to now his sister did her work in relative safety. Her casualty clearing station sat behind the medium-sized German town of Patersdorf, while so far, the enemy probed with as-yet insufficient forces to break through. But Mark knew this meant the night's business had only just begun. With waves of his hands and flicks of his wrists, he flitted around the digital sky, observing all of the kit required for NATO forces to fight this war.

"Good evening, Babyface."

Mark groaned at the sound of Captain Joe Neely-also-known-as-Shithead in his ears. "Oh, God. What do you want?"

"You sound almost as pleased to hear from me as I am to have to sink to the depths of stupidity to be able to communicate at your level."

"Where did Lieutenant Cho go? You smiled at her and she decided life was no longer worth living, right?"

"If I decided to, I could make the lieutenant a very happy woman; unlike you, with your dick no doubt as miniscule and as shrivelled as your brain."

"You certainly know what a woman looks for in a man, Captain Shithead. And in your case, what a woman looks for is someone else."

Shithead's voice lowered and became businesslike, "Okay, I'll let you have that one. The enemy's probing all along the front tonight; not only your sector."

With a wave of his hand, Mark pulled up Squonk's latest forecasts. He said, "The stats are fluctuating slightly more than usual. Odds still favour another massed attack overnight."

"Oh, it's coming, Babyface."

Mark reassured himself that Maria would not be in immediate danger. In any case, he would send her a warning if the situation in her sector deteriorated suddenly. He said, "Your crystal ball-gazing isn't up to much, is it? We have attacks almost every night."

"I hope they do. I hope they throw everything they've got against us tonight. You know what? I can't wait, in fact."

Mark heard something different in Shithead's voice. "Why do you say it like that?"

There came a pause, then Shithead replied, "They're going to get the shock of their bastard shitty lives."

Mark couldn't help himself but make light of the situation. "What are you going to do, sir? Wag your index finger at them sternly?"

To Mark's surprise the captain laughed. He replied, "Nothing so effective. I can't tell you what's going to happen, Babyface, because you're simply not important enough and you don't have clearance. But I will give you one piece of advice: whatever you do tonight, don't blink."

Chapter 22

23.56 Thursday 1 November 2063

Rory drew in a deep breath and opened comms to his squad, "Prepare to fall back. We've almost certainly got a cube on the way to clear the ground for the ragheads. Usual drill, people: full mag and do what your Squitch tells you."

He turned back from the dark hillside facing him, cradled his Pickup, and began the fastest trot he could. On either side, the sound of army boots plodding in the dirt followed him.

Sergeant Heaton spoke in his ear on private comms, "Nay drama, laddie. We've done our patrol. If things go wrong, we'll have air or ground transports to evac us afore you know it."

Rory muttered his agreement, but it wasn't his own safety—or even the safety of his squad—that concerned him; it was Pip's. Since she and her battalion had been reassigned to his sector on Attack Group South the previous Sunday, he'd spent the most time with her since that claustrophobic metal coffin called *HMS Spiteful* rescued them from the Spanish coast at the beginning of the war.

He thought he'd let her go. They'd been through so much separately, he thought those feelings he'd harboured before the war had gone, withered and died like so much of his previous life, before the fighting, before the injuries, before poor George.

But now, Pip seemed to need him. They talked about the comrades they'd lost, to keep the memories of them alive. They talked about why they should've survived this far when so many had not. Pip wanted to know how he went on. But he did not want to discuss it, lest the admission of some element of fortune caused it to desert him and in result he should die. Alternatively, he knew how Pip felt—he understood that peculiar confusion of continuing on this Earth when so many around them had been so violently removed from it—so he wanted to comfort and console, but dare not allow his emotions towards her the free rein they demanded. Fortunately, their day-to-day duties came between them.

"Warning," his Squitch announced. "You must accelerate your pace."

"Christ, again?" Rory hissed in frustration. "Why?"

"The probability of a concentrated enemy attack on this sector has increased to over ninety percent."

"Why here?"

"The terrain in this location is most suited for the enemy to advance."

"Shit, that's not good." As he lumbered more quickly up the gentle incline to the nearest track, Rory twitched his eye to zoom the map in his vision to check the other patrol squads' locations. All were returning to the forward operations base, but they were spread out over a line nearly three kilometres long. He contacted Heaton, "Grandad, my Squitch is giving me some kind of bullshit. I reckon we should get the transports out from the base to take us back." His boot slipped when he tried to use a protruding root to push himself up. He recovered and reached the dirt track. "But we don't have enough ATTs for all of us. So, who do we prioritise?" He turned back to check on his squad.

"Aye," Heaton called. "The super AI will likely put the Falarete teams first. I think we need to order a retreat now and not wait to be told."

"Roger that," Rory answered, noting the young men and women who made up his squad as each of them clambered onto the track.

Pip spoke in Rory's ear, "Attention, all squads. Looks like we've got nasties inbound. We're assured of sufficient air cover so don't just leg it; make sure you're good to go: secure your kit and make your way back to base for evac. I want everyone back there in under three—"

Pip stopped in the same instant a vast explosion erupted to the northeast, on Rory's left. He knew at once it was a Spider.

Rory froze. "Pip?" he said.

A tall plume of smoke with orange flames flashing rose up in a gout, spewing chunks of debris outwards like an evil fountain.

"Report," Rory ordered, sure that a Spider had detonated and terrified that Pip had triggered the explosion, in which case she could not have survived.

"Fuck," he breathed, feeling the panic in his chest. "Fucking report."

His Squitch said, "The highest probability is that a dormant enemy Spider has detonated. Rescue measures have been implemented. You should continue to withdraw."

Rory resumed jogging, cradling his Pickup, the weight of his kit on his back forcing him to make more effort. He hurried towards the site of the explosion, dismay sweeping over him; not only for Pip, but for all of them. The ragheads must have left dormant Spiders behind weeks ago. The first NATO troops to advance through this sector had certainly used Pathfinders to clear their route, but somehow, they must've missed this one. Worse, there might be others given the vast area the foothills of the Pyrenees covered.

He hurried on, leaving the designated track and moving into low scrub to try to get to the site of the explosion sooner. Sweat prickled his skin, making his uniform irritate his shoulders, waist and thighs. Heaving for breath, he said, "Location and condition of Captain Clarke?"

His Squitch replied, "Captain Clarke was in the vicinity of the detonation and is currently unaccounted for."

This impossible answer forced Rory to stop running. "What?" he exclaimed. "How can you not know her condition? Explain, now."

"Advancing enemy formations are attempting to jam communications in the battlespace."

He cursed and resumed leaping onwards, around dry shrubs and withered trees. "Could you please stop them?" he asked with as much sarcasm as he could muster.

"Enemy jamming will be defeated in approximately twenty-nine seconds."

He reached the crest. Ahead, the dull orange glow of flames now lit the way, black shadows dancing over the uneven terrain. At least it would be easier to spot divots and other pitfalls.

The air above him suddenly split with the hiss of NATO Scythes racing to meet the approaching enemy. He estimated over a hundred of the machines, which his lens identified as X–7s. But instead of relief, dread crystallised inside him: everyone knew the X–7s and X–9s were no match for the Siskin. In addition, their arrival meant that the attack could only be moments away.

As if in confirmation of the increasing danger, his Squitch said, "You must seek cover now or withdraw from the battlespace."

He resumed jogging and hissed, "Location of Captain Clarke—now."

Abruptly his display came alive with the details of the casualties. Pip was three hundred metres on his left.

His Squitch said, "Medics are inbound to retrieve the wounded when the battlespace is secured. You must seek cover or withdraw from the battlespace."

He searched the dark, shadowed ground as his display guided him to her, avoiding smouldering debris, climbing over mounds of freshly exposed dirt, and nearly gagging on the stench of burned vegetation. Overhead, sounds of the distant clashes of ACAs carried on the air.

Heaton spoke in his ear, "Laddie, where are you?"

"Assisting the wounded."

"That's nay your job."

"Don't argue, grandad. Get clear. I'll follow."

"I'm half a klick to your north. We've got transports on their way—"

"I can see that."

"I'm coming in to get you—"

"Negative. Help the other wounded if you want, or collect some pieces of the bodies in case we're not able to come back this way again."

"You nay have the time, lad—"

Rory terminated the connection when he reached Pip. She lay on her side. At first, he assumed she must be unconscious or dead, but the one eye he could see blinked. He put his Pickup on the ground and crouched beside her. She looked incredibly fragile.

"Hey, mate?" he asked.

Her body didn't move but her eye looked at him and she tried to smile.

"I see you're slacking on the job again, captain. I'll put you on report if you keep this up."

Pip didn't speak. Her eyelid fluttered and closed.

"Squitch? Status of Captain Clarke."

"Blunt force trauma to internal organs and minor shrapnel damage to lower limbs."

An impossible weight formed at the back of Rory's throat. "Will she live?" he croaked.

"The casualty must receive medical attention within seven minutes. An autonomous troop transport is inbound with GenoFluid packs on board. ETA, two minutes."

Rory breathed a heavy sigh of relief. "Thank God for th—"

"Approaching enemy ACAs have targeted this section of the front. You should seek cover until friendly forces retake the battlespace."

Pip coughed suddenly.

Rory unclipped his webbing and let it and the pack on his back fall to the ground. This allowed him to get closer to her. Despite being unsure whether he could or should move Pip, he sat in the warm dirt and lifted her shoulders. At once, she stopped coughing. No blood escaped her mouth.

He smiled and said, "We're well in the shit now, mate."

With an effort, she said, "Cube… In seconds."

Rory said, "What?" in reaction, even though he knew what she meant.

She frowned and said, "Leave me. Please."

His Squitch repeated, "Overwhelming enemy forces have entered the battlespace. You must seek cover."

He looked into Pip's pleading eyes. "Not a chance, captain. We always were the best team."

She said, "I'm so tired."

"Yeah, me too." He turned his head to see the sky above them filled with a vast cube of Siskins advancing on their position. Waves of tiny white dots that his display told him were X-7s flew in to join battle. The cube undulated and warped like a graceful, liquid polyhedron, as it fired invisible laser shots to defeat the NATO machines for no loss. The Scythes flashed and twisted and spun, burning, back to earth. The base of the cube sagged like a bellbottomed tear, the Siskins there flying closer to the ground, ready to burn any target.

Rory knew what would happen next and cleared the data in his display so he could look at Pip and only Pip. He held her in the dirt, wisps of smoke curling around them. He wished he could take her pain from her and endure it for her. He looked up at the cube as it loomed hundreds of metres over them, higher than the mountains beyond, and saw now that it was made up of thousands of enemy machines. It struck him as the deadliest machine-made work of art it was possible to imagine.

His Squitch abruptly said, "Danger, seek cover from falling debris."

The announcement made no sense to Rory.

Pip tugged his sleeve. He lowered his head to hers and she said, "We're okay."

"You bet," he replied, assuming she must be delirious.

She coughed, swallowed, and said, "You don't unders—"

A powerful gust of wind bore down on their position. Rory shielded Pip with his free arm against a rush of small twigs and bitter dust. The air stilled again. Rory looked back at the sky. The cube now retreated. Its centre undulated backwards as though punched by an invisible fist. Green flashes spoke to the impact of laser shots against the Siskins' shielding. From the middle, bright white light erupted, revealing other, different specks in the sky.

Realisation hit Rory at the same time the first destroyed Siskin came whirling out of the sky to crash into the ground.

He held Pip more closely and almost shouted, "The Omega."

His Squitch repeated, "Danger, seek cover from falling debris."

The cube above them began to dissolve. Siskins flashed green as their shielding burned out after what seemed to Rory to be a very short time. They exploded under the onslaught, popping and screeching and twisting earthward, reduced to scrap metal.

Rory raised the digital display in his lens. An elevated map showed him that hundreds of the new Scythe Omegas descended on the Siskins. Outmanoeuvred and outgunned, the enemy machines had no option but to retreat. But most were being removed from the battle with breathtaking efficiency. He focused on individual groups in the sky, amazed to see Siskins burst into flame and fall after being hit by only a few laser pulses. The laser the Omega carried must be an order of magnitude more powerful than the one on the X–7.

Any fear Rory had that a falling ACA might hit them receded as the seconds passed. The Siskins that made up the cube broke formation and fled the battlespace, chased by the new Omegas.

His Squitch announced, "The battlespace is secure. Prepare to advance."

Rory replied, "I'm not going anywhere. I have a casualty to take care of."

The continuing hisses, pops and metallic screeches of the ACAs fighting each other faded.

He glanced at Pip but her eyes were closed. He had a flash of panic and asked, "What is Captain Clarke's status?"

"Unchanged."

"Where's help?"

Before his Squitch replied, a large autonomous troop transport heaved into view, having climbed the slope to reach the area where the dormant Spider had detonated. It rolled to a halt and a side door slid open. Four troops leapt out, one following another, each clutching small, battlefield GenoFluid packs. The second figure out ran to them. The name, 'Medical Orderly Kamilia Meyer' resolved in Rory's vision. He watched the young woman's eye twitch as she looked Pip over.

"Okay," she said. "Let's get her comfortable."

Rory extracted his BHC sleeve from its pocket on his calf, opened it, then scrunched it up to form a makeshift pillow. Once Pip's head was supported, Meyer undid Pip's tunic and placed the small pack on Pip's throat and upper thorax.

"What does your Squitch say?" Rory asked, knowing the orderly would have more details of Pip's condition.

Meyer replied in a professional tone underlain with an edge of urgency, "There's a piece of shrapnel in her liver, that's the only moderate concern; her other injuries are pretty unpleasant but superficial. The bots are on their way to the site to assess the damage and begin repairs. Bots are also going to her heart and her brain to ensure nothing worsens until we can get her to a proper facility."

"Good," Rory said.

Meyer looked at him, "There's nothing for you to worry about, Sergeant Moore. Your comrade will be fine. I'll get a stretcher from the ATT and we'll get her to the nearest casualty clearing station."

Rory caught the faintest trace of dismissal in her words. He replied, "Right, yeah. Thanks." He stood, pulled his webbing back on, heaved his kit onto his back, and collected his Pickup. He stared at Pip, reluctance to leave her rooting him to the spot like a sentry standing guard over his monarch.

Meyer also stood and then returned to the ATT.

Heaton's voice broke into his thoughts, "Laddie, are you nay coming along?"

"What? Yeah, give me a minute to get back to the line."

"You don't want to miss this," Heaton said.

"Miss what?"

"Shitloads of barbequed ragheads, lying all over the place, that's what."

The news made Rory nod in approval.

Heaton went on, "The Omegas have done us proud, laddie. Them bastards can nay stop us now."

Rory twitched his eye to raise the map of his squad's location. Once orientated, he paused and took a last look at his beloved Pip lying on the ground, the small GenoFluid pack ensuring her safety.

He turned away and, cradling his Pickup, hurried to catch up with his squad and the rest of the platoon.

Chapter 23

08.59 Friday 2 November 2063

Terry Tidbury strode around the large desk in his private office in the War Rooms. In the main screen on the wall, thumbnails of his generals flashed into existence as they joined the sitrep. He concentrated to rein his emotions in and not display the burning urgency he felt.

After what seemed like an eternity, the time on the screen advanced to '09.00'. He stood still in front of it and reminded himself that, now more than ever, he had to lead. He began, "Ladies and gentlemen, the new Scythe Omega ACA has exceeded all of our expectations. According to our computers, the Omega's ability to defeat the enemy's ACAs has given us an unassailable advantage."

The expressions of satisfaction that greeted this opening only heightened his determination. He feigned an angered disposition and went on, "However, this remarkable advantage is strictly time-limited. Even now, as I speak, the enemy must certainly be aware of the superiority of the Omega. He absolutely must redeploy his forces currently occupied on his border with India into the European theatre.

And when he does, our advance will be slowed, stopped, and possibly even reversed. If his superiority in numbers can do that, then we can expect him to gain sufficient time to design and deploy new weapons that will, in turn, be able to best ours."

Terry paused, drew in a deep breath and said, "I've instructed our computers to accelerate advances wherever possible, and I want now to order you all to do the same. It is highly likely forward units will come across many more harrowing scenes than they have to date. The further we drive the enemy back, the longer he has had to work his especially dark talents against the local populations. However, we cannot pause. We will, of course, bring up support units to offer assistance, but, as we have all seen since Repulse commenced, they already have much to do.

"Nevertheless, I want to impress upon you all the utmost urgency of the situation we now face. We must use this advantage to the maximum and regain as much of our territory as we can before events, as I strongly suspect, take yet another turn and this most problematic of enemies comes back at us, potentially even stronger."

Terry unfolded his arms and stuck his clenched fists on his hips. "According to the original plan, Operation Repulse was forecast to be accomplished before the end of this year. However, the arrival of the Siskin put paid to that. Now, we must use this brief window of opportunity to advance Repulse to the maximum extent. Any questions?"

There came a pregnant pause, as though none of his generals could decide who should speak first. The Polish General Pakla enlarged to cover the screen, his forehead creased in concentration. He said, "Yes, field marshal. If, as you say, so much now depends on how quickly the Third Caliph can redirect his forces from the border with India, what is your opinion on this? What I mean is, do you have any new intelligence that gives you knowledge of our requirement for urgency; or, rather, is it just your opinion that he can fix the situation on his border with India?"

Terry refolded his arms and replied, "To answer the first point, I have no better intelligence than the daily reports that go out to each of you. Yes, from time to time, some very sensitive figures may be redacted, as you have seen, but there is very little you are not provided with. We could hardly prosecute this war effectively if that were not the case. The covert intel-gathering process that began when we captured the very first wounded enemy warrior still continues where practicable. Not all of you might be aware, but some battles over the last few weeks have yielded more wounded enemy combatants than we can transport to America for scanning. In those cases, they are transferred to holding centres in the rear.

"Regarding the second point, the imperative is driven by military necessity. You are all accomplished and experienced soldiers who have served your country's armies for decades. While for all of us, the bulk of our careers occurred during peacetime, it's important we recall and adhere to the core military principles of combat. Remember that when this unprovoked war began, the enemy was so successful due in part to our complacency."

Terry raised a calming hand in anticipation of any murmurs of discontent. He said, "Yes, we had little advance notice of his intentions and, at the beginning of last year, his arms were far superior to ours, but we must not allow even the slightest trace of a similar complacency to negatively affect our reactions now. Standard military doctrine insists he must react to stymie our advantage, and I want all of us to be fully aware of that fact. Any more questions?"

Pakla's face shrank back to thumbnail and the darker-skinned complexion of General Genevieve Joubert enlarged. Her piercing almond eyes spoke of Asian ancestry. She said,

"Respectfully, field marshal, there are still nearly three million square kilometres of European territory held by the enemy. Does this fact not place certain limits on what we can realistically achieve if we might have only days before we must face an even stronger enemy?"

"No, it does not," Terry replied at once. "Given modern technology, it is impossible for us to have to face outdated military issues such as overextended supply lines or similar problems. In addition, our computers are more than capable of managing advances across all types of terrain. We must exploit this ability as much as we can. Is that clear?"

"*Oui*, field marshal. Thank you."

"Any further questions?"

General Joubert's face shrank back to a thumbnail. Silence followed.

"Very well. Thank you, ladies and gentlemen. I will speak to each of you individually during our scheduled meetings."

The faces disappeared and the screen became blank. Terry let out a long sigh. He clenched a fist and punched his desk to expel the frustration. General Joubert had made a good point that he felt he might've dealt with a little too brusquely.

He looked through the windows into the central area, at the screens above the stations with the range and depth of data they displayed. Would it be possible for NATO forces to become somehow overextended when the inevitable enemy counterattack came? How many lives might be lost if he pursued this course instead of advancing at a more measured pace? He realised he could not afford to second guess tactics at this stage of the war, after nearly two years. Only one certainty remained: Terry asked himself how much time they had before the enemy struck back.

Chapter 24

21.10 Sunday 4 November 2063

Crispin Webb took a tumbler from the drinks cabinet in the sideboard and filled it with orange juice. Then, in consideration of the fact that his lens told him he was not in imminent danger of another heart attack, he grabbed the bottle of vodka, unscrewed the metal cap, and added a hefty glug to the glass. After all the media enquiries he'd fielded in the last couple of hours, he'd earned it.

He glanced around the expansive living area of the boss's flat in Ten Downing Street. He would enjoy this illicit drink and then go home, but he took a moment to savour having to himself the room in which so much had happened. The boss was on her way back from some gladhanding at a smattering of barracks in the north of the country, sensibly making sure that as much martial glory as possible should be reflected back onto her and her government.

He shuddered at the implications of the weekend's events on the wrecked battlefields of Europe. If this new Scythe Omega really did mean—

A comms signal broke into his thoughts, the latest of many on this Sunday evening. He raised it in mild irritation when he saw it was the front of house. A young female voice he didn't recognise said, "Hi. I've got Defence Secretary Liam Burton here, requesting to come up."

"But he must know the boss isn't at home," Crispin replied, wondering why on earth Burton hadn't contacted him directly.

His confusion cleared when the woman responded, "He says he'd like a quick chat with you about something he thinks you should know. If you have the time, of course."

"Sure, send him up," Crispin said. He put his drink on the marble mantle and made for the door. He recalled arranging Burton's security file for the boss the previous week, but it contained nothing that might compromise the man. Crispin made for the door. He strode along the corridor and arrived at the lift just as the doors opened and the young defence minister emerged.

Liam Burton stuck his hand out and said, "Hi, Crispin. Thanks for seeing me."

Crispin shook it and noted Burton's smooth skin. The man's blue eyes shone wide and friendly and guileless. "Come into the living room." When they entered, Crispin closed the door with the question, "Drink?"

"Yes, thanks. Scotch, if there's any left."

Crispin walked over to the drinks cabinet and decided to divert any small talk. He said, "I'm a little surprised you didn't contact me directly before just turning up here." He turned to see Burton's reaction, but the man's face didn't change. Crispin spun back and poured the scotch.

Burton replied, "I want to talk to you about something you might be interested in."

Crispin handed Burton the glass and then collected his vodka and orange from the mantlepiece. "Curiouser and curiouser," he said. "Cheers."

Burton echoed, "Cheers," and drank. He nodded to the walls and ceiling and asked, "How secure are the comms in this place? Since that debacle with the Chinese SPI last year, I find it difficult to believe any government building is secure."

Crispin replied, "This is. You know, the PM will be back in a couple of hours. You could speak to her directly then."

Burton shook his head. "No, I wanted to sound you out first."

Crispin shrugged, "Go ahead."

"Have you noticed anything different in the way Charlie Blackwood has been behaving lately?"

"No. You?" Crispin fired the doubt back at Burton while trawling his own memory for anything out of the ordinary from the foreign secretary that he might've missed.

Burton replied, "My people have heard that there's some chatter about the upcoming Paris conference."

"Oh?"

"And now, given what the Omega has shown us it can do, the Paris conference is, A: certain to go ahead, after all; and, B: also certain to be, let's say, a frank and open debate."

"And your point is?"

"There is some concern in the foreign secretary's camp that the PM may not perform as well as required when she comes under the pressure she most surely will."

"What?" Crispin asked, failing to keep the shock from his voice.

"Our relationship with the Americans has never been worse. Dahra and Coll clearly hate each other's guts, and that's not good for England's interests. The leaders of the other

191

Home Countries are already sucking up to the Yanks hoping to curry favour—"

"No, no, wait a minute," Crispin broke in, holding out a hand. "You're telling me that ministers of the crown are actually dissatisfied with the performance of the most successful wartime prime minister since Winston Churchill? Have I got that right?"

Burton's smooth face dropped and his mouth curled in anger. "Don't be an arsehole, Crispin. Her performance to date is not the issue; her performance at the Paris conference is. There are going to be representatives from every European country as well as the Yanks. We have to make sure we get the best result not only for England, but for Europe as a whole."

"And what makes anyone think the PM can't do that, never mind one of her closest political allies?"

"Listen, I've been in the army, and if I learned anything at all, it's that in a war like this, surprises always happen. Yes, we've got the initiative with the Omega, but that won't last. It can't last. This war might drag on for months or even years yet. It might even evolve into some godforsaken frozen conflict still in Europe. What we need to do as soon as possible is establish our joint aims for the resolution, so that they do, in fact, become established. More and more backbenchers are getting concerned that the PM is not the person to do that. She's been under a ridiculous amount of pressure for almost two years, and, frankly speaking, the cracks are starting to show."

Crispin's eyes narrowed. "Why are you telling me this?"

"I think that the general consensus among many MPs in the parliamentary party is that we push for unconditional surrender to be adopted as a formal policy at the Paris conference. Equally, the belief is that the PM will not do so, that she will yield to a more flexible position. I wanted to let you know that dissenters are talking to Charlie Blackwood to either persuade the PM, or—"

"Or what?" Crispin broke in, incredulity growing.

Burton shrugged and said, "Or mount a leadership challenge."

Crispin threw the insult back at Burton: "Don't be an arsehole, Liam. No one wants a leadership challenge right now, unless…" Crispin's words trailed off as he realised. He took a swig of his drink, which was now nowhere near strong enough, and said, "Unless by coming here and telling me this, you are actually delivering a threat."

Burton put up a defensive hand. "Steady on, fella. Absolutely no one's talking about threats to anyone."

"Glad to hear it," Crispin said, having made up his mind about the level of threat involved. "And what do you think the PM will say when I tell her what you've told me?"

"Come on, you know how it works. Charlie or me or any other minister can't say this kind of thing out loud at cabinet. The PM needs to know that there are some strong feelings about what the government's objectives at the Paris conference need to achieve. We can't have the Yanks dictating to Europe where the endpoint is, and we can't have the Europeans strongarming us into putting their reconstruction ahead of ours."

"Really?" Crispin said.

"But no drama, okay?" Burton said with a wink that irritated Crispin. "She should just know what's been going on while she still has a couple of days to think about it. It's no good to anyone if she and Coll are giving it their ridiculous, bitchy stilettos-at-dawn confrontation bollocks."

Crispin drained his tumbler and said, "Well, you've delivered your message. If there's nothing else, I'll show you to the lift."

Burton finished his scotch and put the glass on the coffee table next to him. "It's okay, I know the way. Thanks for the drink." He strode to the door and opened it. But before he left, he turned and said, "It's nothing personal, you understand. It's about getting the best deal for England. See you."

The instant the door closed, Crispin shook his head, muttered a curse, and began running comparisons in his lens for all press articles and interviews since Operation Repulse had begun to see if a pattern revealed itself that might give any credence to Burton's ridiculous assertion that Charles Blackwood would cause the boss any unnecessary trouble.

As he expected, a few seconds later the super-AI comparison of thousands of press articles and spoken interviews over the preceding three months yielded no evidence that Blackwood had publicly let slip any hint of betrayal.

As Crispin left the flat, he recalled his meeting with Blackwood the previous year in St. James's Park. Charles Blackwood: sartorial, educated, erudite, and the boss's closest political ally for many years. And that little working-class ex-soldier expected Crispin to believe that Blackwood was engineering some kind of conspiracy. Crispin decided he knew exactly who was really thinking about challenging the boss.

On the other hand, he found it oddly comforting to have some traditional political betrayal to deal with

Chapter 25

08.14 Tuesday 6 November 2063

Field Surgeon Maria Phillips pushed the last gurney into the black interior of the AAT. In the darkness within, she heard Orderly Igbe Kalu secure the casualty. Maria backed away and Igbe emerged, breaking into a trot. The morning sun flashed off the bulbous side of the aircraft and a warm autumnal breeze ruffled Igbe's hair.

Maria's Squitch said, "Move clear to allow the autonomous air transport to take off."

The hatch slid down and the aircraft's engines emitted a faint whine.

Igbe reached her and asked, "Do you think we will have time for a brew?"

Maria gave her an ironic glance as her Squitch said, "Enemy casualties are inbound and will land in one minute at LZ Sierra."

"Come on," Maria urged, turning left and heading towards Landing Zone Sierra. "That's the last of the most urgent NATO casualties." A comms notification flashed in her view. She raised it.

"Hi, Field Surgeon Phillips," an impatient male voice said.

"Hello, Corporal Eastcott," she replied. "I and one of my orderlies are heading to meet you at the LZ. How many casualties are you carrying?"

"Seven."

"All enemy?"

"Roger that."

"Okay." She terminated that connection and opened another. "Ranni?"

"Yes?"

"We need some elbow grease out here."

"Sure," he replied with a chuckle.

Maria and Igbe reached the landing zone as the AAT descended. It landed. The hatchway slid up and a gurney emerged and rolled onto the dusty ground. Igbe collected it and pushed it towards the designated field hut where wounded enemy warriors were kept.

Maria took the next one and called into the aircraft, "Corporal Eastcott?"

"Yes?"

"How many are walking wounded?" she asked, knowing it was the only reason the corporal travelled with the aircraft. If they'd all been critical and unconscious, they would've arrived without an escort.

"Just one."

"Let's get him in a bed and sedated now, then." She took a few paces back and remembered she didn't have her small arm on her. She hoped she wouldn't need one.

An enemy figure shuffled out of the aircraft, tall and thin. His kept his face cast down. Blood and dirt stained his simple tunic and military trousers. As he stepped past her, she noted the restraining tie that bound his hands behind his back and which went up and encircled his neck.

Ranni approached them and said, "Oh, we've got one that's awake. And he doesn't look like his injuries are too severe, either."

Corporal Eastcott exited the aircraft. Short and pugnacious, he insisted, "Can we get on with it, please?"

Maria looked at him pointedly and replied, "Welcome to my field hospital, corporal. In a rush, are we?"

The man's frown deepened on his otherwise handsome face. "Let's just say I got the short straw for this job."

Maria gave him a half-smile and said, "It'll only take a few minutes."

"No, it won't," he complained. "This bird's got to go back for more, so I'm going to have to wait here."

Maria couldn't be bothered to respond. She walked off to lead them to the long, single-storey hut where they kept the wounded enemy until their evacuation. Ranni proceeded with the next gurney, and in the distance, Lyla and Grayson hurried towards them. Maria heard a grunt from the warrior behind her but ignored it—the corporal could treat the warrior how he wanted, as long as he didn't try to kill him.

Maria led them into the hut, where the air smelled of dried blood and weak bleach. Inside lay two rows of ten gurneys, either side of a central walkway. Ahead of them, Igbe was checking the casualty she'd pushed in. The far end of the hut was bare, ready to host more casualties, and four empty gurneys were bunched up against the far wall. Maria strode the length of the walkway and pulled one out. She rolled it and lined it up with the gurney next to the one Igbe had just installed.

Maria nodded to Corporal Eastcott. "The casualty needs to get on the gurney."

"He's not a casualty; he's a fucking prisoner," the man replied with venom.

With aggressive grunts and hand signals, Eastcott indicated what the warrior had to do. The taller, dark-skinned man sat on the gurney. Eastcott loosened the restraining tie. With a supressed moan of pain, the warrior lay down on his side, his legs still vertical. Maria lifted the man's legs up.

Eastcott said, "I won't release the restraint until he's fully sedated."

Maria lifted a GenoFluid pack from the shelf beneath the casualty and held it in one hand. She said, more to herself than the others, "I'd like to get this on as much skin as possible."

Eastcott asked, "Doesn't your lens tell you what's wrong with them?"

"Nope," Maria said without looking at him. "That only works with NATO troops or civilians who have either a lens or implant. With these warriors, I have to wait for the bots to get around their bodies."

The warrior muttered something.

Eastcott hissed, "I hope the bastard is saying his prayers."

With her free hand, Maria lifted the man's tunic and tutted as shallow gashes and other cuts across his torso reopened and blood began to seep out of them. She laid the GenoFluid pack over the wounds and dabbed the small panel on it. She said, "Advance to the brain and induce a coma. Locate and disable any unknown implants." Maria sensed those around her exhale. She turned to leave.

Eastcott pointed to the warrior and asked, "Don't you secure them to the bed?"

Maria replied, "Not really required when they're in a coma. Would you like to go to the mess and help yourself to a brew?"

Eastcott looked from Maria to Igbe. "I'll go for a walk, I think."

The corporal strode away as Ranni wheeled in the next casualty.

"Come on, Igbe," Maria said, "let's go and have a brew." She led the young orderly back outside and into the growing heat of the morning. In her view, her lens ran up the list of injuries the warrior had sustained. It confirmed he was sedated and would reach a comatose state in minutes, and that a Caliphate implant had been located and disabled. The data carried a caution that his restraint should be released at the earliest convenience to improve blood flow.

Igbe said, "Do you think the rumours are true? About what happens to them?"

"You can read my mind," Maria said with a smile. "I was wondering the same thing, yet again."

"It is just, well, what is the point?"

"We must follow orders, Igbe. And anyway, who's got any sympathy for them after what they've done to us?"

The women arrived at the mess hut, entered, and each collected mugs of hot, steaming tea. They sat at a trellis table that wobbled under every footfall.

As soon as Maria took her first sip, her Squitch said, "Wounded enemy warriors in Hut Foxtrot are expiring."

"What? Why?" Maria asked in shock.

"Unknown. Highest probability is external interference."

Igbe leapt to her feet and said, "It's Eastcott. I know it." She made for the door.

Maria followed the young orderly, the tea forgotten. When they reached Hut Foxtrot, the plain metal door was ajar. Maria caught Igbe's arm and held her back with a look of caution.

Igbe frowned and said, "He is in there, killing them."

"I know, which means he's armed," Maria answered, conscious that neither of them carried a weapon.

"We cannot let this happen."

"I know," Maria repeated, steeling herself.

Ranni came running towards them, yelling the same observation Igbe had just made.

Maria entered the hut. Eastcott stood over one of the comatose warriors, muttering indistinctly.

"Stop what you're doing and leave my patients alone," she demanded in the most authoritative voice she could force through her constricted throat.

Eastcott ignored her. She looked at the nearest gurney where a casualty lay dead, blood spatting on the floor, mixing with the thicker liquid of the split GenoFluid pack. She stepped forward, unsure of herself. Eastcott appeared calm and methodical. She twitched her eye to open a special comms channel and said, "Emergency at Casualty Clearing Station Sierra Zero-Four. Request immediate MP assistance."

At once, a measured male voice replied, "Key details, please?"

"Corporal Francis Eastcott is killing my patients."

"Roger... Military police have been assigned and will contact you directly. ETA eight minutes."

"Damn," Maria said.

Eastcott moved onto the next sedated warrior. He lifted a short scimitar and again muttered words Maria could not hear. He drew the blade across the GenoFluid pack and then across the warrior's neck. He seesawed the blade a few times and nodded as the blood dribbled off the gurney. He proceeded to the next warrior.

Ranni entered, brandishing a sidearm. He held a bony arm aloft and yelled, "Stop, or I'll shoot."

Eastcott glanced back at Ranni. He gave a mirthless chuckle and said, "Sure, whatever."

"I mean it," Ranni said in a tone that convinced Maria.

Eastcott arrived at the next gurney, faced them, and with the scimitar poised above the next comatose warrior, said, "This one is going to be for my kid sister, Tricia. These bastards murdered her along with the rest of my family last year. I've been waiting a long time for this. And you're not going to stop me."

Eastcott's faux justification enraged Maria. She wanted to scream that she'd lost family, too; likely everyone in this war had. But that didn't justify his actions.

Ranni yelled, "Last chance, Corporal Eastcott. Stop and put the blade down or I will shoot you."

Eastcott turned back to the warrior and muttered indistinctly again. He sliced the GenoFluid pack open.

"Right, you asked for it," Ranni said. He pulled the trigger. Nothing happened.

Igbe said, "Are you going to shoot or not?"

"Shit," Ranni cursed. "My Squitch has blocked it. Shit." Ranni's hand began shaking and his breathing became shallow.

"Override," Maria said.

Ranni shook his head and looked at her, "Only ranks of lieutenant-colonel and above can do that."

Maria said, "We need to stop him. This isn't right. Igbe, can you get me a battlefield pack?"

Igbe nodded and exited the hut.

Ranni asked, "What are you going to do?"

She looked at him and asked, "Can you grab his blade arm and hold it away from me?"

Shock suffused Ranni face, "I can try. Wouldn't you rather just wait for the MPs?"

"He will've killed them all by then."

"I know, but do we really care that much? He's getting his revenge, can—"

"If we treat them the way they treat us, then we're no different than them. Don't you see that?"

Ranni shook his head, "No. And they're going to die anyway."

Igbe rushed back in through the door, a small pack in her hand.

Maria said to Ranni, "Then I'll do it myself." She thanked Igbe, took the pack, and broke into a trot down the narrow walkway.

Maria heard Igbe ask, "What's she doing?"

Eastcott had his back to Maria, having moved onto the next in line. She tried to move quietly but her boots thumped heavily on the thin, flimsy floor.

Eastcott turned to face her. He held the bloodied scimitar up and put his other hand out. "Leave me alone."

Maria shouted, "No." Closer to him, his cool demeanour vanished. His face trembled and his hands shook.

Maria immediately reassessed the situation. "Look, just stop, okay? You've done enough, right?"

Eastcott blinked a few times. He lowered his arms.

"That's good," Maria encouraged. "Let's just go—"

With a yell, Eastcott turned and brought the scimitar down on the prone warrior behind him. He hacked at the man's throat, shouting, "No, they should all die."

Maria leapt and crashed into him, pulling his empty arm up behind his back and slapping the GenoFluid pack on the back of his neck and hissed, "Sedate this individual, now." To her immeasurable relief, Igbe appeared next to her and grabbed his other arm. Eastcott grunted in frustration; then Ranni arrived on the other side of the gurney and forced Eastcott's head down onto the dying warrior.

"Hold him," Maria urged.

"How long?" Igbe said.

"The bots are already working; he's getting weaker."

"Christ, he's a strong one," Ranni said.

Maria gasped in air while all of them pinned Eastcott to the Gurney. The soldier's resistance faded and he became limp with a sigh.

Igbe said, "I'm covered in blood. Again."

"Okay," Maria said, "he's done now. Ranni, pull one of those gurneys out over there and let's get him on it."

Maria held Eastcott to stop him collapsing on the floor. "And hurry up, will you? He weighs a ton."

Igbe came away with the scimitar in her hand, covered in blood. "Don't we have enough drama in this place as it is?"

Ranni wheeled the gurney over and said, "Maybe put that blade down, Iggy. You look like a butcher."

Together with the others, Maria heaved Eastcott's inert form onto the gurney. When the soldier's limbs were on it, Maria said, "Okay, the MPs will be here in a couple of minutes. I'll let them decide what to do with him—"

"Maybe he planned it all along?" Ranni broke in.

"What?" Maria said.

Ranni gave her an ironic look and stretched his arms behind his back. "He's going to get court-martialled, but there's no way they'll lock him up when the story gets out."

"God, you're cynical," Igbe said.

Maria stifled a yawn and said, "Doesn't make much sense to me. The fronts are moving ahead faster than when Repulse started." She looked down at Eastcott, his face relaxed in sleep. "We've all been through so much. Some of us are bound to lose it, I suppose."

"I just wish they'd 'lose it' somewhere else," Ranni said.

Maria sighed under the weight of running a casualty clearing station and seeing wounded NATO soldiers die and injured warriors being shipped off to God-knows-where. "Come on," she said to the others. "Eastcott's AAT is coming back with more enemy wounded."

Chapter 26

10.21 Thursday 8 November 2063

Crispin Webb stomped back and forth around his room in the Ritz hotel in Paris, trying to ignore the aroma of fresh paint that lingered. He fought to manage the data feeds in his lens. He'd known busy days before, but now the hotly anticipated Paris conference had begun, this busy day had taken a draining turn for the worse.

He cursed when the home secretary, Aiden Hicks, tried to contact him. He raised the icon in his lens and feigned the most professional tone he could, "Good morning, home secretary, how can I help—"

"My PPL has just sent me an updated speech schedule in the grand ballroom, which says the PM is going to make her speech after the French and German presidents, not before. What's changed?"

Crispin stopped himself from slapping the plain desk in frustration. He said, "The PM has agreed to address the reconstruction committee meeting in the green room at eleven, so it was better to swap the main speech running order."

"Oh, I see."

"It got us some gratitude from the French and Germans, and we still can't have her being near Coll in the running order."

"Yes, but we fought quite hard to make sure the PM is front and centre as the defender of Europe."

"She still has that kudos, sir. Anything else I can help you with?"

"No, unless you can do something about the standard in my room. I'm quite surprised the Ritz should be like this. Never mind," Hicks said, and ended the connection.

Crispin shook his head and said to the window, "That's because it's just been completely rebuilt, you idiot, sir."

He grabbed his sports jacket, put it on, and left the room. He strode along the corridor hardly able to concentrate on walking due to the notifications he had to deal with in his lens. Every major and minor dignitary had descended on the war-shattered French capital for two days of speeches and negotiations spread throughout the rebuilt hotel's seven conference rooms. The building heaved with politicians, diplomats, high-ranking military personnel, bodyguards, PAs, security staff, interpreters, journalists, porters, and all of the people needed to create an event—a spectacle—that would show the rest of the world that Europe would win this war.

After a frustratingly slow journey in a packed lift that stopped at every floor, Crispin arrived in the main lobby. He cast his eyes at the ornate cornice and ceiling roses from which chandeliers hung at equidistant intervals. On yet another notification in his lens, he steered left around people dressed both well and indifferently.

He found the boss.

"Crispin, good. You're here," she said with a welcoming smile.

Crispin eyed the two personal protection officers, but neither appeared to be giving off any signals other than strictly heterosexual. Pity; the taller one's jaw was chiselled like an Adonis. "Yes, boss," he said.

"What do you think of the latest version of my speech?" she asked, walking off towards the green room.

"It's fine, boss. I think we might even ramp up the rearmament passage."

"So, deal with that, would you?"

"Sure," Crispin replied automatically, again handling requests and notifications in his lens while trying to walk as part of a group of people that made way through the throng.

They came to the entrance to the green room. Crispin managed a peek over the heads of the assembled attendees to see a ceiling of green struts that might have been wood, steel or hemp.

"Crispin," Napier said, "go to the main ballroom and listen to the speeches there. I will want your opinion afterwards. Especially the one by the President of the United States. Let me know if she says anything derogatory about me or England."

"Sure," he said, keeping the dismay from his face.

Dahra disappeared through the doors while her security detail lingered, standing aside to allow other attendees to enter.

Crispin moved closer to the one with the chiselled jaw and asked, "Does it ever get a little dull, all that waiting around?"

The man's blank eyes held no flicker of interest. "No," he replied.

With his gaydar thus untroubled, Crispin gave both of them a nod and strode off to the grand ballroom.

He entered a vast, circular area furnished with about fifty round tables that each seated over a dozen people. At the far end, a stage the colour of teak stood higher than the floor, with a speaker's podium in front of a black background. Via his lens, the hotel's super AI guided Crispin to one of the few remaining free seats. He nodded hellos to some the other figures and took no interest whatsoever as their names and positions resolved in the air next to them.

A waiter appeared at Crispin's elbow with a look in his eye that conveyed something more than professional service. Crispin smiled with warmth and ordered an orange juice.

He spent the next ninety minutes listening first to President Coll and then to the leaders of each European country whose lands were now free of Caliphate forces. The speeches soon became repetitive and tedious. At the same time, Crispin had to manage press coverage as well as stay in touch with Number Ten.

As the war moved further away across the European mainland, English political business again returned to normal. For Crispin, this meant having to perform juggling acts on two fronts: domestic and European. For all the destruction in London and England, returning English MPs exercised themselves the most over whether the Houses of Parliament should be rebuilt according to its original designs, allowing for modern improvements. The English press also returned to its prewar combative approach to domestic issues, forcing Crispin to be more vigilant in defending the boss.

At the same time, western Europeans were coming to terms with the results of an overwhelmingly horrific occupation that England and the Home Countries had escaped by a hair's breadth. Up on the stage, each president or prime minister or chancellor described how their country and people had suffered since February the previous year, while also praising NATO and the resilience of the survivors.

Despite the distractions in his lens, he noted that none of the luminaries mentioned anything about the future. This had been pre-agreed to allow the first day to concentrate on expressing solidarity and the need to secure Europe's borders, but Crispin still thought one or two leaders of the smaller countries might not adhere to the agreement.

He fine-tuned the boss's speech to add or omit any references based on what the other leaders said, and sent it to her. After ten heads of state had been applauded and listened to and cheered and applauded again, his lens told him the boss had entered on the far side of the ballroom. She mounted the stage to a surge of applause that Crispin imagined was slightly louder than for the other leaders.

The boss's image appeared on the huge screen behind her. She tucked a strand of auburn hair behind her ear and said, "Thank you, ladies and gentlemen. Twenty-one months ago, an unimaginable catastrophe befell our continent. Since then, the peoples of Europe have endured the worst kinds of suffering; and, indeed, still do. Today, we meet here in Paris to acknowledge all that has happened and, hopefully, to help begin the long healing process by sharing our experiences…"

As the boss continued, and with his work on her speech complete, Crispin's thoughts drifted to the flirtatious waiter, and he resolved to make a pass at him when he returned. A sudden tap on his shoulder made him jump.

"Hi, Crispin," said Liam Burton.

Crispin turned around, romantic images shattered by the young defence minister's face mere centimetres from his own. "What do you want?"

The glare in Burton's eyes urged caution. Crispin caught the unmistakable smell of alcohol on the man's breath. He said, "I've been speaking to a couple of the PPEs and they seem to be of the impression that unconditional surrender is definitely off the table. Is that true?"

Crispin pulled his head back from Burton's and said, "What are you asking me for?"

"Come on, you're in the know. Remember what I told you in London, about Charlie Blackwood, eh?"

Crispin calculated in an instant that he had the opportunity to give Burton the rope to hang himself. He lied, "I haven't spoken to Blackwood since then, so I don't know if what you say is true, but this isn't something that will be decided here, either today or tomorrow. We're nowhere near winning the fucking war yet."

"This conference is going to issue a communique tomorrow afternoon before we all go home. It's going to state—for the benefit of the rest of the world—what our objectives are. And it needs to state that we're going to demand unconditional surrender. The PM has to push for this. Do you understand that?"

"It's hardly my choice, or hers. There must be fifty or more leaders and their flunkies who will negotiate the final wording tomorrow." Crispin glanced back up at the image of the boss on the stage screen. She'd moved on to talking about the millions of stories of personal sacrifice that had inspired her to remain in England when the future looked bleakest.

Burton concluded with, "There's a vocal minority in the party, representing a strong groundswell out in the constituencies, that unconditional surrender is the only way to teach those bastards a proper lesson and stand any chance of getting appropriate reparations. Let me know if the PM has a spare five minutes to discuss."

Crispin watched the young man thread his way among the tables and smothered a curse. According to reports, the war might yet be turned against them, and all that little prick could think about was manoeuvring for the sake of his career. Crispin said aloud, "And the way that's going, his career won't last much longer."

He turned back to concentrate on the boss's speech and caught the waiter's eye. The elegant man hurried towards Crispin with an inviting smile that Crispin reciprocated.

Chapter 27

07.11 Friday 9 November 2063

Geoff Morrow awoke with a headache that threatened to split his skull open and an overpowering sense of a loss of time. The sheets in the bed caressed his skin, causing a recollection of a luxury he'd not experienced for some time.

In the early morning fog of dissipating sleep and obstinate hangover, the war seemed somehow ghostly, indistinct like a memory from an imagined alternate reality. He opened his eyes to focus on the beige ceiling and the memory came to him that he'd moved to the Ritz, along with Buckley.

He forced his legs out from the warmth and comfort, and sat up. The pain in his head seemed to flop over like a damp pancake, from his forehead to the back of his cranium.

A comms signal flashed in his lens. He selected audio only and said, "Hi, Dan. I hope your head hurts as much as mine."

"Morning," Daniel Buckley said. "We've got a busy day today, Geoff."

"Don't remind me."

"See you in the restaurant in ten?"

"God, can we make it fifteen?"

"I thought you Limeys could hold your liquor?"

"Yeah, well, it's been a while."

"Shape up, dude. Big day coming up."

The contact ended and Geoff stood, realising that he had to keep Buckley happy to keep Alan happy to keep a job that would help him write the book that would be the ultimate account of this war. Shit.

Twenty minutes later, he sat at a table in the Ritz's restaurant, using a torn piece of white bread roll to mop up the last of the egg's benedict on the plate in front of him.

From opposite, Buckly asked, "Do you want to take the bonds issue forum and I'll cover the tech distribution debate?"

"Sure," Geoff said, stuffing the yolk-soaked bread into his mouth. He chewed and added, "But then, I usually agree with you, don't I?"

Buckley murmured his confirmation as he finished his bacon and fried eggs. He swallowed and said, "US readers will be more interested in how much tech Europe's gonna need in the first one-to-three years, post-war, so that's where I'd rather be."

"Fine, but we've both got to be at the field marshal's address."

"Sure."

"And the big one: the communique at four this afternoon."

Buckley said, "They won't agree the wording before seven at the earliest. It's gonna be a long day."

"I still don't get how everyone is behaving as though the war is already over."

"Like I told you—"

"I know what you told me," Geoff broke in. "But there's still a long way to go, both figuratively and literally."

"Latest forecasts are saying it'll all be over in a few weeks, if it stays like this."

"And that's a big 'if'. I know these mad bastards, Dan. I can still see them coming back at us with something stronger."

"Why?"

The question surprised Geoff. "What?"

"I said, why? We're taking back a wasteland. Fewer than twenty percent of the buildings that existed two years ago are still standing. The survivors we're finding are traumatised and emaciated. Anything of value has been looted."

"So, you're saying the Third Caliph has had his fun and doesn't care anymore?"

Buckley shook his head and said, "Nope. You're making the same mistake as quite a few of those folks out there. You still think Europe is real important, and it just ain't."

"I don't think you're being fair—"

"This war was always a training exercise for him. He's got his sights set on much bigger prizes."

"Yeah, which China is going to slap him down for. You said so yourself: Beijing is not going to risk nukes going off anywhere near their borders."

Buckley drained his orange juice, shook his head, and said, "But what if China doesn't have the control over the Caliphate everyone always thought they did?"

Geoff shrugged, "Does it matter now? That mad bastard in Tehran no longer has the most advanced weapons. His great advantage from almost two years ago isn't worth shit anymore."

Buckley replied with a noncommittal tilt of his head.

Geoff finished his tea, stood, and said, "Let's catch up in the main ballroom ahead of TT's speech."

"Sure. Is that what you call the field marshal?"

"Yeah," Geoff replied, nonplussed at the question. "Well, not everyone. But a lot of people in England call him that."

"But he's a knight of the realm."

"So? I really don't think he gives a shit about that."

For once, Geoff noticed, the dour American's face expressed an emotion. He turned away without further response and left the restaurant, making eye contact and offering half-smiles to many of the other hacks at the tables, some of whom also looked the worse for wear. He shuddered to think of the volume of booze the newly rebuilt Ritz must be getting through at the first big gig of its new incarnation.

Geoff made his way to the busy meeting room for the bonds issue forum, taking a complimentary bottle of water with more gratitude than required. The chairs were arranged schoolroom fashion in straight rows in front of a raised stage. He took his ascribed seat and noted which other hacks were given better or worse locations than him.

Over the next two hours, the eight panellists on the stage explained and discussed a multi-country bonds issue that planned to raise over a hundred trillion euros for reconstruction. Geoff tried to stay interested but struggled. Once he established the primary news angle—that it was hoped Americans would purchase the vast majority of the bonds—his mind wandered. Via his lens, he flitted around the other meetings and forums and debates taking place in the hotel. When the lawyer on the panel began describing the legal challenges to the bonds issue, he left in fear his headache would become even more painful.

Outside, he sent a summary audio report to Alan, then made his way to the grand ballroom. The throng to enter buffeted him; here, the interest in what the field marshal would say ran through everyone like an electrical current. Geoff scanned the room for Buckley. His lens located the American in the middle of a mass of bodies of all heights and skin tones.

At one o'clock, an imposing, broad-shouldered figure lumbered onto the stage and took the podium. In the air next to him resolved the words, 'Bjarne Hasselman, Secretary General of the North Atlantic Council.'

In accented English, Hasselman said, "Ladies and gentlemen, thank you for coming. In a moment, I will introduce our main speaker. However, he will not be taking any questions today because, as we might assume, he is a little bit busy with other, slightly more important matters." Hasselman threw the room a smile; several chuckles floated on the air. "However, after this speech, I will be available to answer your questions. So, without any more delay, from the War Rooms in London, here is Supreme Allied Commander, Europe, Field Marshal Sir Terry Tidbury."

A ripple of applause grew into a wave when the screen behind the podium came alive with an image of TT. He stood, arms folded, leaning against a desk behind which windows offered indistinct views of screens beyond. Geoff smiled; he'd never seen the inside of the War Rooms.

Light from above glinted off Terry's bald head as he spoke, "Hello, everyone. Thank you for requesting me to address this important conference. Firstly, I will appraise you of the current state of NATO forces. Then, I will make my recommendations regarding future objectives."

Geoff cast his eyes around the grand ballroom. Almost everyone stared at TT's image with expressions of awe. He reflected that the vibrant acoustics in the vast room did not hurt the field marshal's cause.

TT said, "NATO forces are currently regaining territory at the greatest rate since the commencement of

Operation Repulse in August. With the introduction of the Scythe Omega to the battlefield, the enemy is both outmatched and outgunned. Therefore, he has only two options: withdrawal in order to preserve his forces, or to introduce more and better weapons to turn our advance.

"Intelligence tells us he does indeed have the available forces currently deployed on his eastern flank. However, it appears that for whatever reason, there are no signs of their redeployment to Europe. Although it is not my role to speculate why this should be the case, I want to make it absolutely clear that the danger that remains to Europe is still very much there. If at any time the enemy changes his plans, that could have devasting effects on our frontlines."

Geoff knew that tensions between the Caliphate and India were sky high and showing no signs of easing. So, he assumed, as long as that remained the case, Europe should be in the clear.

TT went on, "Regarding NATO's military objectives, little has changed. Operation Repulse will be deemed to have succeeded if and when all enemy forces have been expelled from the European mainland and our borders are as they were in February 2062. I have been asked to give this conference my professional opinion on the possibility, in the event Repulse does succeed, of further offensive action against the enemy's territory to guarantee the security of Europe's borders.

"In my opinion, any such attempt would be doomed to failure. The reasons for these are many, but I will give the conference a few examples. One, the extent of the enemy's domain. To subdue it would require an army of from twenty to thirty million troops, from which, even in the best-case scenario, we might expect up to seven million casualties. Furthermore, our computers indicate a very high probability that the enemy would resort to using nuclear weapons in any defence of its key lands, even if that were to involve millions of casualties among his own subjects."

In the following pause, Geoff muttered, "So, we'll take that as a 'no', then."

TT scratched his forehead and went on, "I'm not generally given to delivering history lectures, but that scenario shares parallels with the end of the Second World War. In 1945, the allies drew up plans for an attack on Soviet forces with the aim of ensuring a free Poland. It was appropriately called Operation Unthinkable. You may wish to review its details. In my opinion, any attempt to invade the New Persian Caliphate would face comparable barriers: it would be an extremely long and costly campaign certain to cost us millions of casualties with no guarantee of victory."

Geoff called up the relevant operation in his lens and began reading.

TT concluded, "Ladies and gentleman, thank you for letting me speak directly to you. If you have any questions, the Secretary General of the North Atlantic Council will take them now."

TT vanished from the screen and more applause rippled around the room. Geoff read about Operation Unthinkable as Bjarne Hasselman walked back across the stage to the podium. When the clapping died down, he said, "On behalf of the field marshal, thank you. Now, we have a few moments for questions. I will choose from the notifications in my lens."

In Geoff's view, dozens of notifications flashed into existence in the air overhead. He listened while accredited hacks were given priority, but, as Geoff had expected, there was little to be gained from the answers: most were either subject to op-sec while others concerned issues of legality and reparations that were not strictly military in nature.

Hasselman closed the session and the audience dissipated. Geoff contacted Buckley. They met up and headed for the hotel's terrace bar at the rear. They arrived in the spacious area that overlooked the resurgent Paris, and both sat on stools at one end of the bar.

"Scotch?" Buckley asked Geoff.

"Yeah, why not?"

"Did you get what he said about... what was the name of that Second World War op?"

"Unthinkable. Yeah, I read up on it. Made a lot of sense. Even if the ragheads roll over now, there's no way on Earth NATO can invade the Caliphate and expect to survive."

"Well, one step at a time, I guess."

A harassed-looking barmaid plonked the two scotches on the bar in front of the men.

Geoff lifted his glass and said, "Here's to the communique."

"Bottoms up," Buckley replied.

"Reckon there'll be any surprises in it?"

"Nope... Damn, that's a good scotch."

"Just as long as they don't say anything about the useless UN."

"That's exactly what they'll say," Buckley insisted.

"So, we're expecting something like, 'the objective is the reclamation of European territory and a claim for reparations made with the International Criminal Court'."

Buckley chuckled and shook his head. "We shouldn't laugh—"

"I know."

"But yeah, they'll stand up proud and go on about their legal certainty and all the rest of it."

"And none of those dictatorships out there will give a shit."

"You bet."

"How long do you think we'll have to wait for the final wording?"

Buckley drained his glass, slapped the tumbler on the bar, and said, "Long enough for another drink."

Geoff followed, although he wished he didn't feel the urge to keep up. As he waited for the barmaid to return, he asked, "What's next for you?"

Buckley shook his head, "Not sure. Guess my editor will keep me here awhile. I'll sneak around the bigshots and see what I can dig up. You?"

"I get a feeling mine will send me back nearer the frontlines, if not actually to them. You're not keen on embedding with your troops?"

"Are you kidding? That's what we've got the juniors for."

"Lucky you," Geoff said, as the barmaid arrived and refilled their glasses.

Buckley smiled, "I'm not strictly a war correspondent, anyways—"

"Neither am I," Geoff protested. "But needs must when the devil drives."

"I'm sure not going to miss your idioms. No, I do investigative stuff. This has been a bit like a vacation."

Geoff had to choke down a flash of jealousy. He lifted his refilled glass and said, "So, let's enjoy it while we can."

Buckley said, "Agreed. It might be hours before they settle on the final wording."

Geoff replied, "I hope it is," and he meant it.

Chapter 28

11.59 Friday 23 November 2063

Head of MI5 David Perkins looked at the screen on the wall in his office, waiting for it to come to life. He preferred briefing the regular COBRA meetings—when he had anything to brief them on—over one-on-one conversations like this. And in the two weeks since that particularly useless Paris conference, the intel coming into MI5 had shrunk from a trickle to a slow drip.

The hour turned and the screen came alive with an image of the field marshal. "Good afternoon, Mr Perkins," he said, leaning back against his desk.

"Good afternoon, sir."

"I wanted to have a chat with you about the current level of intelligence your office is receiving."

"I thought that might be the case."

"Can you add anything to the information you gave to the COBRA briefing three days ago?"

"The short answer is 'no'," Perkins said, deciding he had nothing to gain by attempting false optimism, which was hardly his forte. "All of our stations, contacts and undercovers are reporting the same thing: no one is certain what is happening inside the New Persian Caliphate, only that it involves violence."

"How about Beijing? What is coming through from our embassy there?"

"Again, very little, once we discount planted stories and false flags," Perkins said, opening his palms. "Our operatives lack the top-table contacts that might provide genuine, useful information. And that goes for the Americans, as well."

"And what about our key contact? The one that delivered the original data-pod warning of the enemy's threat two years ago?"

Perkins shook his head but hid his own vast frustration. "Nothing. They vanished after their last delivery in September."

"Do you know what happened to them?"

"No. I strongly suspect they have been liquidated. If they'd simply been pulled in to have new, er, restrictions, placed on their conduct, they would've resurfaced by now. As it was the last time, I keep a deep-clean team on standby in Beijing in the unlikely event they do make contact. But given that it's been two months... well, I only hope it was quick."

"My problem, Mr Perkins, is that I need to know what's going on inside the enemy's country."

Perkins replied, "I understand, sir. But the current situation is in line with the intel we have. The last data-pod in September confirmed China's objective that the New Persian Caliphate and India should go to war—a position of which, incidentally, very few people outside China are aware."

"Indeed. And what of intel from the brain scans of injured warriors?"

Perkins frowned and said, "You do receive daily updates on that in your files, sir."

Terry shook his head and replied, "I don't have the time to read every single thing I'm sent, Mr Perkins. Besides, I would prefer to hear your assessment, as it is to MI5 that this intel is first provided."

"The scanning results are insufficiently recent, sir. The *Institut Neuropsi* facility in America requires more recent casualties. However, I am hearing rumours of political pressure to stop these scans."

"Where from? Number Ten?"

"There are two or three junior ministers in Napier's cabinet who are, shall we say, being a little lax in how openly they are discussing what still remains a top-secret process."

"Hmm, such rumours among the ranks are also filtering up the chain of command."

"I find, sir, that the longer a secret has to be kept, the more likely those who know of it will begin to regard it as 'open'."

"And what of protocols in the government?" Terry asked, folding his arms.

Perkins shook his head and replied, "In relation to what, sir?"

"If a private or corporal or other lower rank discusses something they shouldn't, their Squitch will advise them accordingly and block the affected comms."

"There are no such restrictions on government ministers, sir."

"So, they can chat about whatever they like?"

"They are bound by the Official Secrets Act, of course."

Terry paused and Perkins hoped the conversation would conclude. It wasn't his fault the best contact they had for providing intel had gone missing for two months, and in all likelihood permanently.

Terry said, "Mr Perkins, I see something happening that causes me concern."

Perkins didn't reply.

"And that is complacency. As you will have seen in your own reports, the armies now have the wind at their backs. We are making quite remarkable progress in regaining territory. My concern is that it can still change. We do not know what is going on inside the enemy's territory; specifically, we do not know why he still allows us this advantage."

Perkins wanted to say that he thought NATO's superior weapons were the reason for the progress, but he thought better of potentially antagonising the field marshal.

Terry went on, "We know he has millions of ACAs tied up on his border with India, and since we deployed the Omega, he has chosen not to release any of them into the European theatre to stymie our advance. I need to know why, Mr Perkins."

"I see."

"Good. If any intel arrives on your desk, from whatever source, from whatever part of the world, that might give me the answer to the 'why', contact me directly. Is that clear?"

"Yes, sir."

"Thank you."

The screen went blank but Perkins kept staring at it. Whatever he thought of the field marshal, he could not fault the soldier's logic. You didn't need to be a military genius to realise that NATO would push the Caliphate out of Europe in a few weeks unless it reassigned its available forces on the border with India.

He turned away and went to a window to look at the drab grey cloud that hung low over central London. He said, "Computer? Send a quantum-encrypted message to all monitoring stations. Message reads: new priority. All intel on or related to internal state of the enemy to receive top priority. Imperative control knows what is happening. End. Oh, and send a copy—no, wait. Send message."

"Confirmed," Squonk replied.

Perkins checked the time in his lens and said, "I suppose it is too early to wake them up. Computer? Schedule a call to *Institut Neuropsi* for two o'clock. Perhaps it's time the urgency of the situation was impressed upon those slackers across the ocean."

Chapter 29

07.28 Wednesday 12 December 2063

Pip steeled herself as the autonomous air transport descended. The map in her view brought back many memories, but she remained focused on the objective. She opened comms to her team sitting on either side of the fuselage, "Conditions are looking fair this morning, team. But keep sharp. Same as usual: Pathfinder team out first followed by the Falarete team. We're showing ninety-eight percent probability of clear territory. Keep a lookout for any local civilians who might've survived. They could be confused and misunderstand why we're there."

Through the porthole opposite her, Pip glanced at the rugged, precipitous terrain of the day's objective: a specified zone in the Sierra Nevada mountains. But in addition to her orders and the platoon's military aims, she had her own personal goal.

Her Squitch announced, "Prepare to disembark."

She made eye contact with her troops opposite and confidence in them made her smile. This confidence came from the fact NATO's superior ACAs had reduced the level of casualties to the lowest in the entire campaign. Along with many units, her platoon now regarded that proper preparation could not only minimise casualties, but eliminate them altogether. And given that the enemy were withdrawing all along the contact line, a sense prevailed that only slack performance or bad luck would prevent these troops from making it to the end of the war.

The end of the war.

Pip found it difficult to comprehend the phrase and its meaning. A gentle jarring brought her back to the moment when the AAT landed. Her troops freed themselves and collected their arms. The hatchway slid up and the teams disembarked in the designated order. Pip followed them, the last one out of the aircraft. The clean early morning air chilled her throat. She cradled her Pickup and took in the clouds clinging to the mountaintops like lovers reluctant to part.

No threat presented itself. In keeping with their training, teams moved out to secure the area. The AAT had set down on a former sports pitch on the edge of a village—one of the few level spaces in the area. The Pathfinders were sent out and triggered no dormant Spiders. The Falarete team took up a defensive position and stood by for a danger that did not materialise. Pip overlaid her tactical map to confirm that the SkyMasters stood watch over them, far above the mountains. Below them, Scythe Omegas patrolled, ready to deal with any detected threat, which themselves were supported by thousands of X–7s and X–9s in the broader battlespace.

Her squads called in confirmations that their locations were secure. The empty aircraft lifted off.

Pip said, "Okay, I want two teams to clear this LZ. We're going to have a lot of gear coming down in the next hour."

"Yes, ma'am," echoed in her ears.

"Secure your weapons over there," she ordered, indicating one corner of the playing field. "Have a scout around for any equipment that might help, then get rid of all the debris at the perimeter and clear a path into the village."

Eight of her troops ran to follow her orders.

"Private Hines?"

"Yes, ma'am?"

"Go into the village and see what's left. Have you got more Pathfinders?"

"Yes, ma'am."

"Take care around cellars and places like that, just in case. I know our Squitches are saying it's clear, but there's always room for a surprise."

"Right you are, ma'am."

"Good. Let's crack on then, people, and be like Royal Engineers." Pip strode to the edge of the flat area and peered into the valley below. To the south lay the next village in a chain of habitations that straddled the descent on this side of the mountains. She glanced back at the higher ridgelines and watched as the rising sun warmed the air and made the clinging cloud roll away like spray from the tip of a wave.

She twitched her eye and said, "Good morning, Sergeant Moore. How are things on your side of the line."

Rory's voice answered, "Our objective is secured and it's not even mid-morning yet."

"How soon can you be here?"

"The vehicle says seven minutes."

"Great, see you." Pip checked on her troops and helped one of the squads move the charred ruins of a shed to clear the path to the village. She met Barney Hines coming back from it. His square head and grim countenance didn't fill her with confidence. "Report?"

He scoffed and replied, "Nothing doing, ma'am. No live ones, at any rate. Most of the remains look pretty far gone."

"Ok, it's not such a surprise. Listen, I need to leave the area for an hour and you're in charge."

Hines's eyes lit up.

"Just make sure everyone keeps busy. I should be back in plenty of time before the kit starts arriving."

"Right you are, ma'am," Hines repeated, with a movement of his lumpen arm that might have been a wave or a salute.

Pip collected her weapon and made her way up to the road. A mobile command vehicle drew up. She stowed her Pickup and got in.

"Hi, mate," Rory said.

"I can't believe we're back here, where it all started," she said, without looking at him.

"I know."

Pip strapped herself in as the vehicle took the most direct route to the cave. It bumped down into the valley, tilting to one side.

Rory said, "I remember being on secondment to that Spanish unit when the shit came down. I only just got out of there before Spiders blew the whole place sky high, and then one of those bastard things came down on me."

Pip said, "But we worked it out, didn't we? How long did it take you to realise what you had to do to stay alive?"

"And I've had the better part of two years to think of all those poor bastards who never even had a chance."

"Me too," Pip replied, melancholy settling on her with the memories. "That night was awful. We were being pulled out. I remember speaking to Pratty just before his transport got hit. God, it shattered like a smashed egg."

"We had no idea what was coming, mate."

"You know, the only reason I wasn't on it was because I helped a young girl, a teen, with a sprained ankle. There has not been a single day when I haven't thought of her and her family."

The vehicle began to climb, forcing Pip to grasp the restraining straps. It levelled out and carried on along a gravel track, turning hard right until sheer rockfaces rose up all around them. At length, it rolled to a stop.

"This is it," Rory said.

Pip glanced at him and saw in his eyes some of the reluctance she felt. She said, "Do we really need to go in—?"

"I'm going," Rory said in determination. "You coming?"

Pip unclipped the straps and opened the door. She extracted her weapon and went to the rear of the vehicle, where she opened a small hatch and took out a Pathfinder.

Rory said, "My Squitch is showing a ninety-eight percent pro—"

"So's mine," Pip broke in. "But I want to be sure."

She activated the Pathfinder and the little device trotted off into the cave. It returned a minute later, ready to be put back in its storage space.

Pip entered the cave side by side with Rory.

He said, "Locals found me in a cave over the back there. They brought me here. An old man fed me soup."

Pip said, "There's no one here now." She hurried on and turned into an area on her right.

Rory said, "There's Crimble."

A threadbare blanket covered the remains of their erstwhile comrade, identifiable only by the scraps of NATO uniform lying around the whitened bones.

Pip pointed and said, "There are more remains over there."

"Some of them must've escaped."

"At least a Spider didn't get them."

"A Spider would've been quicker."

"I suppose so. What was the old man's name?"

"Pablo."

"Come on," Pip said. "I'll flag this location for forensics. Third-wave investigators can return his remains to his next of kin." She turned and walked out of the cave. Outside, the sky shone blue and wide and open.

Rory joined her and said, "I'll give you a lift back to your sector."

"Thanks. How did you snag this vehicle, anyway? Same as before?"

As he strapped himself in, Rory winked at her and said, "You bet. My name still carries a bit of clout. A perk of surviving."

Chapter 30

14.07 Tuesday 1 January 2064

Field Surgeon Maria Phillips sat back on the bed in her small room in the semi-permanent field hospital near Pécs in southern Hungary. She clenched the hot mug of tea in her hands and fought to contain her hope. She closed her eyes and twitched her eyelid.

Jamie's faced resolved in her vision. "Hello, you dear lady," he said with his winning smile. "Happy New Year."

"And a Happy New Year to you. Have you made any resolutions?"

"Only those you already know about. It won't be long now, you know?"

Maria sighed, "It often doesn't feel like that at the front."

"When are you going back?"

"I don't know for sure," she said, and sipped her tea. "My schedule says tomorrow, but the front lines are moving so quickly that deployments change all the time."

"I know. Wonderful, isn't it?"

"We're still taking casualties," she pointed out. "And the further we go, the worse shape the refugees we find are in."

That seemed to dampen Jamie's exuberance, even though she hadn't meant to. He said, "Beats me how anyone could've survived for nearly two years in those conditions."

"Their stories will come out. In some of the rural areas we've regained, we've had emaciated farmers coming to us with bottles of booze they'd been saving for just that day." She changed the subject, "You remember I told you about that guy, Eastcott, who went berserk and killed all those ragheads in November?"

"Of course," Jamie said.

"He got ten years."

"He got off lightly."

"He had a lot of support from the local people in his town, but what he did was wrong, Jamie. I told you: it makes us no better than them."

"I'm on your side, sweetheart," Jamie said. "But his supporters really made a noise that he was being singled out for special treatment."

"That doesn't surprise me. But it will never make what he did right. Murder is still murder."

"Yeah, it looks like he picked the wrong place to do it."

"What do you mean?"

"I hear a lot of stuff from my former comrades-in-arms, Maria."

Memories of her dead brother Martin surged into her mind's eye, Jamie's former CO.

Jamie went on, "They're all getting their revenge in, but being discre—"

"Can we talk about something else, please?"

"What? Yes, sorry, sweetheart. I didn't mean to—"

"It's okay," Maria said, wishing he would understand that she'd chosen the profession of field surgeon to help

234

people, not kill them. "We've all suffered and we all deal with it in our own ways."

"I suppose so."

"How is your work?"

"Good, like always. The latest implants are working wonders."

"That's nice," Maria said, happy for him.

"Most of the amputees insist it's no different from having the original limb back. Of course, that's usually the case with the clean cuts, so to speak, while the more complex artificial limbs tend to include some joint irritation." There came a pause, then Jamie said, "I miss you. I can't wait for you to come home."

A lump formed in Maria's throat. She didn't want to think so far ahead. "There's still a long way to go."

"They're running away now."

"But we still have to be careful."

"Did you hear about the earthquake?"

"What?" Maria asked, shocked.

"Inside the Caliphate. Somewhere in the south."

"No, I didn't."

"Well, everyone's calling it an 'earthquake', even the ragheads, but the smart money is on a nuclear explosion."

"Oh God, that's awful."

"For them, maybe; for us, it's good news. Let them kill each other if they have to, instead of people in other countries."

"Can't argue with you there."

"Okay, I have to go now, sweetheart. My next patient is in the waiting area and he's a tricky one."

"Be in touch soon, Jamie."

"You can count on that. Stay safe."

She blew him a kiss and his face vanished. She smiled and drank her tea. She resolved to go for a walk but a new comms indicator flashed. She raised it.

"Hi, Maria," Ranni said. "Sorry to bother you on your day off."

"You're not bothering me. I was going to check in with you today anyway. How is *your* casualty clearing station?"

"First, Happy New Year; second, we have actually done our jobs and cleared all of our casualties."

"You're kidding?"

"Nope," Ranni said with a note of pride in his voice. "That's why I called. As of ten minutes ago, Casualty Clearing Station Sierra Zero-Four has a free capacity of one hundred percent."

"First time ever."

"I don't know what's going on at the front lines, but it is so good to see our troops have got their act together so well."

"What's it like further along our line?" Maria asked.

"Yeah, there's still enough trouble. Clearing Station Sierra Zero-Five is dealing with the aftermath of a couple of dormant Spiders further east that caught some new recruits off guard. Really, amazing some of them still seem intent on learning the hard way. Anyway, you rested now?"

"Sure, is Igbe helping you?"

"She's a star."

"Great. See you tomorrow morning, Ranni."

"You bet."

Chapter 31

09.51 Thursday 17 January 2064

Terry stepped out of the autonomous air transport into the bright, blue morning air that had a chilly edge to it. Bjarne Hasselman, Secretary General of the North Atlantic Council, stepped forward to shake the field marshal's hand.

"Welcome to Brussels," he said.

Terry shook and said, "Thank you. It's good to get out of London."

Hasselman's deputy, Wolfgang Eide, stuck out a slenderer and much longer arm. Terry shook the hand.

Hasselman said, "We are honoured to have you here in person, to mark the opening of the new headquarters for SHAPE."

Terry looked up at the sweeping glass and steel structure that he'd seen from the air a few moments earlier. He found the curves pleasing, as though the architect had copied lines from the racing cars of old, but otherwise he regarded buildings primarily from their functional use rather than any aesthetic quality. He observed, "I'm impressed with how quickly this has been designed and built."

"You know," Hasselman answered, "many people here are very keen to rebuild, to move on. I think it helps them, yes?"

"I'm sure it does."

Terry followed the men into the building's huge entrance that aped the exterior's gliding features. Along the back wall, letters a metre high spelled out the facility's full title: Supreme Headquarters Allied Powers, Europe.

Eide leaned in and said, "We have a luncheon prepared for after the conference and would be honoured for you to join us."

Terry said, "Thank you, it will be a pleasure."

Eide's face beamed. "Excellent," he replied.

They ascended a transparent escalator to the first floor.

Hasselman said to Terry, "Shocking news from our enemy yesterday, do you not think?"

Terry replied, "It might go some way to explaining his European strategy over the last couple of months, if true."

"Yes, I am in agreement with you there," Hasselman said. "There may be much more to it than we see. Perhaps this 'Fourth Caliph' is an imposter and the Third Caliph is still in charge, really?"

Terry nodded his agreement, preferring to keep his opinions to himself. The news the previous day, when an individual completely unknown to anyone outside the enemy's territory, suddenly announced that he was the Fourth Caliph and in complete command, had kept Terry busy half the night. He'd run simulations through the computer in the War Rooms in as many variations as his puny human brain could cope with, but the result was always the same: no matter what the enemy did now, he could not stop NATO forces regaining Europe.

They entered a large conference room half-full with figures in civilian dress and military fatigues. The background chatter stopped when Terry walked in. There followed many handshakes and greetings, as Terry met several of his generals in person for the first time since Operation Repulse had begun.

When pleasantries had been exchanged, Hasselman cajoled, "Please take your seats now, thank you. We have a schedule to keep to and many more attendees will be joining remotely. Thank you."

When everyone had finally shuffled to their high-backed chairs and sat, Hasselman reminded the participants of the top-secret nature of the material that would be divulged. He then introduced General Sir Patrick Fox, commander of British First Corps.

Fox made his way to the front of the room. Terry watched him and saw the general twitch his eye. The wall behind him came alive with a map of Europe.

Thin and upright, Fox stood off to the side and began, "Good morning. The situation of the entire campaign improves day by day, I'm pleased to report. To begin in the south, the entire Iberian Peninsula is now under our control."

The map enlarged the area of Spain and Portugal, and indicators of various shapes and colours flashed into existence.

"As many of you will have already heard or read, we have a provisional plan entitled Fortress Europe, whereby all coastal regions will have stationed a number of defensive arms. These begin with the Scythe Alpha, which will remain on constant patrol in the skies above our territorial waters. On land, we are already deploying next generation Pulsar battlefield lasers and one very important—and extremely secret—weapon."

Fox paused and scanned the room. Terry smiled to himself, pleased to have delegated this presentation to the man who was becoming Terry's successor in all but name. Now, on this big reveal, Terry could ease back in his chair and enjoy the moment.

Fox went on, "In the weeks before Operation Repulse commenced, a secret operation was undertaken by an elite squad of troops, to penetrate into enemy territory and disable one of his most important ACA manufacturing plants. A special new weapon was created for it, called a 'sonic mine'. This device utilises the power of sound waves to cause a quite remarkable level of destruction. And, as far as we are aware, knowledge of this device has not gone beyond NATO. Thus, Fortress Europe will also use this weapon in coastal regions to prevent any attempt by an enemy to gain a foothold."

Terry noticed several faces around the table lift in surprise, but no one spoke.

"To return to the current situation, we know that the enemy made little effort to penetrate the Alps, preferring to advance further north, presumably for easier spoils. Units there are reporting greater numbers of survivors in those regions. Currently, forward units are this morning approximately fifty kilometres north of Rome and meeting no resistance. Our advance is limited only by the caution required to ensure there are no dormant Spiders or other boobytraps. Otherwise, we have more than enough troops and the logistic infrastructure to advance as quickly as we can. In any event, we expect to secure the whole of Italy within the next seven to ten days."

The map shifted to the left, bringing central Europe into view.

"If we look to the east, we can see that Polish First Corps has already secured NATO's eastern flank, and now our forces are concerned with the drive south to regain the Balkans, Romania, Bulgaria, and, ultimately, Greece. Progress is accelerating here given the availability of greater forces now the eastern flank is secure. In sum, Operation Repulse is on track to be completed by the end of the month."

A smattering of applause greeted this announcement. Terry wondered if Fox would ask if anyone had a question when the general gave him the answer.

Fox said, "Now, I won't be taking questions at this juncture because we do have quite a lot of ground to cover this morning, as it were." The general threw his audience a wan smile as he realised his double meaning. He went on, "In addition, we now face growing political pressure to minimise casualties wherever possible. You have all, I'm sure, had to field enquiries from your country's leaders concerning the issue of minimising casualties, as if NATO did not already do that in combat operations involving flesh-and-blood troops.

"There is a tendency that we should allow fleeing warriors time to leave Europe and we should stand down our submarines in the Mediterranean. However, it is important to note that there has never been any official declaration of war. Thus, until some document or other communication exists that sets out an official cessation of hostilities, the conflict goes on and every warrior remains a legitimate military target. In addition, the feeling among the chiefs of staff is that whether or not hostilities take place should not be exclusively in the purview of the Fourth Caliph. If any of you feel differently, please let me or the field marshal know."

A ripple of chuckles rolled over the table. Terry heard someone on his left call, "Hear, hear."

Thus buoyed, Fox smiled and said, "Thank you. Anyway, that is the current position for us, but what of the enemy? I think I also speak for all of us when I say the shock announcement yesterday gives us an indication of the chaos that must have been prevalent inside the enemy's territory recently. While I do not wish to conjecture, latest intelligence reports suggest that the alleged 'earthquake' on 19 December was in fact a low-yield nuclear detonation, somewhere in Saudi Province."

The map behind Fox moved up to bring the lands of the New Persian Caliphate into view, with internal borderlines denoting its constituent provinces. It zoomed south towards the Red Sea. Fox said, "Given the history and myriad linguistic and cultural forces at play in the southern regions, it comes as no surprise there are constant tensions. In particular, there is a warrior group called the Rashidun Army. Much of this has been deployed to Europe, but some of these units appear to have mutinied in a desire to return home due to an uprising that began against the Third Caliph in the later part of last year. But what might have caused this uprising?"

The map moved upwards and tracked right to bring Persian Province into view, with its capital Tehran in the centre.

"We have obtained remarkable new intelligence from the *Institut Neuropsi* via England's MI5. And to present it to you, I will now handover to the head of that agency, David Perkins."

Fox strode back to his seat. On the wall, the face of Perkins replaced the map. He sat at his desk, hands clasped together in a fist in front of him. He said, "Good morning, SHAPE. I will be as brief as I can. However, I give you notice that my materials include unaltered images of fatal injuries."

Terry thought that was a considerate, if dated, thing to say: they had all seen many unaltered images of fatal injuries.

Perkins went on, "For some time, we have been faced with the mystery of why the Third Caliph took no action when NATO introduced the Scythe Omega. We know he had the weapons to cause us trouble, but it appears he chose not to use them, preferring to maintain his standoff with India instead of finding a diplomatic way to calm tensions and release those armaments for use in Europe.

"The most recent scans of injured warriors' brains and the memories extracted reveal some interesting happenings. Last October, there occurred an event of notable destruction close to the Third Caliph's capital, Tehran."

Perkins shrank back to the top-right of the screen. The map of the Caliphate zoomed to bring Tehran to the fore. Coloured indicators followed Perkins' description.

He went on, "In this western suburb, on the night of 15 October, a large palace and its grounds were completely destroyed. The palace was the residence of the House of Badr Shakir al-Sayyab, an educated man who seems to have risen in the Third Caliph's favour for reasons unknown. The order sent out to the local militia and other, regular military units based there was that every single person who had been to the palace or who had any contact with it was to be killed without delay and without mercy. The palace was initially destroyed with Spiders, but for several days afterwards, many more enemy subjects were executed. We have cross-referenced this intelligence with a number of warriors whose brains have been scanned, although for now I would like to share just one with you."

In the top-left of the screen a picture resolved of an oval face with dark skin, a low forehead, and small, black eyes. Perkins introduced him, "This is Mahbod Dabiri, whose rank was equivalent to corporal. He was wounded in a contact on the Polish/Czech border on 3 November, just after the Omega had come into use. He was flown to the *Institut Neuropsi* in America and his brain scanned. In October, he was stationed in this district, in a police station-cum-military observation post, part of the Third Caliph's multilayered internal security apparatus. When the House of Badr Shakir al-Sayyab was destroyed, a general alert went out to the local population that if they found anyone from the palace, they should hand them over to the authorities for a reward.

"In the afternoon of 16 October, a mother and daughter entered Corporal Dabiri's station to deliver two servants from the palace. However, the servants were European. What is of interest here is that the local women who delivered the Europeans were first stunned and then shot. And then, the two European women were also stunned and shot."

In the screen appeared images of Serena's and Tiphanie's bloodied corpses, lifted from Mahbod Dabiri's memories.

Perkins went on, "There are a couple of remarkable things here. The first is that such an order was even given. We have now scanned the brains of thousands of wounded enemy warriors, garnering millions of hours of memories from all over the New Persian Caliphate, and despite its rigid discipline and harsh criminal punishments, we could find no trace whatsoever of any similar order being given before. Therefore, we can surmise that whatever happened in the House of Badr Shakir al-Sayyab on that night, nothing like it had ever happened before.

"The second remarkable thing here is that European abductees were members of such an illustrious house. With cross-referencing, we know that the House of Badr Shakir al-Sayyab certainly enjoyed the Third Caliph's favour. To be a member of the staff would have been a prestigious position for the local population, never mind Europeans."

Terry asked, "Do we know who those women were?"

"Yes," Perkins replied. "The first was a trainee nurse at the Santa Maria hospital in Rome called Serena Rizzi. The second was a beautician from Lyons called Tiphanie Paquet. When all of the available data is taken together, the most probable reason for the destruction of the palace is an attempt on the Third Caliph's life. Whether this attempt was successful or not, we will probably never know. But whatever happened on 15 October in that palace, the other two brothers decreed that it should be razed to the ground and everyone connected with it, killed. When taken together with what we know about the Third Caliph's movements before that date, and events inside the Caliphate since that date, the most likely conclusion is that the Third Caliph was either seriously injured or killed. In turn, this led to infighting inside the Caliphate that paralysed an already inefficient decision-making structure. This in turn appears to have contributed significantly to our enemy's prevarication in responding to our new attack. Does anyone have any questions?"

"So," Terry said, glancing at the shocked faces around the table, "we have the answer why the enemy did not respond as he should have when we deployed the Omega."

No one else spoke. Fox stood and said, "Thank you very much, Mr Perkins. Good work."

Perkins replied with a trace of disdain, "I did little. I will pass on your thanks to the *Institut Neuropsi*. Will that be all?"

"Yes, thank you," Fox replied.

Perkins disappeared.

Fox turned to the table and said, "Very well, let's take a ten-minute break there. Afterwards, we will discuss reconstruction and using military personnel to assist with civilian infrastructure."

Chapter 32

01.01 Friday 1 February 2064

Officer Mark Phillips of 3rd Airspace Defence reclined in his usual pod, headset on, and monitored his assigned sector. Over the last two weeks, a sense of boredom had crept in. The pride from helping to protect soldiers' lives had dissipated as it became clear the war had nearly reached its conclusion. Tonight, his sector covered most of southern France and its border with Spain.

He toyed with his altitude and aspect to observe hundreds of autonomous air transports cruise through the safe sky unmolested. They included all makes and models from the western world, ferrying supplies and water replicators and food replicators and construction replicators as well as returning refugees. Such was the demand, the AATs were flying constantly, bringing a flood of materiel and people back to their reclaimed countries.

His supervisor broke into his thoughts, "Good evening, Babyface. How is the most pathetic officer in the corps this night?"

"I was just about to ask you the same question, sir. Might I suggest you look in the mirror?"

"Guess who's going to be out of a job soon?"

"The way the war is going, most of us, I should think," Mark replied.

"Not me, Babyface."

"Oh? What will you do, sir? Go back to being a rent boy in Kensington?"

"If I did, I'd earn more than you, you ugly scrotum. No, my little amoeba-brain. I am a career soldier. And when this war ends, I will get to decide who stays and who gets kicked out."

Mark hovered his view at an altitude of six thousand metres and enjoyed the geometric elegance of the super-AI controlled aircraft as they sped past him; some descended, some climbed, but all were safe. Above them, the SkyMasters stood guard, while Scythe Omegas patrolled below them, ready to swoop in at a moment's notice. But now, they didn't need to.

"Holy shit," Captain Shithead said abruptly.

Mark's senses sharpened at once. "What is it?"

"Wait one, Babyface," Shithead replied.

Mark held his breath as Shithead spoke with other operators. He used the time to pull out from his localisation and rise up to see his entire sector. All of the data streams around the image showed nothing untoward.

His supervisor returned, "You're cleared to open a secondary pane. Go to sector tango foxtrot three-nine, right down at almost sea level."

Satisfied his area of responsibility would not see any enemy action, Mark splayed out a new pane and followed Shithead's instructions. Suddenly, he found himself in the middle of a vast battle. Dozens of Tawny Owls, the enemy's huge warrior transport aircraft, were trying to escape from southern Greece and return to enemy territory.

Shithead observed, "Their Siskins can't save them." His voice increased in pitch with a sense of righteous justice with which Mark felt compelled to agree. "Look," Shithead hissed, "the bastards are finished. Our subs are going to kill the fuckers."

With efficiency and elegance, squads of Scythe Omegas destroyed the wings of enemy Blackswans that screened the Tawny Owls. The choppy surface of the water broke as missiles from NATO submarines fired on the enemy warrior carriers. The aircraft released tens of Spiders to dive into the waters below.

Mark said, "But what about those Spiders?"

"Jesus, Babyface, don't you keep up with our armed forces' latest developments? Those subs have got underwater Falaretes."

Mark stammered, loathe to admit he wasn't up to speed with current naval warfare standards.

"In three minutes, each sub can fire off enough Falaretes to take out two hundred Spiders."

"How?" Mark asked, as the digital feeds around the battlespace showed explosions under the water almost as soon as the Spiders splashed into it.

"Through the subs' torpedo tubes. Each torp holds a full shit-ton of Falaretes. Those Spiders won't get anywhere near them."

"Shit."

"Yeah, that's just what those fuckers are in if they think they're going to run away now."

Mark shared Captain Shithead's opprobrium. The enemy's protective screen of Siskins was destroyed. The Tawny Owls' shielding was breached. And then the aircraft themselves broke apart under the impacts of laser shots fired by Omegas that conducted a lethal dance around their prey. He watched and imagined the thousands of warriors being burned to a crisp and blown to pieces and those not dying in the explosions drowning with no one coming to help them. He thought of his dead parents in East Grinstead and his dead brother Martin and his sister Maria, still helping people in Europe. Mark had never felt such satisfaction in his life.

Mark muttered under his breath, "Bet those fuckers wish they had a navy now."

Chapter 33

11.10 Friday 1 February 2064

Terry stood at the main console in the War Rooms, hands clasped around a warm mug of tea. The holographic display in front of him described southern Greece and the thousands of islands in the Ionian Sea. Indicators of assets that denoted NATO's complete dominance of the battlespace clouded the image.

He spoke to his adjutant, Simms, without taking his eyes off the display. "Quite something, isn't it?"

"Remarkable, sir."

Terry pointed to various indicators as they changed colours and said, "There are the confirmations going up the chain of command."

Squonk announced, "Information: major combat operations are complete."

Terry couldn't stop himself blowing air through puffed cheeks. He asked, "What about outlying islands in the Adriatic and Ionian Seas?"

Squonk answered, "Inhabited islands have provisionally been assessed as secure, although there are a range of probabilities of dormant Spiders remaining. Uninhabited islands are in the process of being secured, although there are as yet no reports of any enemy activity."

Terry noted the data: currently, NATO had over three thousand, one hundred Scythe Omegas patrolling over Greece and its islands. He reflected how the operation had gained momentum. The more territory the armies had reclaimed, the more machines were deployed; the more machines deployed, the more were produced. Production plants were rebuilt. Millions of refugees returned from the British Isles and the Nordic countries, eager to reclaim their lands and reconstruct their homes and societies. The wave had become unstoppable.

Terry said, "Audio comms to Number Ten."

Dahra Napier's voice sounded in the War Room. "Terry?"

"Good morning, PM. I would like to let you know that major military operations are over. Operation Repulse is… complete."

There came a pause. Terry thought he heard a trace of breathlessness in her voice. She said, "Thank you, Terry. Thank you very much. I invite you for a celebratory glass of champagne and a debrief when you have time."

"Very good, PM." Terry took a long pull on his tea. He ordered, "Open red-level comms to all generals and field commanders at the rank of major and above."

"Confirmed," Squonk said. "Open."

"Attention, this is London. Operation Repulse is complete. The enemy has been removed from Europe. Encourage all ranks to remain vigilant. Dangers and threats still lurk in our territory, and it will likely still be some time before we can be certain that all of the lands are, finally, ours once again. Please pass on my thanks and inform all ranks that extra rations of rum will be delivered directly."

Terry caught the smiles on the faces of the others in the War Room. The flaxen-haired operator at the comms station announced, "Sir, I have fifteen generals wishing to speak to you. Sorry, make that forty-six; er, plus eighty-one lieutenant-generals, and—"

"Request them to leave a message," Terry said, also smiling.

Simms observed, "I suspect you're going to be dealing with a substantial number of congratulatory messages, sir."

Terry shook his head in dismissal. "In all honesty, we did so little here, you and I, Simms. We didn't face a Spider or a warrior. We haven't collected the remains of the enemy's victims or listened to the horror stories the survivors have to tell."

Simms said, "Quite so, sir. But without appropriate leadership, none of what you've just mentioned could've happened. With respect, field marshal, I submit you played a pivotal role."

Terry scoffed and replied, "I have always appreciated your unerring ability to know when to be quiet, Simms. I'm beginning to think you might be losing it."

"Possibly," Simms answered, smiling.

"Sir?" the flaxen-haired operator called. "You have over three hundred congratulatory messages, increasing constantly."

Terry nodded his acknowledgement at the young woman, noting for the first time the tears running down her cheeks despite the smile on her face.

"I'll deal with them later." He cast his glance around the War Room and said, "So, I suppose we'll have to take all this to pieces and all move it to the new SHAPE HQ in Brussels?"

"It is in the post-war plans, sir," Simms confirmed.

"It's for the best. At least we were there when the rest of Europe needed us."

"Indeed, sir."

Chapter 34

14.07 Monday 4 February 2064

Geoff Morrow decided that the dry forests of southern Croatia were no place to go exploring. Gulping for air, he made his way around the low hills interspersed with settlements, intending to reach the town of Grabovac before nightfall. The emaciated locals in the previous village had set him on this track, with a clumsy-worded warning not to deviate, lest he become lost. But while local super-AI systems might not have been restored, Geoff still had access to his benefits as an embedded journalist, and could use NATO comms to guide him.

He hadn't intended to leave the trail in any case, until the relentless cawing of crows someway off to his left aroused memories along with curiosity. Among so much else, the war had given Geoff a keen sense for death. He turned onto a narrower path towards the avian din. The map in his lens showed another settlement a few hundred metres ahead. He threaded his way through an avenue of gnarled ash and oak trees, branches twisting over as though the hot, dry climate were too much for them to cope with.

He arrived at the settlement, unsurprised to find the buildings of the sole farm in burnt and blackened ruins. The track widened into a road and swept around a gentle curve to the left. As he rounded the bend, he saw several bodies hanging from tree branches. He hurried towards them, at once opening a feed back to London. As he approached, many of the crows took off to circle, still cawing.

At once, his journalistic sense for the dramatic kicked in. He said, "Here in the Croatian countryside, we can find a less palatable side of NATO's victory over the New Persian Caliphate."

He reached the bodies, glad that the birds had flown off because it meant less interference in his audio. The second body along had a crude sign scrawled on some kind of packaging or wood. His lens gave him a translation at once.

He continued, suddenly aware that those locals might not appreciate their handiwork becoming global knowledge, "The bodies look to have been hanged recently. The sign on the second one along says that this is what will happen to all enemy who try to surrender. This corroborates and adds to the growing evidence of liberated locals who've decided to take matters into their own hands. Although not the worst atrocity to come to light so far, summary executions like these are nevertheless illegal. In addition, such barbaric acts beg the question: why? To whom is this kind of kangaroo justice directed? If more enemy warriors did go into hiding in Europe rather than return to the New Persian Caliphate, it is unlikely they will come across these kinds of summary executions. In addition, without modern technology, they will also be unable to communicate, so we can assume their options will be limited."

He walked around the bodies while talking. Some of the birds got used to his presence and returned to their feast. He glanced behind him, his imagination placing the locals heading his way. But he was still alone. He went on, "More importantly, is this yet another sign of law and order breaking down? It seems clear that more and more authorities all over Europe now have to deal with the challenging task of reinstating the rule of law."

He turned away and increased his pace, eager to return to the track towards Grabovac.

His editor, Alan, spoke in his ear, "Good content, Geoff."

"Thanks. You'll edit and publish, right?"

"Yeah, soon."

"What do you mean, 'soon'? This is red hot. Nine ragheads who likely tried to surrender got strung up by angry locals. It's a great story."

"Yeah, yeah. But, you know, here in London and western Europe, the war is over and there's a lot of relief."

"Oh, I get it. How quickly the old east/west divides reassert themselves, eh? Anyway, I don't have time for that now. I need a break, Alan."

"You had a week in Paris."

Geoff reached the main track and his concern eased. He turned left towards his destination. "Paris? That was months ago. Since then, I've been sending you solid copy, and I need a break."

There came a pause. Geoff kept glancing behind him, but no one followed. He already knew the day would not end for him without a stiff drink.

Alan said, "You sure you can't stay until you get down to Greece?"

"No," Geoff said. "You know what? Danny Buckley offered me a temp gig at the *WSJ* a while back. He told me they'd assigned him to cover southern Africa and offered that I could go with him."

"Good that you didn't take him up on his offer."

Geoff mistook Alan's tone for belligerence and snarled, "Oh yeah? Why?"

"You haven't heard?"

"Heard what?"

"Buckley's dead."

Geoff hadn't been in touch with the American for a couple of weeks, but put it down to workload. "Yeah? How?"

"He was tailing some Chinese diplomat in Mozambique. You know how loyal those African nations are to the Chinese? I don't have the whole gen, but Buckley thought he could prove the Chinese knew more than they were letting on regarding what was happening inside the Caliphate. Turns out the CIA thought the same and a trigger-happy agent shot him."

"Fuck."

"So, good you weren't with him."

"The shooting might've stopped but there's still enough shit going around."

"Right. Come back to the Smoke and we'll have a chat."

"I need to write the book, Alan. And I'd really appreciate a bit of support, if you can manage it."

"You and every other hack this side of the English Channel."

"Let me pitch you, okay?"

"Yeah, yeah. Just get back."

The connection ended. Geoff strode on, the cawing of the crows gradually fading behind him.

Chapter 35

11.23 Wednesday 6 February 2064

Dahra Napier stood by the marble fireplace in the flat at Number Ten and addressed her ashen-faced defence minister, "Therefore, I will be pleased to accept your resignation."

"Er," Liam Burton stammered, "Do you really think that's quite necessary, PM?"

Crispin Webb watched in dark satisfaction as the boss proved to everyone in the room why she was the PM, and not them. Blackwood, Hicks and two junior ministers sat or stood with neutral expressions.

The boss said, "I will not tolerate my ministers briefing the press against me."

The finality of her statement left Burton not knowing where to look. Then, as Crispin expected, the young man stood, face flushed with anger. He said, "You're making a mistake, PM."

"You deny briefing against me?"

"Unconditional surrender was—and still is—the path we should be pursuing. To stop like this, at this half-arsed

'Fortress Europe' compromise, will only lead to an even bigger war a few years down the line. You mark my words."

"I'm not going to have the same discussion again, Liam. I expect your letter of resignation by the end of the afternoon. Thank you for your sterling work during the last couple of years. Goodbye."

Just to make the point, Crispin walked to the door and opened it for the former defence minister.

Burton looked from the boss to the door and back again. "As you please. Just remember that the history of this war is yet to be written. I'm not going to be the only one publishing my opinion on your leadership."

"Which you are quite welcome to do," the boss said.

Burton scoffed and stomped out of the room. Crispin closed the door.

"Thank you," Napier said to the room. "Annabel, take over Liam's responsibilities for now. It'll be good experience for your future career. Just until George is back on his feet."

"Very good, ma'am," said a young woman standing by the far window.

From one of the couches, Foreign Secretary Charles Blackwood brushed the thigh of his pressed trouser leg and said, "Duplicitous little toad. You can expect him to write a damning account of his time in office, PM."

Napier smiled, "I would not expect anything less."

Home Secretary Aiden Hicks added, "And he won't be the only one."

"Ladies and gentlemen, I still wanted to thank you all personally here. Like Liam, you played important roles in this administration and worked very hard to ensure we did not become overwhelmed. Now that the only unpleasant task is out of the way, I suggest we all go downstairs and have an early celebratory lunch."

Murmurs of agreement greeted Napier's offer and her audience stood. Crispin reopened the door for the others to leave. They did so and Napier indicated with a nod of her head to close the door again when they were alone. He did so.

She said, "Do you think I did the right thing, forcing Liam to resign like that?"

"Absolutely," he replied.

"It was a little Sun-Tzu," she said in a wistful tone.

"You'll always be a war leader now, boss."

"Yes, I hadn't thought of that." She looked into Crispin's eyes, "It has been quite the journey, hasn't it? There were times I was certain we had only hours left to live. I can't quite believe we've made it to the other side."

Unsure of what he could say, Crispin didn't reply.

Napier smiled, "And now, once again, my biggest problem is irate ex-ministers who will try to score points to burnish their own credentials." She paused and stroked Crispin's shirtsleeve. "Thank you, most of all. Did you never think of throwing the towel in, even after the heart attack?"

"Honestly?"

"Honestly."

"Not for a second, boss. It was history in the making. How could anyone just walk away from that?"

"Plenty enough ran away, though, didn't they?"

"Cowards are everywhere," he said with a shrug. "But we didn't run away."

She tucked a strand of hair behind her ear and replied, "No, we didn't. Come on, I'm hungry."

Crispin opened the door again. As soon as the boss went through and out of his line of sight, he puffed his cheeks and rolled his eyes. He thought of the secret diary he'd been keeping almost every day since this bloody war began, and how its publication would provide amply for him in his old age.

Chapter 36

10.10 Saturday 9 February 2064

Turkish engineering student Berat Kartel stepped off the gangway and onto the dockside in Hamburg. Over one shoulder, he carried a heavy rucksack with his belongings, including his handwritten journal. Behind him, the vast container ship, bringing irreplicable supplies from the Nordic countries, towered over the low buildings and metal cranes.

He stopped, labouring under a pain above his right hip that had begun two days before. He located the way to the exit and began walking, avoiding making eye-contact with the workers and other passengers. The chaos he sensed around him matched his mood. He felt adrift. He understood now he would never be able to return home, to his apartment in Usak, Turkey. Memories of his flight two long years ago assailed his mind's eye. He couldn't stop wondering what had become of all the poor souls he had passed as he travelled alone across Europe.

He made his way to a building where the authorities offered help to new arrivals. One of the kind families who had lodged him in Sweden had given him an old, spare lens, but the infrastructure in Hamburg still needed much work. And that was the reason he'd come here: to take a job with a construction company that had recruited him the previous week. They sent him outline plans to rebuild Hamburg's central monorail station. Looking at them and thinking of improvements was the sole activity that could keep Berat's memories at bay.

He had to queue for over two hours before his turn to approach an emaciated elderly lady, who appeared to take pity on him. She allocated to him a loft apartment in a building in the old redlight district, sight unseen. He signed his name, aware that any roof over his head was better than none. She gave him a coded card to enter the building and told him it would be weeks before civilian super-AI infrastructure would return to pre-war levels. Until then, he should be grateful for whatever worked. She drew him a crude map to guide him to the street and block, and indicated an emergency shelter where stores such as bedding, food and water might be available.

The journey to his new abode took a further two hours. On the way, Berat stopped at the shelter and collected a rolled-up single person's mat and linen. Knowing he would at least sleep well, Berat's mood lightened. As darkness fell and the air chilled, he reached the imposing block. He entered and trudged up the five floors to his loft apartment, the dust carrying the stench of despair, as though the building itself felt guilty for remaining intact when so much of Hamburg had been destroyed.

He reached the wooden door, above which a circular symbol of some kind was embedded in the wall. He went in and closed the door behind him, sighing in tired relief. The area was bare apart from some broken furniture stacked in the far corner. Berat dropped his things and sipped some water from a bottle he'd been given on the ship. The stabbing pain above his right hip intensified and he was at a loss as to why something as simple as water could produce such a reaction.

Darkness fell and the single-phase power in the building meant the lights offered too little illumination for him to consider the plans for the central monorail station.

He unrolled the mat-cum-bed and wanted nothing more than to collapse in it and sleep. But first, he rummaged in his rucksack and withdrew his handwritten journal. He extracted the pencil from the spine, now less than half the length it had been two years earlier, and limped over to the nearest window sill. He sighed and wrote: *Finally, I am back in Europe proper, heartbroken that I will never see my homeland again nor find out what happened to everyone I left behind. I should not complain, for the German authorities have given me temporary accommodation for which I am grateful, probably as a result of the employment contract I have. Perhaps I might yet be of some use to someone? However, I have had some severe pain in my stomach, above my right leg, which comes and goes but which makes drinking very painful. Medi-scan points have yet to be reinstalled on public transport. I think I should go to a doctor, but I am wholly absorbed by the initial plans for rebuilding the central monorail station. I must sleep now, but will go to a doctor if the pain is still there tomorrow.*

He closed the journal, and despite the pain, collected a cheap dining chair from the pile at the back. He climbed up on it and placed his journal on top of a dusty crossbeam for safekeeping. He got down and decided to sleep. He considered taking another sip of water but decided against it. Berat lay on his mat in his clothes and pulled the cover over himself.

He fell asleep unaware that the peritonitis caused by his burst appendix had worsened to sepsis. In the early hours of the following morning, Berat briefly regained consciousness, coming to in a sea of confused agony before the shutdown of his internal organs killed him.

Chapter 37

15.09 Friday 15 February 2064

Pip stared at her boots as they scrunched through the small stones on the Spanish beach. On her right, the slight swell made small waves curl and flop down in an exhausted white spray, as if the effort of turning over were almost too much for them. By her side, Rory's boots made heavier going than her own, and he stomped along, taking longer strides than she.

He said, "It was somewhere around here. I'm sure."

"It's odd. I can still recall really small details, like the house I hid in and the colour of the rowing boat the Spanish special ops guys were trying to push into the sea, but I can't remember anything general that would help me be sure we'd found it now."

"I remember when the contact started going off. At first, I thought you were alone, trying to defend yourself. Then, I realised there was way too much fire for one person."

"I lost count of how many Spiders those guys shot down."

"Me too. When it kicked off, I hid and waited for the Spiders to clear off. I thought about it and had to know if you'd been involved. When I got to the beach, I actually expected just to be looking for bits of you."

"I tried to warn them," Pip said, the memory hurting her chest. "But they thought they could beat the Spiders."

"I shudder to think how many good troops we lost in those first few weeks."

"And yet we managed to survive, to make it to the end of the whole thing. You know, it's almost two years to the day since we got the sub that took us back to England?"

"It still bothers you, doesn't it, mate?"

Pip shrugged, "It always will. For the rest of my life. And you're okay with it, yes?"

Rory let out a mirthless chuckle. "Not 'okay with it', mate. Not at all. Listen, when I was on my sergeant training course, we learned about this French guy called Marbot. You heard of him?"

"Nope."

"He fought with Napoleon through all of his campaigns. He spent forty years fighting in almost every battle the French army was engaged in. He got injured loads of times. But he survived, living into old age. The thing is, before each battle or contact with the enemy, no one knows who's going to die and who isn't, right? For a guy like Marbot, for troops like you and me, every contact is a toss of the coin. For the Frenchman, he made the coin land heads every single time for forty years. All we've had to cope with is a two-year war."

Pip stopped walking and turned to face Rory. "Come on. Nineteenth-century warfare didn't have ACAs and smart bullets and lasers that can burn a person to death in two shots."

"Fair comment," Rory conceded, "but then they also didn't have water replicators and GenoFluid packs. Two hundred years ago, a rifle shot or cut from a blade could easily go manky like Crimble's arm did, and that was the wounded soldier's lot."

Pip resumed trudging along the beach.

Rory went on, "My point is that some of us had to survive. Some of us who began this war were bound to make it to the end. And it's not just you and me, is it? Look at old granddad Heaton. He was due to retire from the army with his pension in April '62. I swear the poor bugger thought he wouldn't make it out the other side."

Pip smiled.

"But why stay in the past, mate? It's over. It's Fortress Europe now. What are we doing back here, on this beach where so much happened two years ago?"

Pip nodded, "Being engineers."

"Right."

"That's the other thing."

"What?" Rory asked.

"The future. Suddenly we've got one. I've spent so long living one day to the next, one retreat after another, the next day's advance and objectives. Somehow, it seems incredible that we now have some kind of future."

Rory's next question surprised Pip. "Do you think you'll leave the army?"

"Not a chance," she replied at once. A gull overhead cawed, and Pip wondered if it might be some kind of sign or omen.

"Me neither," Rory answered. "Fortress Europe is going to need experienced soldiers like us."

"I suppose so," she conceded.

He suddenly changed the subject, "Do you remember when we first worked together, on the flood defences in England?"

"Oh, yes. Those 3D ultra-Graphene ribbons."

"I was crazy about you then. I adored you."

His admission made Pip think of Martin Phillips, killed like so many of her comrades. She still missed him. She would always miss him. "Thank you," she said.

"But, you know, after Dover, when you were injured, I sort-of got the message."

She stopped walking and looked up at him, feeling both flattered and annoyed. "There was no 'message' for you to get, mate."

"I know. It's fine, really. But I want you to know that if you ever need anything..."

Pip decided to lift the mood, and replied, tongue in cheek, "Your outdated chivalry is appreciated, Sergeant Moore. But as the only commissioned officer present, I should like to point out the same goes for you, as well, if you ever need anything."

Rory laughed.

Pip said, "Shall we get on with what we came here to do?"

"Sure," Rory answered. He indicated ahead, "There's the headland at the end of the beach. Up there is where the first line defences are supposed to go."

They stopped walking. Ahead of them, the stony beach tapered off as a rocky outcrop rose out of the sea. At the top of it, yellow grass flopped back and forth in the breeze.

Pip stopped walking and said, "So, are you going to tell me?"

"Tell you what?"

"If the rumours I've heard about these 'earthquake bombs' are true?"

Rory tutted and replied, "Captain, are you asking me to breach the Official Secrets Act?"

Pip gave him a sarcastic look and replied, "No, I'm ordering you to."

Rory shrugged, smiled, and said, "Fair enough. If you insist, ma'am."

"Well?"

He walked over to a dry tree trunk lying on the stones and sat on it. "They're called 'sonic mines'; but yeah, you could call them earthquake bombs, if you like. These things, they're not much bigger than a small block of wood. I saw half a dozen of them flatten a massive ACA production plant and the city next to it. No explosion. No blast wave. No fuss. Just brought the whole lot crashing down."

"How?"

"Ultra-low sound waves. If you can generate them strong enough, they break everything to bits."

"Wow."

"Yup. And if the boffins can tweak them to make air-burst versions—which, I think, we can assume they have—then if a fleet of Tawny Owls were to fly over our heads right now, the sonic mines would shatter them into tiny pieces. Pretty good defensive insurance, if you ask me."

"And it's our job to make sure the defences do what they have to." Pip motioned to the outcrop and said, "Come on, race you to the top."

"Hold on," Rory said, twitching his eye.

"What is it?"

"Oh, shit."

"What?"

"I've just got a summons to go back to London."

"What for?"

Rory shook his head. "Maybe it's a joke, although it looks pretty genuine."

"Go on."

Rory looked at her and said, "Quote: 'Field Marshal Sir Terry Tidbury, Supreme Allied Commander, Europe, requests the pleasure of your company at the Twenty-Eight club in central London, at 13.00 on Monday 18 February 2064. Transport from your current location will be provided'."

Pip clapped. "Well done, you," she exclaimed, beaming. "And he didn't even order you—he *requested* you."

Rory puffed air out through his cheeks. "Yeah, I know. Bloody hell. Probably a good thing I won't be able to drink, isn't it?" he said with a smile.

Chapter 38

13.23 Saturday 16 February 2064

Maria Phillips stood outside her reconstructed home in East Grinstead. In her hand, she grasped the blackened wooden foot of Billy the Rabbit that her brother Mark had given her. She glanced up at the roof but Billy was not there. She felt a selfish twinge when she wished her mother and father and brother Martin would emerge to greet her and welcome her home, but a voice inside chided her: how dare she dream of such things when she'd seen so many people die in the last two years?

She pushed the front door open and dropped her kitbag in the narrow hallway. Traces of exotic herbs invaded her nose. She walked through into the kitchen. On the table sat a vase with fresh flowers and a note of deepest thanks from the refugee family who'd been living in the house. They had now returned to their own home in the Czech Republic to rebuild, like so many thousands of others. The note implored Maria and her family to visit so that the people she'd helped might show her their gratitude.

"That would be nice," she said to the kitchen.

A noise in the hallway made her smile. Jamie burst into the kitchen with a breathless, "Sorry I'm late."

She took a moment to enjoy his straight blond hair and wide face: Jamie, one of the last people to see Martin alive and part of her brother's squad. She ran to him and they embraced. She pulled back and asked, "Did you see Mark on your way? He should be here, too."

"Don't think so, although I did pass a couple of guys. Maybe your brother was one of them?"

"He wouldn't be with anyone," she said dismissively.

"You did say he was a loner."

"Oh, yes. He was a gamer before the war. Never had any real-world friends at all."

Jamie's handsome face creased in a concerned frown. "Ah, I had a friend who got into that. Convinced himself that he could win one of those 'Bounties' and he'd be set for life."

"That's it. Such a con."

Jamie clapped his hands. "Right, where did your refugees leave the kettle?"

"Just there," Maria said, indicating the work surface under the window.

"Great." Jamie moved past her and filled the kettle from the tap.

"I'm not sure the tea—"

Mark appeared in the doorway. "Hello, sister," he said.

"Mark." She crossed the kitchen, hugged him, and was pleasantly surprised when he responded without awkwardness.

"Er, I hope you don't mind," he said, "but I brought a friend. His name is Joe. Well, actually he's a shithead, but I took pity on him."

Confusion settled on Maria like the shadow of a cloud on a sunny day.

Mark moved into the room. Behind him stood a tall, lithe man who carried himself with confidence. He strode forwards and offered his hand, "Delighted to meet you, Maria. And you, sir. My name is Joe Neely."

Maria shook his hand, impressed with his mannerisms. "Nice to meet you, Joe."

Jamie leaned over the table and also shook Joe's hand.

Maria looked from Mark to Joe, saying, "And you two—?"

"Work together at 3rd Airspace Defence," Joe explained. "And given how utterly useless Mark is, not only at his job, but also at everything else in general, I decided that I would like to meet his big sister and offer you my heartfelt sympathies. You must have had to put up with so much from him."

"Well, he's my brother so I don't really see it as a prob—"

"Don't listen to him, sis," Mark broke in. "Poor Joe can only feel good about himself by believing everyone else is even stupider than he is. It's a conundrum and I thought some interaction with normal people might help cure him of these ridiculous delusions."

Joe tutted, looked at Mark, and said, "My God, Babyface. If shit was made out of rubber, you'd bounce to the moon and back."

Jamie put out a calming hand and said, "Guys, guys. How about a cup of tea and we have a nice game of cards, eh? Then we'll go and get something to eat, all right?"

"Yes," Maria concurred. "Mark, did you read the instructions. And did you share them with Joe?"

"Of course," Mark said. "But I expect Joe will struggle, as always. He really is as thick as mince."

Joe said, "My dear Maria, if it's a game Babyface can learn, then I would imagine an orangutan could play it."

"You should know," Mark said.

Maria said, "Right, okay," unsure how she felt, sensing only that both her brother and Joe enjoyed the banter.

Ten minutes later, Maria sat at the small, plain dining table shuffling the new pack of playing cards she'd brought with her. In front of her sat a paper pad and pencil to keep the score. She looked at the three men around the table. Relief that the war, and with it the danger, had passed lightened her breaths. "Good," she said. "First jack deals." She spun the cards over from the top of the pack. The first jack landed in front of her.

She scooped the cards back up and gave the pack one more shuffle. "We used to play this so often before—" Maria stopped herself. She was going to say, 'before the war', but then realised that, from now on, everyone's lives would be divided into 'before' and 'after' the war. She decided she did not want her life to be delineated like that. She heaved in a breath and said, "We used to play this a lot." She dealt each of them seven cards. "Okay, hearts are trumps. Jamie, your first call and lead. How many tricks do you think you can win?"

Chapter 39

07.12 Sunday 17 February 2064

Geoff Morrow stood at the window of his small flat and gazed out at the London skyline. The distant construction replicators stood immobile, like sentinels guarding the piles of rubble that they would sift and sort and reuse as aggregate to rebuild the ruins around them. But they wouldn't begin until nine o'clock, so Geoff had risen early to take advantage of the relative quiet. Broken clouds hurried through the blue sky above the buildings, as though in a rush to be somewhere else.

Geoff closed his eyes, still slightly disbelieving that he had returned to his home, to the flat he'd shared with Lisa, the flat where he and she and their child should be, together. But lately, her constant refrain, "You're a bastard, Geoff Morrow," had begun to fade from his memory. He recalled all of the conversations they'd had before The Day: 2 June 2062, when a Spider had blown up St. Barts hospital and crushed Lisa and their baby.

He slapped the window frame in frustration and said, "I don't have time for this." Now the war had ended, every hack in Europe would be racing to get an account, a history, published, and Geoff had determined long ago that his history would be the definitive one—the account future students and commentators and historians would turn to for reference.

And it started now, on this Sunday morning.

"Computer?" he called. "Begin new project."

He considered the title. He wanted something powerful but not overwhelming; something appropriate to the book's scope, but not trite.

"Title page: 'The Great European Disaster, by G. K. Morrow'." He paced back and forth in the confined living area. "Page one, foreword: 'No one would have believed, in the last years of the 2050s, that Europe's fate had been decided by beings with vastly inferior intellects. No one could have dreamed that the distant, isolated New Persian Caliphate had decreed that Europe was to be put to the sword in the ultimate act of revenge for centuries of colonialism. Even as ordinary Europeans went about their day-to-day business, three-hundred-and-fifty kilometres distant on the other side of the Mediterranean Sea, minds consumed with petty hatred for perceived historical wrongs intended nothing less than the complete destruction of Europe and the eradication of its peoples and cultures'."

He murmured to himself in satisfaction. It might not be perfect, but that's what editing was for. He continued, "New paragraph. 'This work will detail every facet of the 2062 to 2064 war between Europe and the New Persian Caliphate. Each military engagement and every victim of this most unjust conflict is described herein'. No, scrub that. Makes me sound like a bloody lawyer. Rewrite: 'Each military engagement and every victim of this most unjust conflict is described in these pages.' There, that's better."

He went into the kitchenette and pressed a button on the coffee machine. He sighed and said, "This is going to take a lot of coffee…"

Chapter 40

12.12 Monday 18 February 2064

Terry brushed the fine dust from the Budda he had finally returned to carving in his garden shed. He frowned in disapproval as he struggled to form the curvature of the figure's belly to his liking, each tap with a chisel seeming to cause more problems than it solved. He put the chisel down and rubbed a piece of fine-grade sandpaper to soften a ridge and try, in vain, to give the plump belly the correct shape.

From the back door of the house, his wife Maureen called, "Terry, your car is here. You haven't forgotten, have you?"

"Rats," he said. He wiped his hands on a cloth that itself had seen cleaner days and left the shed, calling, "I can't get the blasted curves right." He crossed the lawn and entered the house. He patted his white shirt. "Do I look passable?"

"You'll do," Maureen replied with a smile.

He grabbed a sports jacket from the back of a chair at the kitchen table.

"Will you be long?" Maureen asked.

"I don't expect to be. But it is an important lunch at the Twenty-Eight gentlemen's club."

"'Gentlemen's' club?" Maureen queried with a raised eyebrow.

"Anyone can be a member; man, woman or hermaphrodite. It's just a throwback to tradition," he replied, putting the jacket on. "Anyway, I'll be in touch so you know." He gave her a peck on the cheek.

Maureen followed him to the front door. "Why's it called the Twenty-Eight club?"

"That was the year it was founded, 2028. A group of English politicians who wanted to reintroduce decency and responsibility to public life established it as a place for likeminded people to meet."

The autonomous car sat on the drive. The door opened upwards for him.

He turned back to his beloved wife, took her hands in his, and said, "Now it's over, I need to acknowledge the one contribution that really did make all the difference. Without Hastings and Operation Thunderclap, Repulse could never have succeeded. And the Twenty-Eight was his club. The least I can do is give everyone involved in Thunderclap the opportunity to remember and salute Hastings and those of his team who never came back."

Maureen's features softened. She said, "I think these won't be the last fallen comrades you'll be remembering."

Terry nodded in sombre acknowledgement, left her, and got in the car. The door closed and the vehicle trundled off along the local road. When it reached the motorway, it accelerated. Terry watched the countryside roll by, a strange sense of redundancy close to him in the confines of the vehicle. Now the war was over, he struggled to avoid reviewing his decisions and whether he might or should have done anything differently.

The car broke into his thoughts, "Field marshal, the British Army's super AI is requesting urgent contact with you. It wishes to communicate a message of the utmost importance. Do you agree?"

Terry replied, "Yes."

Squonk's voice filled the vehicle, "Information: early warning systems are reporting powerful explosions on the border between the New Persian Caliphate and India."

Dread formed in Terry's stomach. "What kind of powerful explosions?" he asked.

"The highest probability is the detonation of several medium-yield thermonuclear warheads."

Terry said nothing. He recalled the most recent deployments for Fortress Europe and felt confident that no enemy weapons of any sort could threaten the peace in Europe now. But the rest of the world? That was hardly his responsibility.

Squonk asked, "Do you wish to change your current travel arrangements?"

"Absolutely not," Terry replied at once, seeing no reason not to honour Hastings and the other members of his team. "I will proceed as planned."

"Confirmed."

He cast his glance out at the barren English countryside rolling past. He spoke his thoughts aloud, "But how secure can Europe ever really be in the midst of such global chaos?"

THE END

For the latest news and releases, follow Chris James on Amazon

In the US, at:
https://www.amazon.com/Chris-James/e/B005ATW34C/

In the UK, at:
https://www.amazon.co.uk/Chris-James/e/B005ATW34C/

You can also follow his blog, at:
https://chrisjamesauthor.wordpress.com/